SACRIFICE

T0321497

THE TRAGIC CULT MURDER OF
MARK KILROY IN MATAMOROS

SACRIFICE

A FATHER'S DETERMINATION
TO TURN EVIL INTO GOOD

JIM KILROY

AND

BOB STEWART

THOMAS NELSON PUBLISHERS
Nashville

SACRIFICE: THE DRUG CULT MURDER OF MARK KILROY AT
MATAMOROS

Copyright © 1990 by Jim Kilroy and Bob Stewart. All rights reserved. No
portion of this book may be reproduced in any form, except for brief quotations
in reviews, without written permission from the publisher.

Scripture quotations used in this book are from the following sources:
  The King James Version of the Bible (KJV).
  The New American Bible, translated from the original language by members of
    the Catholic Biblical Association of America; copyright 1968, Catholic Book
    Publishing Company, New York.

Library of Congress Cataloging-in-Publication Data:

Kilroy, Jim.
    Sacrifice : the drug cult murder of Mark Kilroy at Matamoros / Jim
Kilroy and Bob Stewart.
        p.   cm.
    ISBN 0-8499-9098-X
    1. Murder—Mexico—Matamoros (Tamaulipas)—Case studies. 2. Human
sacrifice—Mexico—Matamoros (Tamaulipas)—Case studies. 3. Drug
traffic—Mexico—Matamoros (Tamaulipas)—Case studies. 4. Kilroy,
Mark James, d. 1989. 5. Murder victims—Texas. I. Title.
HV6535.M43M384 1990
364.1′523′097212—dc20   90-42079
                                                                                      CIP

Printed in the United States of America

012349 MV 987654321

In loving memory
of
MARK JAMES KILROY,
a caring young man who touched the
hearts of many people during his life—
and even more since his death.

We know that Mark is safe now. God is taking
good care of him, much better than we ever
could. For this and for the happiness we have
known with Mark, we are eternally grateful.

—JIM and HELEN KILROY

CONTENTS

ACKNOWLEDGMENTS

I want to express my deep appreciation for the countless people who have been a part of our story. First of all, without my wife's help, this book could not have been written. Helen's loving insight and special attention to detail have been invaluable contributions. Her support has always been important to me. In times of emotional crisis we automatically turn to each other. And since the day Mark disappeared, Helen and I have leaned heavily on each other. Together, we faced a tragedy that possibly neither of us could have faced alone.

Also it is with very special pride that I acknowledge our son, Keith. As he endured the deep sorrow of the loss of his brother, his courage strengthened our family. He may never fully realize how much he bolstered us.

Even though we have given a very detailed account of the search for Mark, his death, and the outpouring of love and support which sustained us throughout our ordeal, space limitations have made it impossible for us to individually recognize all of the people who are a part of our story.

Our old friends and neighbors in the Santa Fe area were a comfort and strength to us. In Brownsville and Matamoros strangers who soon became new friends reached out to us, and we did not feel alone in the Rio Grande Valley. The concern shown for us by people from across the state of Texas, really from all over our country and Mexico, gave us tremendous encouragement. For the kind words and gentle touches of all these people, we are indebted.

It was this love from afar, a reflection of God's true love, which showed that good people united can overcome evil. Because of their efforts and especially their prayers, we found Mark and brought him home.

—JIM KILROY

PRINCIPAL CHARACTERS

THE FAMILY
Mark Kilroy, kidnapped and killed in Mexico.
James Kilroy, father.
Helen Kilroy, mother.
Keith Kilroy, younger brother

THE FRIENDS
Billy Huddleston
Brent Martin
Bradley Moore

THE LAWMEN
Oran Neck, U.S. Customs agent-in-charge, Brownsville.
George Gavito, lieutenant in the Cameron County Sheriff's Office.
Juan Benitez Ayala, comandante, Mexican Federal Judicial Police.
Alex Perez, sheriff of Cameron County.
Ernesto Flores, deputy in the Cameron County Sheriff's Office.

THE DRUG CULT
Adolfo de Jesus Constanzo, the gang's *Padrino* or Godfather.
Sara Maria Aldrete Villarreal, the gang's *Bruja* or Witch.
Elio Hernandez Rivera, Constanzo's second-in-command.
Ovidio Hernandez Rivera, Elio's brother.
Serafin Hernandez Garcia, Jr., Elio's nephew.
Sergio Martinez Salinas (*La Mariposa*).
Malio Ponce Torres.
David Serna Valdez (*El Coqueto*).
Alvaro de Leon Valdez (*El Dubi*).
Omar Francisco Orea Ochoa.
Martin Quintana Rodriguez.

THE CARETAKER
Domingo Reyes Bustamante, the caretaker at Rancho Santa Elena

<!-- faint mirrored bleed-through text from facing page, illegible -->

PROLOGUE

It was drugs that killed Mark James Kilroy, although he was not a drug user—drugs and a vile, unspeakable evil done in the name of religious worship. The twenty-one-year-old pre-med student died in a scene that even the most nimble mind in Hollywood would have difficulty articulating—although, ironically, in the final analysis it was a bit of Tinseltown celluloid that would help determine the details of his murder.

Pick an adjective to describe the horrors uncovered by investigating law-enforcement officers: gruesome, macabre, terrible, beastly, horrid, grisly. They all seem inadequate to describe the atrocities found under manure-saturated haystacks behind a small, one-room shack in Mexico. There, on a few acres of farmland, which the news media would tag the "Devil's Ranch," human body parts had been used in ceremonial activities that were supposed to make cult members impervious to the police and bodily harm, and give them wealth beyond their dreams. There, too, more than a ton of marijuana a week was shipped to eager drug users in the United States.

Juxtaposed against this background of incredible evil, a family's love of God and their determined search for their son stirred the passions of the world for twenty-eight days in the spring of 1989. When the search ended, the contrasts between good and evil were stark. Two young men had met. One was an example of the American dream: Mark, a former high school sports star, was studying to be a doctor. The other was an example of the American nightmare: Adolfo de Jesus Constanzo, twenty-six, was the spawn of twisted cult worship in a Cuban-dominated area of Miami.

Two young men met—and one of them died as a pagan sacrifice at the hands of the other.

This is the story of that death, inspired by evil. But it is also the story of a beleaguered family, inspired by love, working together to unravel a mystery as first a city, then a nation, and finally, the whole world clasped them to its heart in a moment of shared grief.

It has been a staunch belief in God that has sustained the Kilroys and defined their acceptance of this hideous tragedy. But theirs has not just been an inward search for consolation. Mark's family stunned the world with their plea to "pray for the men who did this."

The contents of this book are based largely on the recollections of four people, Jim and Helen Kilroy, George Gavito, and Oran Neck. Keith Kilroy also gave unstintingly of his time. Other law-officers, officials, and friends—both new and old—have been interviewed in an effort to achieve the most accurate presentation of the facts as possible. In some instances, dialogue has been recreated from memory and is as accurate as memory allows.

Despite worldwide media attention, the unique depths and ironies of this story of love and evil have not been completely revealed—until now.

—BOB STEWART

BOOK ONE

THE DISAPPEARANCE

SPRING BREAK

Mark James Kilroy had finally arrived!

After months of anticipation, Mark stood on the beach at South Padre Island where the cool breeze sweeping in from the Gulf of Mexico converted the shimmering Texas sun into a glowing warmth. It was a perfect day for fun in the sun.

Spring break 1989.

Ubiquitous, logo-decorated T-shirts, posters, and even hand-lettered signs proclaimed the season. Everywhere he looked Mark saw thousands of students enjoying the annual break in their studies.

Spring break has to be experienced to be understood. In Texas it is as traditional as a rodeo and as necessary as barbecue to feed the pounding hormones coursing through the eclectic group of college students drawn to the Rio Grande Valley for a celebration of youth.

Mark was no different than the thousands of other students who jammed the beaches on this slender island that is known for its beauty and its proximity to Mexico. On that Saturday morning after an all-night trip with three buddies from his hometown of Santa Fe, Texas, Mark was just another face in the crowd.

On the same day the carefree college students plunged into the celebrating crowd, Adolfo de Jesus Constanzo packed a suitcase at his Mexico City home. He frequently flew to the border to check on a drug-smuggling operation he controlled through occult superstitions. Each week his small band of outlaws methodically moved two thousand pounds of marijuana across the Rio Grande into the United States.

3

Constanzo had come to the gang two years before when he met
Sara Maria Aldrete Villarreal. She had introduced him to Elio Hernandez Rivera, twenty-two, who had taken over the drug-smuggling
gang several years earlier after his brother, Saul, was shot down in a
Matamoros restaurant. Carefully, Constanzo had taken control of
the outlaw group. And at the Hernandez family ranch he skillfully
wove occult activities into the drug-smuggling operation. Eventually,
Constanzo wielded such power that the gang members referred to
him as *El Padrino* or Godfather. Without question, they obeyed his
every command.

On Sunday, he would be met at the international airport at
Harlingen and taken to the Holiday Inn in Brownsville, where he
would stay in a room registered in the name of Sara Aldrete.

The next day Constanzo would issue an order that would eventually shake the sensibilities of the civilized world.

The sequence of events that would lead to a meeting between
Mark James Kilroy and Adolfo de Jesus Constanzo began several
days earlier, on Friday, March 10. Mark had spent an exhausting
semester tackling the complex subjects required of pre-med majors
at the University of Texas at Austin. Since the first day of classes in
September he had been dreaming of the traditional spring-break
holiday at South Padre Island, a strip of sandy, sun-baked beaches
running along the South Texas coast. There, for five weeks in early
spring, the beaches would reverberate to the beat of rock music and
the youthful exhilaration of college students at play. More than
450,000 young men and women from across the nation usually make
the annual pilgrimage to the white beaches for fun and sun, and a
chance to visit Old Mexico, where the beer is cold, the tamales are
hot, and the excitement throbs.

Mark would make the trip with three childhood buddies. Bradley
Moore, twenty, would drive from Texas A&M University at College
Station to pick up Mark at his efficiency apartment four blocks from
the University of Texas at Austin. In Santa Fe, the two would be
joined by Billy Huddleston, twenty-one, and Brent Martin, twenty,
for their Easter holiday. The four young men had played sports
together in Santa Fe High School, where Mark graduated fourteenth
out of a senior class of 210 in 1986. Mark, Bradley, and Brent had
played basketball together. Mark and Billy had been on the baseball
team.

The break would be a rare treat for Mark, who spent much of his
time cramming. In the latter part of his junior year, he had already
begun cramming for the crucial Medical College Admission Test he
was to take that summer.

Mark was ready when Bradley threaded his Mustang through the entrance and into the courtyard of the apartment complex at two o'clock that Friday afternoon. It took only a few minutes for the two men to throw a few things into the trunk.

"You sure have a lot of shoes," Bradley laughed as they loaded Mark's gear into the car.

"I want to look preppie like you," Mark teased, knowing that remark would be a gentle jibe to his soft-spoken friend.

Bradley shook his head and laughed.

"Get in the car," he demanded.

"Just a minute," Mark said, disappearing into the apartment. "I have something to do."

In a few minutes Bradley saw Mark crawl out the kitchen window, carefully pull the window down and then replace the screen. Mark saw the quizzical look on Bradley's face.

"I had to set a roach trap. And then I put the chain on the door. That way if someone tries to break in, the chain will stop them and they'll think someone's in the apartment since it's locked from the inside," he explained.

"Oh," Bradley said, used to his friend's often-convoluted way of doing things that was always coupled with studied self-assurance. It was one of the traits that had forged the boys' friendship when Mark's family moved to Santa Fe in 1974. Bradley and Brent had been best friends since early childhood and Mark's happy-go-lucky personality was a welcome addition to their youthful circle. But his friends soon learned that beyond the lively grin and practical jokes lay a pensive mind that was quick to offer encouraging solutions to daily problems.

"Let's get something to eat," Mark suggested as he stepped into the car.

After a quick hamburger, the two headed out of town. "We're finally on the way," Mark laughed as they left the city limits of Austin behind them.

Bradley, too, had spent the last months in arduous study. Throughout the spring term, he had called Mark once or twice a week to discuss the pending spring-break trip.

"Do you realize that this trip is all we've talked about this semester?" he asked his friend.

Mark nodded. "It's been a hard semester and I'm ready for a break."

The four-hour drive to Santa Fe was not unlike other trips the two had taken together. They talked about grades, school, girls, and especially the fun of spring break. Both had gone to South Padre Island the year before, but not together. The buddies agreed that if this trip together was half as exciting as last year, it was going to be a trip to remember.

Because it was spring break, they tried to put thoughts of study and school behind them; but it dominated their conversation.

"I'm sure having trouble with physics," Bradley said at one point during the trip. "I just don't like it."

"If you don't, then you'd better change your major," Mark replied. "How can you be an electrical engineer if you don't like physics?"

"I don't know," Bradley said.

"Don't worry about it," Mark reassured him. "You'll think of something else. You have to find something that you're good at—something that you like," he encouraged his friend.

"You know," Mark said after moments of silence. "You are in College Station, Billy is at Galveston, Brent is at home driving over to [nearby] Alvin, and I'm at Austin. We're all going to graduate from college in a year or so. I'll be going to medical school. This might be the last time we get everybody together."

"You mean our last summer at home?" Bradley asked.

"Yeah."

"Then we'd better make this summer a good one," Bradley laughed, reaching across to punch Mark on the arm. "Santa Fe is going to know we were there."

"Listen, I heard about a new way to go through Houston that will cut miles off the trip," Mark said, giving instructions.

"I don't recognize any of this," Bradley said, as unfamiliar landmarks swept by.

"Don't worry, I know where I'm going," was Mark's confident reply. "Dad showed me this route."

Within a matter of minutes, the two were completely lost.

They were more than an hour late getting home when they finally pulled into town at 7:30 that night.

The rural community of Santa Fe, just southeast of Houston, still retains the aura of small-town America although it lies in the shadow of a major metropolis. Worthy of a Norman Rockwell canvas, Santa Fe has one main strip through town, lots of wide-open spaces for children to explore, mom-and-pop restaurants and groceries, and a general sense of isolation from the turmoil which usually accompanies city life. Crime in Santa Fe is typical of most small towns; there is not much traffic and not much trouble of any kind. It's just a good place to grow up and learn those treasured American values.

The Kilroy family—Jim, Helen, Mark, and Keith—had lived in the Santa Fe community for fifteen years in a modest brick and wood home tucked away on five acres where Jim keeps a few cows, goats, chickens, and his prized garden. They moved there from Illinois, where Jim spent his childhood watching the outskirts of Chicago turn from farmland into suburbs. Helen grew up in the city of Cicero, located only six miles from downtown Chicago. Both attended Catholic schools in their hometowns. Jim courted Helen for three-and-a-half years. They married in 1967 shortly before he earned his degree in chemical engineering at the University of Illinois. Mark was born a year later, and Keith arrived twenty-one months after his brother's birth.

During their early years of marriage, Jim's employment called for extensive travel. At first the family accompanied him on each trip. But when Mark reached school age, the family settled in Santa Fe, Texas, and soon became part of local church and community activity.

Jim, forty-five, has worked twenty-eight years for UOP as a technical advisor at numerous refineries and plants which dot the Southeast Texas coastal area, West Texas, and New Mexico. On occasion he travels outside the United States to troubleshoot or to teach a technical school.

Helen, forty-four, is a homemaker who has worked as a hometown volunteer paramedic for the past five years. For a time, Helen was a public school volunteer to help children develop skills in reading and math. She also taught religious education classes at Our Lady of Lourdes Catholic Church.

Mark, a handsome, blond six-footer, was the kind of clean-cut, sober young man who had never been in serious trouble of any kind in his life. He had his feet on the ground and his nose in his books, eager to eventually earn the coveted title of medical doctor. After graduation in 1986, Mark spent one semester at Southwest Texas State University in San Marcos, where he made the dean's list. He transferred to Tarleton State University in Stephenville when offered an academic scholarship and a chance to play basketball. But after two years there, Mark decided he should give up college athletics and transfer to the University of Texas in Austin to concentrate on his pre-med studies.

Younger brother Keith, nineteen, is also a college student, but is living at home. The popular honor student plans to become an accountant.

The Kilroy family attends Mass regularly at Our Lady of Lourdes Catholic Church, in the nearby town of Hitchcock, just a few minutes down the road from Santa Fe. From time to time, the family shares its home with foster children from Catholic Charities.

In March 1989, theirs was an idyllic American family, unaware that tragedy was just a half-step away. Keith had asked that his mother keep Mark home until he had a chance to visit with him.

"It's been four weeks since I've seen him," he said in a telephone call from school. "Tell him not to leave until I get there."

Keith also had another motive. He had just purchased a used bright red sports car, and he was anxious to show it to his brother. In November Keith had been involved in an automobile accident that nearly claimed his life. Although it had been four months since the accident, Keith's battered body was just beginning to spring back from the serious surgery.

Mark knew that the past few months had been difficult on his brother, whose injuries had forced the young man to confront the reality of death. Always close, the brothers had been drawn even closer after the accident.

So, it was no surprise when adventuresome Mark had called one spring day to invite Keith to join him and a friend on a snow skiing trip the weekend of March 5.

"You can help me celebrate my birthday," Mark suggested to Keith. "I'll be twenty-one years old. It's my treat. You come on up and stay with me and we'll go."

"I'm afraid I might break something open," Keith said, his body still aching from the surgery. "And if I did, Mom would really be mad—at both of us."

"You don't have to ski. You can just go up with us to celebrate," Mark pressed on.

"No, I don't think I'm up to it," Keith had said.

But when he hung up the telephone, Keith paused to reflect upon his brother's offer. One of Mark's friends had told the younger brother that as he lay under the surgeon's knife following the accident, Mark had said, "I don't think my brother will ever know how much I love him."

Keith smiled as he thought of his secret: *You'll never know that I know.*

Helen was not surprised when Mark began unloading bags of dirty laundry out of Bradley's car shortly after the two arrived that Friday night.

"I need to get these washed and dried before I leave," Mark said, holding up several pairs of pants as Bradley drove away to visit his family.

This was a rare reunion for the Kilroys, because Jim's job kept him on the road much of the time, and Mark was in college in Austin. All four family members seldom were together except for special events such as the previous Christmas.

At that time, Keith, the family mechanic, had finally gotten Mark's old car to run. When the holiday season ended, Mark had been gone about thirty minutes on his return to Austin when the telephone rang.

"This is your son. I'm back from the dead," Mark began the conversation.

A tire had blown out only a few miles from home, and his vehicle had swerved violently to the right, nearly clipping the rear of an automobile in the next lane.

"I'm lucky I didn't get killed," he said.

One of the lug bolts had frozen on the rim, so Helen had to drive him back to Austin.

Mark returned home February 12 for a family outing to the National Basketball Association All Star game in Houston.

"It might be the only time I'll get to see some of these famous basketball players on one court," Mark told his dad.

Mark's last visit with his family was a spur-of-the-moment decision. At first he and Bradley had planned to drive straight to South Padre Island from Austin, but they changed their plans so they could meet Brent and Billy in Santa Fe.

Helen began washing the laundry as Mark and his dad settled in, waiting for Keith to join them.

"Dad, when I come back Wednesday I'll practice up for the golf tournament, and if you can get home in time, we'll play," Mark suggested. "You, Keith, and I can practice together."

"That sounds good to me," Jim said, looking forward to the two-man tournament with Mark the next weekend.

Keith came in and the three firmed up the golf date before the brothers took Keith's car for a spin. After a few minutes of idle small talk, the two discussed their plans to share an apartment next year when Keith would also be attending the University of Texas at Austin. When the brothers returned, Helen brought out a birthday cheesecake—Mark's favorite—with one single candle to mark his twenty-first birthday on March 5 the week before.

"Why don't you four consider sleeping in tonight and leaving in the morning?" she suggested.

"It's okay, Mom," Mark smiled. "We won't fall asleep and we'll be careful driving."

"Are you sure that's what you want to do?" Jim asked. "Maybe you want to get some sleep and leave in the morning."

It was not long before Bradley returned with Brent to pick up Mark.

To help the boys get on the road, Helen packed Mark's clean clothes straight from the dryer, carefully folding several pairs of damp pants which had not had time to completely dry.

Bradley remembered that he did not have a pair of black socks. Jim solved that by lending him a pair.

Keith hugged Mark goodbye.

"Have a good time down there," he said.

"Make sure that the guy in the front seat with the driver stays awake," Jim said, unable to resist one last warning.

"Give me a call," Helen asked Mark as they embraced.

"It's not easy to find a phone on the beach," Mark teased.

But you and I both know you will call, Helen thought to herself. Mark hugged his dad.

"Be careful," Jim admonished.

"Love you, man," Mark said to his dad.

"Love you, little buddy," Jim replied in his best Skipper's voice from "Gilligan's Island."

Mark turned back to his mother.

"I love you, Mark," Helen said, then kissed her son. It was the way they always parted.

"Love you, too, Mom," Mark said as he walked into the dark night.

The three set out in Brent Martin's Cutlass to pick up Billy, who was not ready to leave. It was after midnight when the four traveling companions began the long drive to the southernmost tip of Texas, a legendary land of good times along the Mexican border.

Fog slowed the friends' journey as they followed the meandering Texas coastline down two-lane highways through small towns similar to Santa Fe. As Billy and Mark slept in the backseat, Bradley helped Brent peer through the dense fog which at times cut visibility to only a few feet past the hood of the car. Later, refreshed after a nap, Mark regaled the three with stories about a trip to Australia where the Kilroy family had ridden in a vehicle called a Moke.

"Not likely," Bradley laughed, convinced that his friend was teasing them with yet another tall tale.

The poor driving conditions delayed their arrival until mid-morning, and when they stepped out of the car on Padre Island, they found that the gigantic party was just beginning.

Weariness was washed away by youthful adrenaline and a quick shower after they checked into the Sheraton Hotel on the island. Anxious to hit the beaches, mischievous Mark ended Billy's long, hot shower by dousing him with a bucket of ice water.

When the quartet stepped onto the beach that Saturday morning, Mark James Kilroy had finally arrived at his long-anticipated spring break—and the beginning of his special place in history.

The day was a blur of activity. The men watched the Miss Tanline contest, then relaxed on lounge chairs beside a pool. Mark and Bradley used free telephone service to phone home. Bradley talked to his mother, but there was no answer in the Kilroy home.

The two buddies browsed through a few shops before spotting a pair of sunglasses.

"Those are for me," Mark said.

"No, they're just right for me," Bradley shot back.

Mark grabbed them.

"I'll take these," he told the clerk.

"I don't think he will," Bradley smiled, before turning to Mark. "You forgot your money. It's in the room. Remember? I had to loan you a buck."

"You can always go get your money and buy a pair," the helpful clerk suggested.

"No. I wouldn't wear a pair of sunglasses like he would wear," Mark teased.

Late that night, as the weary men were returning to their room, they discovered that girls from Purdue University were sharing the room next door, so the party continued until nearly dawn.

They finally caught some sleep before hitting the beach to soak up a few rays. Next, the daily Miss Tanline Contest could not be passed up, so it was top priority right after lunch. Then there would be a few more rays, a little flirting, and a short nap to revive them for that night's entertainment—a trip across the border.

The crowd at South Padre traditionally drives the twenty or so miles each evening to the Texas-Mexico border at Brownsville to cross into the Mexican city of Matamoros, famous for night life, cheap drinks, and good Mexican food. A strip on the main street, not far from the International Bridge over the Rio Grande, is lined with small shops, bars, and restaurants up one side and down the other. Each night during spring break this boulevard is wall-to-wall humanity, mostly college students; a few high school teens blend into the crowd, too.

The foursome from Santa Fe was among the throng that Sunday night. On their way they had stopped at a fast-food restaurant in Port Isabel and noticed a group of girls from the University of Kansas.

"Go talk to them," Billy urged Mark.

"Go on," Brent and Bradley joined in.

Mark looked at them.

"You want me to go get the girls?" he asked.

"Sure," Bradley challenged.

Mark considered it a second, opened the door, and walked over to the girls' car. Within a matter of minutes it was decided to party together, so the women followed the men on the twisting, two-lane highway that cuts across the tip of Texas to Brownsville, where they parked in a lot on the U.S. side of the border.

The group walked across the bridge into Mexico, strolling along the street until they spied a club called Sergeant Pepper's about half a block off the main drag. They partied until the clubs closed at 2:00 A.M. and then returned to their hotels on South Padre Island to recuperate.

Monday was the kind of brilliant day that memories are made of. No clouds blocked the sun's rays; the sky was bright and clear, and you could see for miles across the blue Gulf of Mexico as the waves gently rippled ashore. The full spring-break crowd had hit, and nearly every grain of sand supported a sun worshiper, many of them young beauties in skimpy bikinis.

Looking out from their sixth-floor balcony, it was a sight to behold. But why look when you can be a part of it all? Spring break is a prolonged social event. As the four young men followed the crowd up and down the beach they kept bumping into former high school friends from Santa Fe, former fraternity brothers Mark had known at Tarleton State, and Bradley's fraternity brothers from Texas A&M. It was a day of reunion.

Later that afternoon, when Bradley and Mark decided to pick up pizza, Mark once again had no money.

"Pay the man and let's go," Bradley told Mark as he picked up the box.

Mark reached in one pocket and then the other, and finally turned them inside out.

"I left the money in the room," he said, grinning at Bradley.

By the time they got back with the money, the pizza was only warm; but no matter, they would eat it when they got to the room— after stopping at a convenience store to stock up on beer, soft drinks, and snacks which Mark was going to buy with a credit card.

"Pay the man and let's go," Bradley said a second time.

But Mark had forgotten his credit card when he picked up his money for the pizza—and he had left his I.D. back in their room, too.

"Not again," Bradley said, breaking into laughter before adding a humorous threat, "I'm going to let you put everything back."

"We'll go back to the hotel and get my wallet," Mark insisted.

"Anything you say," Bradley laughed.

By now Mark had joined in the mirth. What the heck, it's spring break, why let a little thing like money or credit cards spoil the fun.

By the time they ate the pizza, it was as cold as their drinks.

Adolfo de Jesus Constanzo was also enjoying the clear blue skies and brilliant sun, basking in its rays poolside at the Holiday Inn in Brownsville.

Although drug smuggling provided the money, it was the occult that was his key to power, both in Matamoros and Mexico City. His ability to convince the superstitious that he could divine the future, coupled with his handsome, dark good looks, allowed Constanzo to walk among the rich and famous in the capital city where he maintained a home. Only twenty-six years old, he was habitually consulted by society matrons, entertainers, and even Mexican politicians for his "special ability" to peer into the future. On occasion, even a law-enforcement official or military general would ask Constanzo to entreat his *Santería orishas*, or saints, to allow them a peek into the future through *Obi*, the use of broken bits of coconut shells, or *Diloggún*, the use of cowrie shells. His alleged power to tell the future was a tool that he used with uncanny cunning in controlling others.

His band of drug smugglers was convinced that Constanzo was omnipotent because of his special relationship to the *orishas*, the deities of *Santería* and *Palo Mayombe*. He had carefully forged this diverse group of believers into a quasi-family unit through bloody ritualistic orgies of animal and human sacrifice. He maintained that kinship through a combination of fear and superstition. To each of the men who served him, Constanzo was only slightly below the gods himself.

He claimed to have power to pull spirits from the air, and they believed him. He also claimed the ability to control the spirits of the human sacrificial victims buried behind the shanty that had become the group's occult temple. These spirits were his spies, he said, flying through the air with impunity, their eyes ever watchful, ever on the actions of the true believer.

Easter was the traditional time to replenish the sagging power in the *nganga*, the mystical cast-iron pot that held a warrior spirit Constanzo claimed to manipulate through the rituals of *Palo Mayombe*. Human blood was needed to nourish it and a human brain was needed to revitalize its ability to think, Constanzo believed.

After spending the day at the pool with Sara Aldrete, Constanzo called five men to his room that night. As Sara looked on, the men assembled: Serafin Hernandez Garcia, Jr., twenty, Elio's nephew from Houston; Ovidio Hernandez Rivera, twenty-six, Elio's brother; Sergio Martinez Salinas, twenty-three; Malio Ponce Torres, twenty, and David Serna Valdez, twenty-two, all of Matamoros.

Constanzo understood that death was an ultimate bond among men, since all men die. He knew that, other than love, death is perhaps the strongest element in forging the attitude of men, and he used this basic fear of death to enslave his followers.

All religions focus on death in some way. Christians see it as the last step separating man from God and eternal salvation. Modern believers of Stone-Age religions see it as a means to an end while alive, and simply an end, upon death. There is no reward, no punishment, but perhaps a reawakening should the dead man's spirit be called from the chains of the cemetery to serve a *palero* such as Constanzo.

More importantly, Constanzo understood that a man who controls death, or says he does, controls living men through the legendary power of the devil.

That night in the Holiday Inn, Constanzo looked at the sign of the evil one—*Kadiempembe*—tattooed on his right arm before returning the rapt gaze of his followers.

"Bring me a young, anglo spring breaker who is studying at the university," he ordered softly, looking at the men who already understood that the victim must be male, as had been all the others. "The brain will give the *nganga* more strength to help it think clearly. With more strength it will protect us from harm."

"He will bring us good luck and intelligence."

Early evening found Mark and his friends at a condominium party hosted by some of his former fraternity pals from Tarleton State.

Later when talk turned to going back to Matamoros, the four young men held a powwow. Brent was not feeling well and did not want to go back to Matamoros, nor did Billy; but both realized that was where the girls would be. Bradley wanted to go for another night of fun, and Mark was ready to go along with the majority. For the drive over, the four picked up Zac Creech, a friend of Mark's from Tarleton State.

Once again they negotiated the twisting twenty miles to Brownsville, leaving South Padre Island to drive across a two-mile bridge over the Laguna Madre onto the Texas mainland at the base of the historic Port Isabel lighthouse. Mark drove as they worked their way through the busy tourist district and onto the normally lonely road that leads to the Mexican border at Brownsville. But that night the twisting, two-lane highway could barely contain the vehicles— trucks, cars, vans, virtually anything that moved—as the caravan of high-spirited students wound its way across coastal plains that produced the legendary Texas longhorn. A few miles out of Brownsville the crazy-quilt pattern of hundreds of ships' masts loomed against a moonlit sky.

A celestial marvel set the northern sky aglow that night. The aurora borealis, also known as the northern lights, was creating quite a stir in South Texas. National Weather Service forecaster Jack

Stewart was fielding anxious telephone calls from people who thought a large fire was burning somewhere on the horizon.

"I never heard of it being seen this far south before," Stewart said. "It is an extremely rare event for the southern latitude of the United States. In fact, it would be a quintessential once-in-a-lifetime event," he would be quoted on the front page of a newspaper the next day.

When the revelers shot past a railhead of more than a hundred railroad cars, the winding road straightened somewhat as it took the students past storage tanks where oil and gas are shipped through the Port of Brownsville.

Billboards began to pop up in English and Spanish, touting the pleasures of Mexico. One poignant sign urged runaways to telephone an 800 number for help. Just before crossing the city limits into Brownsville, one large billboard advertised Garcia's, one of the largest curio shops in Matamoros.

As they did the night before, the friends parked Brent's automobile on the American side and walked across the International Bridge into the tourist district of Matamoros.

That Monday night would be much of a replay of Sunday—lots of fun, drinking, and dancing with the girls.

Their first stop was Los Sombreros, a rather benign-looking bar that had a reputation (unknown to spring breakers) as a favorite drinking spot for drug smugglers.

Mark's easygoing personality soon engaged the interest of a table of girls who giggled and flirted with the students. The men drank beer and danced until the bar got boring. Then, they plunged into the living stream of partiers on Avenida Alvaro Obregon. Deeper into Matamoros, they eventually stopped at The London Pub which was patterned after the Hard Rock Cafe restaurants, and had even taken the name Hard Rock Cafe for spring break.

The four men took a table near the center of the bar, then Mark and Billy joined some girls on the dance floor. Within a matter of minutes, Bradley and Brent were dodging beer bottles dropped through a hole in the second floor by high-spirited students.

"Look at that," Brent pointed with the nod of his head at smashed glass scattered all over the floor.

"This could get dangerous," Bradley added. Both decided it was best to stand by the bar and nurse their drinks. Two days with little sleep had taken its toll on Brent, who was feeling worse.

Billy spent most of the evening on the dance floor, while Mark joked with the party of women, occasionally dancing, until Miss Tanline showed up, a beauty in a brown dress. Mark devoted the remainder of the evening to her.

At one point during the evening, Zac checked in with the four buddies to say he was leaving with a group of Tarleton State friends.

Two straight days of partying with little sleep finally hit Billy Huddleston, too. He looked at his watch. It was a little after 1 A.M., time to head back for a little rest.

About that time, Mark walked outside with Miss Tanline.

"Let's go," Billy called out to Brent and Bradley.

At the door, the three spotted Mark leaning against a Volkswagen talking to Miss Tanline.

Serafin, one of Constanzo's gang members, watched the three men come out of the bar and approach Mark. He had spotted Mark when he came out of the club with Miss Tanline. The appearance of the three men frustrated Serafin. They would make it more difficult for him to get to his intended victim. Twice before he had selected a sacrifice that night only to lose him. He had carefully chosen the first victim, then stalked him and was about to make his approach, when the youth had turned and walked swiftly away to join his friends. The crowd had swirled around the unsuspecting victim to become a safety net of human bodies that made pursuit impossible.

The second time Serafin had selected a quarry, he pulled the pickup into position to grab the victim, but a car cut him off and the man walked away, unaware that he had just escaped death.

There was nothing in Serafin's benign demeanor that would send out danger signals to his victim. A chubby, unmarred baby face accented by a neatly clipped mustache, downcast eyes, a soft voice, a submissive, even helpful behavior, all hide a personality that is capable of diabolic deeds.

Serafin would not fail the third time. This time he would seize the opportunity and not let fate stop him. The bars were closing and he did not want to disappoint the *Padrino*.

Nodding his head toward Mark, Serafin looked at Malio Ponce Torres, riding shotgun in the pickup.

"That's our spring breaker," he said.

Malio grinned. He knew that Mark's handsome, blond good looks would please the *Padrino*.

Mark was wearing a black, short-sleeve, button-up shirt atop light-colored pants with alternating stripes of black, brown, and tan, and a gray belt. Black socks and lace-up shoes completed the ensemble. Accessories included a gold-rope chain around his neck and a gold watch given to the student by his grandfather.

Billy, Brent, and Bradley stepped from the building into a whirlpool of partying students on Avenida Alvaro Obregon, making their way across the street to Mark. It was difficult to negotiate the few feet because the thirty-thousand-plus students who had been crammed into the district were now beginning to make their way back to the border in the final frenzy of celebration. Some wanted just one more drink before the thirty-minute ride back to South Padre Island. Many, like Mark and Miss Tanline, were exchanging addresses with new-found friends and arranging to meet again.

Miss Tanline's girlfriends joined her and the men left. Heading back toward the border was like swimming with the tide. As wave after wave of students surged down the street, the four friends became separated by a few feet and fell into unplanned pairs with Bradley and Brent leading the way.

Behind the men, Serafin eased his pickup truck into the traffic, keeping pace with them.

Billy and Mark fell even further behind in the press of the crowd and the other two stopped briefly to wait for them on the edge of the vendors' park north of Garcia's Gift Shop, a large curio store within sight of the International Bridge. They paused for a few seconds, expecting Billy and Mark to catch up to them. When they did not, Bradley and Brent started watching the swarming crowd for their pals, but could not see them.

Serafin kept his pickup even with Billy and Mark, awaiting his chance.

Although he had had little to drink that night, it was obvious that Billy had had enough partying.

"Something wrong?" Mark had asked Billy as they started back to the car. It was not the first time Mark had inquired. Several times he had approached Billy during the evening to ask if he was feeling ill.

"I'm just tired," Billy said, rubbing his head. "I'm just not in a partying mood any more."

As they walked along Billy felt the need to urinate. He ducked into the shadows to relieve himself, but not before he saw a dark figure say something to Mark. Billy's first instinct was that Mark— who, as they say, never met a stranger—knew the person who approached him.

Spring break fosters a sense of brotherhood that is fueled by the giddy exhilaration of youth and sparked by free-flowing spirits. Everyone talks to everyone else. Students from Maine to California and back to Florida all seem to share a common bond. Honors students mingle with those barely passing, all sharing a collective empathy; everyone needs a break from the grind of studies. So, on spring break there are no strangers, just fellow sojourners on the road to diversion.

"Hey man, don't I know you? Do you need a ride?" Serafin leaned across the pickup seat to call out to Mark in English.

Mark paused for a split second, walking out of the mass of humanity to the pickup.

"We'll give you a ride to the border," Serafin added.

"No, man," Mark replied. "My friends are just up the street waiting for me."

"We'll give them a ride, too," Serafin said. "We'll give you a ride up to them and then take all of you across the border."

"No, I don't think so," Mark replied before he was shoved into the truck. Serafin eased the pickup past Mark's friends and around a nearby corner into the cover of a side street, Las Rosas.

They finally had their victim, and it had only taken a matter of seconds.

When Billy came back just minutes later, Mark was gone. He had vanished from sight. Billy called up ahead to the other men, but they hadn't seen anything happen.

At two o'clock in the morning, in the middle of a swirling press of thousands of potential witnesses, Mark Kilroy had disappeared, as if off the face of the earth—and no one had seen anything.

BOOK TWO

THE
SEARCH

THE
SEARCH

FIRST WEEK

Tuesday

Immediately the three young men began looking for Mark, and finally decided he must have somehow gone ahead to the bridge and the safety of the United States.

When Mark failed to show up at the parking lot, his friends became alarmed. Brent and Bradley stayed at the bridge to scan the students flowing north. Billy went back into Mexico, back into the lighthearted, swirling arena of celebration that by now was beginning to thin.

At first he searched with confidence, thinking Mark might have met Miss Tanline again and stopped to talk. Or perhaps he was with his fraternity buddies from Tarleton State, although it was unlike him to leave without talking to his friends first. Billy backtracked the evening, going to Los Sombreros and then to the Hard Rock.

Nothing.

He retraced their steps, stopping at each spot. He was convinced that Mark would not just step into a bar without telling any of them; but Billy checked each bar anyway. Then he headed back into the streets, looking up every alley—perhaps Mark had gotten sick. He checked every restroom on the way. And all the while he was fighting the crush of the crowd. What once had been a carefree throng to Billy was now a twisting, ugly barrier that slowed his search. But he kept looking, even when he wondered if Mark could be waiting back at the car. Long after the bars had closed down and the streets had cleared of celebrating students, he searched.

Nothing.

21

In desperation, Billy found a fellow Texas A&M student from Brownsville who knew the streets of Matamoros and agreed to drive him through the area for one last look around. At four o'clock in the morning Avenida Alvaro Obregon was no longer a street of merriment. It was empty, with only the debris of celebration trashing the curbs. The bars were vacant; most of them had closed down. There were not even any stragglers to ask about Mark. The two talked to a police officer who used his car radio to check with the dispatcher to see if Mark had been picked up.

Nothing.

Driving up one street and down another proved fruitless, so Billy decided to return to the border. The hotel, someone suggested. So the three friends drove the long miles back to the Sheraton. Maybe Mark had gotten a ride with someone. But he was not there. As unlikely as it seemed, they searched the island, driving the streets and looking into any restaurant that might be open.

Nothing.

Finally they went back to the hotel around five o'clock in the morning, and waited, hoping Mark would turn up.

The three bleakly watched the dawn wash away the night. The beach, the laughter, the early-morning sun breaking above the brilliant blue of the Gulf of Mexico now seemed sinister; Mark was still gone.

They finally drifted off into fretful sleep. When Bradley woke up, he looked at the ceiling.

"Man, let him be there," he said to himself before turning on his side to look at the other bed. All he saw was Billy, asleep; Mark's spot was still empty.

It was 2:00 P.M. and a terrible dread began to build in Bradley as fear washed over him.

Something terrible has happened, he thought, fighting down the panic.

They tried to develop a plan of action.

"Where's Mark?" Billy said, inviting each to offer a possible solution. He could be with his buddies from Tarleton State or UT or friends from Santa Fe, or he could be with Miss Tanline. Those would be the best possible solutions.

"But he would never leave without telling one of us," Bradley insisted. "We've been friends too long for him to just take off."

"Or he could have been arrested and put in jail," Brent offered.

They decided to go to the police, and to the American consulate in Matamoros.

They ran into Zac outside the hotel. He had not seen Mark since he left Mexico early the night before.

Their next stop was the International Bridge where they sought help at the Mexican entry. For the first time they had to face the harsh reality of a foreign country where the laws and social mores are different. To their surprise, they discovered they did not even know how to use a telephone in Mexico; they could not figure it out.

"Let's go, we'll find the consulate," Brent suggested. After aimlessly wandering, they found the consulate by chance. But the guard, who spoke no English, would not let them enter.

"I can't believe this," Bradley said. "All we want to do is go in."

Billy spoke a little Spanish. Combining that with English and sign language, he finally persuaded the guard to let him inside. The other two men watched through a window for forty-five minutes before they were allowed inside also.

"Don't worry. He's probably in jail or drunk somewhere or he's run off with some girl," vice consul Michael O'Keefe told Billy. It would become a refrain they would hear over and over.

"Don't worry."

How could they keep from worrying? Their friend was missing. He had disappeared, yet the incident was being treated as if it were a rather common occurrence. Consulate officials assured the men they would check the jails and hospitals.

"We've already called a couple of places and he's not there," O'Keefe told them.

"What does that mean?" Bradley asked.

"Maybe nothing. Sometimes they don't know who is in the jails, so we'll keep calling and checking. You go on back to the hotel," O'Keefe suggested.

All afternoon they looked again, retracing their steps. Dejected by the futile search, the three men were crossing back into the United States when a reporter from the *Brownsville Herald* stopped them for a student-on-the-street interview to be included in a page-one feature story on spring breakers.

"How are you enjoying spring break?" Lisa Baker asked.

"Not too good," was Billy's reply. "We lost our friend last night."

The three poured out their story. They were at least comforted by the thought that an article in the next day's edition of the newspaper would alert fellow spring breakers to their plight.

The South Padre Island police were solicitous, but of little help. Matamoros is in a foreign country and certainly out of their jurisdiction. A helpful officer suggested they contact the Cameron County Sheriff's Office, which at least had jurisdiction in Brownsville.

"And don't worry," the officer told them. "I'm sure he's just in jail in Mexico."

That afternoon in Santa Fe Helen looked out the window at Mark's car, gleaming in the sunlight. He would be delighted to find it waxed and shiny when he returned the next day, a surprise from a loving mother who had spent the previous Sunday afternoon working on it. Keith had repaired the wheel lug which stripped when Mark had guided the car to safety after the blowout at Christmas. It was finally ready for him to take back to college.

About 10:30 P.M. Tuesday, Billy Huddleston made the dreaded call to the Kilroys.

When he answered the phone, Keith immediately sensed that something was wrong, although Billy tried to hide his anguish by acting as if everything was normal.

"What's wrong?" were Keith's first words upon hearing Billy's voice.

"Let me talk to your dad," Billy said.

"He's not here."

"Then let me talk to your mom," Billy replied.

Alarmed, Keith called his mother, his mind racing through possibilities: maybe Mark had been hurt in an accident, or broke a limb or . . . the possibilities were endless. There was a tremble in Billy's voice which convinced Keith that something was terribly wrong.

Brent and Bradley watched Billy take a deep breath to steady his voice as Helen came on the telephone.

"We went into Mexico last night and Mark is missing," he came straight to the point.

Keith saw his mother stagger as she gasped.

"What's wrong?" he demanded.

Dazed, Helen looked at him, still almost uncomprehending.

"Mark's missing. Billy says he's disappeared."

Billy continued, "We had gone to some clubs and were on our way back to the bridge. He just disappeared, Mrs. Kilroy," he told Mark's mother.

"What do you mean, just disappeared?" Helen probed.

"Just that. He just disappeared," Billy stressed before continuing. "It was really crowded, and we tried to stay close together in the crowd. I got ahead of Mark. I looked back and saw someone talking to him. I thought Mark knew him. I ducked into an alley and a few minutes later I tried to find Mark and he was gone," he said. "We just haven't been able to find him."

"Did you go to the police?" she asked, struggling to maintain her composure.

"We went everywhere. We've been to the American Consulate in Matamoros. We reported it to the South Padre Island police. We've looked all day long and we can't find him. But we think it would be best if you called the consulate so they'll take us seriously," he continued. "We want them to know this is serious."

This can't be happening, Helen thought, although outwardly she appeared calm. Slowly her mind began to shake the cobwebs of shock as Billy talked. With that clarity came the chilling realization that Mark could be badly hurt or . . . she didn't want to think it, but it was an instinctive intrusion:

Mark could be dead!

She concentrated on what Billy was saying, trying to sort it all out in her mind. She was still too stunned to cry. The thought of Mark being lost in Mexico was chilling. Neither she nor Jim had given any thought to the possibility that the young men might venture into Mexico.

Billy explained that a story would be in the newspaper. He gave Helen the telephone numbers at the Sheraton and the consulate.

"Call me as soon as you hear anything," she instructed her son's friend.

"One of us will stay by the telephone," Billy promised.

It was March 14, 1989. All three of the college students sensed that their lives would never be the same again.

In Santa Fe Helen hung up the telephone, fighting to keep her composure. She held back her tears as she quickly sketched what had happened to a questioning Keith before fear mingled with a mother's anguish swept over her.

Anger filled Keith as he comforted his mother. Frustration. Disbelief. *If Mark had not gone into Mexico this would not have happened,* he thought. (He would later learn that anger is one of the first emotions at tragic news.) With great effort the teen brought his turbulent emotions under control. He had to comfort his mother. Together, they called Jim, who was on an assignment in the West Texas oil town of Big Spring.

Jim Kilroy:

"Jim, this is really terrible. Mark is missing," is all Helen could get out before she started crying.

Mark is missing!

Those words seared into my brain.

"What do you mean?"

How could Mark be missing? We had been with him just a few days ago. We knew where he was. He was staying at the Sheraton on South Padre Island. Brent, Bradley, and Billy had gone with him. Logic told me where Mark was, but the emotional distress in Helen's voice told me more than mere words could ever say.

Helen outlined her conversation with Billy. She also told me that Billy said we should contact the consulate in Matamoros. That made sense to me.

The Mexican police are notorious for grabbing spring breakers and throwing them into jail. After a few days the students—and their parents—will do anything to get them out. It is an easy explanation, but when it's your son who is missing, there are no easy explanations.

Was Mark beaten and bleeding in some filthy jail cell? If that was so, then I wanted him out, and as soon as possible.

My thoughts were interrupted by Helen's anguished question: "Jim, what do we do?"

"I don't know, Helen. Maybe Ken will know."

I asked to speak with Keith.

"Take care of your mother."

"I will, Dad," Keith paused. "Are you okay?"

Actually, I was sort of dazed from what I had just heard. Keith must have picked up on it.

"I'm okay. I just don't know what to think. They might find Mark mugged or killed." I paused when I realized what I had just said to my younger son. It was something that just slipped out.

"Are you okay?" I asked him.

"Yeah, but I'm so mad," Keith said. "Why did Mark have to go down there?"

"I don't know, son," I answered.

It was the most helpless feeling I had ever known. I didn't know what to do. Maybe my brother would have some suggestions.

"We'd better get off the telephone so Mom can call Uncle Ken."

It was a long, painful night for the family.

When Helen reached Ken Kilroy, an agent with U.S. Customs and Jim's brother, he pledged to use all his law-enforcement connections to start the hunt for his nephew.

"Don't worry," Ken told Helen. "We'll find him."

Later that night Ken, who is Mark's godfather, called Jim and suggested that Helen put a tape recorder on the telephone. Before hanging up he told Jim, "I'm sure they're going to find Mark in jail in Matamoros."

Keith called Tom Davis, the father of his friend Will. A year before, Davis and the boys had discussed the potential dangers that await visiting students in Mexico, and now, his fears had been realized.

"What do we do, Mr. Davis?" was Keith's plea to the man who was familiar with the border area.

Davis suggested that Keith and Helen contact the U.S. Border Patrol, police in Matamoros and Brownsville, the American consulate, and the district attorney's office on both sides of the border.

"And Keith," he cautioned. "You may need to get a Mexican

attorney and have him obtain Mark's release. Do not argue about the amount of the fine once they decide on it."

Helen telephoned the Border Patrol, a division of the U.S. Immigration Service.

"I'm sorry, ma'am, but there's nothing we can do. It's out of our jurisdiction," the dispatcher said after Helen explained the situation. But he volunteered, "Let me call the Brownsville police; maybe they can be of help."

Within minutes the compassionate dispatcher called back with telephone numbers and a disturbing message: "The Brownsville police said they don't have any contact with the Matamoros police. You have to call Matamoros."

It was the family's first forage into complicated territorial conflicts between city, state, and federal agencies in the United States and the even more drastic strife between law-enforcement agencies in the two countries.

"It won't do any good to call Mexico if they can't speak English," Helen reasoned with Keith.

"Why don't you call the Brownsville police and ask?"

The dispatcher assured her that the Matamoros police would have an officer on duty who was proficient in English. He also suggested that Helen call the American Consulate in the morning.

"Bueno," the dispatcher in Matamoros answered.

"Do you speak English?"

A pause.

"Bueno."

"I'm sorry, I don't speak Spanish. Does anyone speak English?"

A burst of rapid-fire Spanish jarred her already-jangled nerves before the line went dead.

"Let me try, Mom," Keith suggested. "Maybe I can use my Spanish to get through to them."

Keith was ready when the dispatcher answered.

"*¿Habla inglés?*"

"No," was the terse reply.

Keith plunged on in broken Spanish.

"*Mi hermano,*" he started, searching for just the right word. "*¡Mi hermano, no está aquí.*"

No, that's not it, he thought. I just told them he's not here. What's the verb for lost? Perdido. That's it!

"*¡Mi hermano, perdido!*" Keith said before repeating. "*Mi hermano, en México es perdido.*"

Does anyone know anything about Mark Kilroy? Have they ever heard the name Mark Kilroy? Could anyone help me find out what's happened to him?

While he struggled to put his English thoughts into Spanish words the connection went dead.

"They hung up on me," he stormed, redialing.

This time he did not even get his explanation out before the telephone went dead again. Keith started to redial when Helen gently put her hand on his.

"There's no sense in it."

Bleakly they looked at each other. It was past midnight.

"We've called everyone Mr. Davis suggested," Helen said, her emotions battered by frustration and helplessness. As the three students had discovered in Brownsville, options are extremely limited and virtually nonexistent when coupled with a language barrier.

"We might as well go to bed," she added. "There's nothing else we can do until in the morning."

It would be a sleepless night for the worried Kilroy family. As Jim lay in his motel bed in Big Spring, he prayed: "God, please take care of Mark, no matter where he is."

Other prayers were whispered that night from beds in Santa Fe. It was the family's first step on a long, lonely journey that would take them through the valley of the shadow of death.

Wednesday

Newspaper editors decided to hold the Kilroy story out of the Wednesday-afternoon edition of the *Brownsville Herald* because it was possible that the student might show up.

John Hensley, assistant regional commissioner for U.S. Customs, Pacific region, picked up the telephone to call his old friend, Oran Neck, U.S. Customs agent-in-charge in Brownsville. The two had worked together for fifteen years and Hensley knew that Oran understood the Mexican border. He had a favor to ask. A fellow Customs agent had told him that his nephew had disappeared in Matamoros. Would Oran look into the case for Ken Kilroy?

"Sure thing," Oran said, hanging up and dialing the Cameron County Sheriff's Office in Brownsville.

It is Sheriff Alex Perez's policy for every officer at the Cameron County Sheriff's Office to work on any case that comes through the door. It was Lt. George Gavito, a specialist in homicide, who answered the telephone the next morning when the South Padre Island police called on behalf of Mark's friends.

"Send them on over; maybe we can help," he said.

He no sooner hung up than the dispatcher buzzed again.

"Oran Neck with Customs," she said.

Why would Customs want me? he wondered. Perhaps they had found a body on a drug bust. It was not uncommon for Customs and the sheriff's office to work together, but other than a casual hello, Gavito had never worked with Neck. He usually worked an investigation with one of Neck's agents.

Puzzled, he picked up the telephone.

Neck went straight to the point.

"I'd like to work with you on a disappearance case," he told Gavito.

"Mark Kilroy?"

"Right. Customs has a special interest. Mark is the nephew of one of our agents in Los Angeles."

"I'll take all the help I can get," Gavito replied. He was also answering an unwritten code that officers in the law-enforcement community look after their own.

"I'll be right there," Neck said.

Within a few minutes Oran W. Neck, Jr., was seated across from George Gavito in the deputy's small, cluttered office. These two men are a Hollywood casting director's dream: fire and ice. The gregarious Hispanic towered more than six feet in his cowboy boots when he stood up to greet Neck who was nearly six-feet tall, himself.

The thirty-five-year-old Gavito was wearing dark pants, a tan button-down-collar shirt—open at the neck—and a leather western vest. A straw western hat was tossed to one side of the desk.

Neck sensed that a fiery temper bubbled just below the outgoing, easy grin that greeted the world of this Brownsville native.

Oran Neck was wearing his distinctive blue jacket emblazoned with U.S. Customs on the back. Ten years older than Gavito, he, too, is a native of Brownsville, but it is doubtful that their paths had ever crossed before due to their age difference.

Fire and ice.

The outgoing Gavito talks as much with his hands as with his booming voice; never at a loss for words, he is a convivial companion for all occasions—unless someone crosses him. In contrast, quiet, soft-spoken Oran Neck has the grace of a boxer and the moxie of a public relations agent. Seldom ruffled, his mind racing to keep track of all that surrounds him, Neck is as placid as Gavito is extroverted. Both are law-enforcement veterans. Neck, a former member of the Border Patrol, had been with U.S. Customs since 1971. Gavito had been with the sheriff's office since 1974, and for the last few years had been a lieutenant specializing in homicide.

An immediate rapport motivated the pair to combine forces. Four sheriff's deputies and six Customs agents would join in the search. The twelve-man team should bring a swift end to the investigation.

So when Bradley and Billy arrived at the sheriff's office that Wednesday morning, they found themselves across the desk from Gavito, a hulking Hispanic with a bushy black mustache and matching hair with a few flecks of silver. Sandy-haired, slightly balding Neck sat quietly nearby during the initial interview.

Brent had stayed at the hotel to field telephone calls.

The students could have ended up with any other investigator in Sheriff Alex Perez's office, but providence gave them an expert in violent death.

Why do these kids come down here and get themselves into such a mess? Gavito thought as he listened to the two pour out their story about Mark's disappearance. It was a familiar tale. Too many youngsters who are used to the freedom of their country, forget that Mexico is a land of different laws.

Spring break is especially difficult for law-enforcement officers. Each year there are adventurous American kids who go to Mexico during spring break, have a little too much to drink, draw attention to themselves, and wake up in jail. Over a five-week period hundreds of thousands of students pour into the Rio Grande Valley's normally peaceful communities for fun and frolic. Each week universities across the nation let students out for holiday, and each week a new batch of seventy thousand or more revelers converge in the Valley. By the time it all ends, half-a-million students leave behind millions of dollars in the business community; but they also leave hotels that have been trashed, and in some instances, lives that have been shattered.

If my kid ever wants to go on spring break I'll handcuff him to his bed, Gavito silently pledged.

Gavito had no doubts that he was dealing with a bona fide missing person; the two students were too sincere. But it was a routine case, one that required time-consuming telephone calls and a check of jails.

Bradley and Billy supplied them with a description of Mark and what he had been wearing the night he disappeared. They filed a missing-person report and arranged for Jim Kilroy to send a telefax photo from Santa Fe. Since Billy Huddleston had been the last to see Mark, he was the subject of a lengthy in-depth interrogation. Then there was nothing more they could do.

"Go back to the hotel," Gavito told them.

There was no cause for great alarm or a massive manhunt, he said. The student had only been missing a little less than thirty hours.

"Don't worry," he reassured them. "I'm sure he's in jail somewhere. We'll check it out."

Neck and Gavito dispatched agents into Mexico; then they immersed themselves into the search with a series of telephone calls. Although Mark's buddies had already talked with officials at the U.S. Consulate, they were contacted again by the lawman. And again, a spokesman insisted that there were no Americans in Mexican jails.

Comandante Juan Benitez Ayala, thirty-five, of the powerful Mexican Federal Judicial Police (MFJP) in Matamoros was sympathetic, but he knew nothing about Mark.

"I'll assign a couple of men to check around," he offered, although his federal police specialized in narcotic cases.

Assistant Comandante Sergio Gonzalez of the State Judicial Police (SJP) in Matamoros, the Mexican state police, had no reports on a missing anglo. He said that he would notify his commanding officer, Comandante Silvio Brusolo, that U.S. Customs agents were looking for a missing student.

The Matamoros city police took a report on the telephone, but knew nothing of a missing student. It was a shot-in-the-dark at best because the city police agency could only take a report; it had no investigatory powers. In the tangled world of Mexican law enforcement, city police were charged with keeping order while the SJP conducted most criminal investigations such as kidnapping or murder. The city police did agree to stay on the lookout for Mark.

Within a couple of hours the routine search had begun; jails and hospitals in Matamoros were being checked. The new team met later that afternoon to compare notes.

But Neck and Gavito knew that the first forty-eight hours were critical. After two days without word of the youth, years of experience told them that the chances of finding Mark alive would decrease as fast as the hours accelerated. And forty-eight hours would tick by at 2:00 A.M. that next morning.

"He's probably shacked up with some girl," Neck suggested.

"That's possible," George agreed.

That's what they wanted: an embarrassed young man and woman who had answered the call of pounding hormones. But too many years in law enforcement made them realists. They went over other possible explanations for Mark's disappearance:

- Mark could be in jail, the victim of Mexican city or state police.

- Mark could be in the hospital, beaten by robbers or Mexican police.

- Mark could be sleeping off the two days of revelry in another hotel on Padre Island, either with friends or a girl.

- Mark could have eloped in a spur-of-the-moment marriage sparked by too much alcohol.

- Mark could have been a closet homosexual who decided to go public or go live where homosexuality would be tolerated.

- Mark could have been beaten and dumped in an inaccessible place. He could be lying there dead or alive.

- Mark could be wandering around, suffering from amnesia.

- Mark could have overdosed on drugs or been involved in a drug deal gone bad.

- Mark could have simply decided to take off, to disappear as a runaway.

- Mark could have been kidnapped and taken into the interior of Mexico for slave labor.

- Mark could be dead, the victim of robbery or some branch of the Mexican police. If this were so, then his body would have been dumped in a remote area deep in Mexico.

- Mark could be dead, the victim of one or all three of his friends.

"Could Mark have been a victim of a sex crime?" Gavito mused. "No. Couldn't be. Sex is so free over there that almost anyone will do anything for a buck. There would be no reason for a sex crime."

Their major concern was that he had been a victim of an unscrupulous Matamoros police officer. All possibilities had to be considered, starting with the most obvious.

"We can't start a big manhunt without more than this," Gavito said.

"Let's give him the benefit of the doubt," Neck added. "He could show up any minute."

Lupe Limas, a retired Brownsville police officer, volunteered to check Matamoros jails. He was joined by Lupe Alderete, a U.S. Customs agent.

"I don't envy you," George said with a laugh. "There are probably three hundred or more of those spring breakers in jail over there."

Gavito found it difficult to believe that not one spring breaker was in jail, as reported by the U.S. Consulate. The law officers believed the case would be wrapped up that night, or at least the next morning. It had been only thirty hours since he disappeared, and they hoped that their speculations would remain just that.

"Don't you think we should run a background check on Mark Kilroy," Gavito asked, "just in case there's anything there?"

Neck agreed.

"And how about his three companions?" Neck added.

A worried Jim Kilroy arrived in Santa Fe that day to the relief of his frantic family. "I'm going to Brownsville," he told Helen. It would not be the first time he would make that decision during that day. His instincts told him to be on the scene; yet, all advice was against it.

"It would be better to wait and let the police work on the case. At this point you would only be in the way," his brother Ken said, passing on word from the scene: "They believe Mark is probably in jail. They expect to find him any time. Neck said he should show up late tonight or early in the morning."

Reluctantly, Jim agreed to stay by the telephone, but not before he telefaxed a recent photo of Mark as requested by Neck.

Meanwhile the investigation escalated in Brownsville.

The background check had revealed that Mark and his friends were clean as a whistle. No drug connections were evident. The people interviewed by telephone painted Mark and his buddies as responsible students with no record.

Billy and Bradley went back into Matamoros with Neck. All Billy could recall was seeing Mark talk to someone who may have had a scar on his face or a scuffed spot which could have occurred in a fist fight. He took the officers to the general area where Mark disappeared, but he could not pinpoint the spot.

Instead of hundreds, Limas and Alderete found only one student in the two main Matamoros jails. He had been held without a booking slip for more than thirty hours after tangling with a police officer, so there was no record of his incarceration. The University of Miami student faced a hundred-dollar fine. Limas informed the police chief that the student had told him that he had a hundred dollars in his wallet when he was arrested. The police chief waived the fine and a grateful student crossed back into the United States with the lawmen.

The lack of American spring breakers in jail was apparently the result of a new city policy. Complaining merchants had caused Matamoros Mayor Fernando Montemayor to instruct police to escort rowdy students to the border instead of throwing them in jail. It was the first year this tactic had been tried.

Neck decided it was time to enlist the cooperation of members of a fellow federal agency, so he went to the U.S. Consulate in Matamoros.

He knew that Mark's friends had already filed a missing persons report with the consulate, but perhaps personal contact on a professional level would help.

"We'd appreciate any help you could give us," he began, filling in Don Wells, head of the consulate. Wells politely listened to a recap of the situation, including Mark's family connection with U.S. Customs—an explanation of why another federal agency was trying to solicit support.

"Since these men are only friends, we need a family member to make the report," Wells said.

"You don't understand," Neck began, upset because his plea for intra-departmental help appeared to him to have been refused. While he did not expect preferential treatment, he did at least expect more than mere lip service.

"I understand that there is no American in jail in Matamoros that we don't know of," Wells cut him off.

"Really?" Neck's anger began to rise. "How do you know that?"

"I have an investigator," Wells countered, calling in an Hispanic woman.

"I have impeccable contacts with all the law-enforcement agencies in Mexico," she said. "I know there is no one in jail."

"That's not so!" Even Neck was surprised at his explosion. "The reason I know it's not so is that my agents just got a kid—an American citizen—out of jail who had been there for thirty hours without a booking skip," Neck continued, deliberately keeping the edge in his voice. "Now we need to press this search a little bit further."

"If you don't find him in several days, then we can get concerned," Wells countered. "It takes the Mexican authorities at least forty-eight hours to report someone."

"Well, we're concerned now." Neck shot back. "And we're going to press it."

It was a clash between diplomacy and investigation that erected a nervous curtain between the two men.

"Let the Mexican policy handle this," Wells stressed. He believed that Neck was responding to the underlying frustration in dealing with diplomacy. *He is a man of action, and time is the key right now,* Wells thought.

"Let's check again," he said as Neck left.

Frustrated, Neck met Gavito back at the sheriff's office.

"Look, we don't know anything about these boys," George began. "In homicide you have to eliminate the people who were there. Let's have someone talk to Billy Huddleston again tonight, and let's interview all three boys in the morning. We might want to put Billy under hypnosis to see what he remembers."

By the end of the workday the Kilroy boy had not been found, but Neck and Gavito were happy with the beginning of the search. All the jails and hospitals on both sides of the border had been checked to the best of their ability and law-enforcement agencies in both countries had been alerted.

The officers had little to work with. Bradley and Brent had seen nothing. Billy vaguely remembered seeing an Hispanic man talking to Mark. The suspect had some type of scar or mark on his face.

One final decision that night.

"We need the press," Neck told Gavito. "We need to get as much publicity out there as we can."

"I know. All the students that could have seen Mark will be gone in a few days," Gavito acknowledged.

"We'll get the boys and go over in the morning and get together with Lisa Baker so she can write a story for the newspaper," Oran concluded, mentioning the reporter in Brownsville.

"And I'll call Jim Kilroy," Neck suggested. "If there is no word by early Thursday morning, I think he should come down."

He paused, thinking about the case.

"From everything we've found out today, this kid doesn't fit the profile of most missing kids," Neck said. "He's from a good family, an open family. He's not the type to go into hiding."

"I see where you're going and I agree. He definitely is a missing person," Gavito said as they walked out the door.

It had been a long Wednesday for everyone. Billy and Bradley joined Brent at the hotel on South Padre Island, impatiently waiting by the telephone, and occasionally watching the festive activities on the beach.

All the reassurances from the law officers had given the Kilroys a glimmer of hope. Although they did not sleep well when they retired that Wednesday night, all three were half-way convinced that Mark would be found.

Restless, Oran Neck drove back into Matamoros, to the area where Billy had last seen Mark. He looked around at the students working their way north toward the International Bridge at the end of a hard day of fun and games. Each was a potential witness. It was going to be a long night. With a sigh he approached a couple, identified himself and held up a picture of Mark.

"Have you seen this man?"

They shook their heads no.

After several hours he checked the time. It was nearly 2:00 A.M. Mark Kilroy had been missing forty-eight hours.

That night Gavito told his wife, Lupita, "What we're going to find is an embarrassed boy."

But in the cold reality of morning, he could not help but wonder if his thoughts were merely wishful thinking or true belief.

Thursday

As hours began to slip away, the days would begin to jumble into one long series of events as the search for Mark Kilroy began to steamroll.

Jim Kilroy and his friend Eddie de la Houssaye traveled the back-roads from Santa Fe to Brownsville, stopping every couple of hours to check in with Helen. Eddie, who had worked on construction sites around the world, had volunteered to accompany his neighbor to Brownsville. His wife, Mary, is Helen's best friend. Jim was grateful for the company of the small, wiry man who is deeply tanned from hours in the sun.

"Mark would do everything he could for me, or to find me," Jim told Eddie as the miles slipped by. "I'll never stop looking until I bring him home."

By the time Jim Kilroy had left Santa Fe early Thursday morning, Neck had already picked up Lisa Baker and the photographer from the *Brownsville Herald* for a story in that afternoon's newspaper. Mark's pals were waiting for them at the International Bridge to show the journalists where Mark had disappeared.

The rest of the morning was not pleasant for Mark's buddies. Neck and Gavito interviewed the three individuals, sometimes vaguely hinting that they knew of foul play.

"I hate to be tough on these boys, but we've got to get the truth," Gavito said during a break as he and Neck sipped coffee.

"They look clean to me. Their attitude is good; their stories agree. You and I know that if you take three people, interview them separately, and then compare their stories that someone's going to slip up," Neck aired their thoughts aloud.

"And these boys haven't," Gavito added.

"They've certainly been friendly and cooperative," Neck said.

The dispatcher buzzed. Ray Martinez, a hypnotist with the Texas Department of Human Services, had arrived. The lawmen hoped that Billy's subconscious would yield an accurate description of the suspect. Under hypnosis Billy described the exact spot Mark disappeared, but he could not pull a vivid description of the suspect from his subconscious.

"There is something on his cheek," he told Martinez. "It could be a scar or a scrape or something like that, like where a ring might cut your face in a fight."

An artist carefully prepared a composite sketch of the suspect.

"Is that what he looked like?" Gavito questioned Billy at the end of the session.

"Maybe, sort of," Billy hesitated, uncomfortable with the results. It had been a fleeting glance. How could he remember exactly, even with the help of hypnosis?

Fearful that the composite might mislead the public rather than help, the officers elected not to use it.

The lawmen decided that a meeting of investigating agencies might speed the search, so a war council was called for 6:00 P.M. in Gavito's office.

At three o'clock that afternoon Jim and Eddie were ushered into Neck's office. The news was discouraging, and the briefing added little to what they already knew. The pictures Jim had sent by telefax from Santa Fe were unacceptable, so he provided fresh photographs. The U.S. Consulate in Matamoros had called and demanded that a parent file a missing-person report.

He was encouraged, though, to find Oran Neck to be cordial and professional, a man who had the appearance of knowing what to do next.

This is a man who thinks things out, Jim mused as he sized up the Customs officer. He was pleased that Neck would be one of the men in charge of the Kilroy family's future.

"What about a reward?" Neck interrupted his thoughts.

Jim felt helpless. Sure, he would gladly post a reward; he would do whatever was necessary. But he did not know what to do.

Let the experts make the decisions, he told himself. *You're a person who needs help, so accept it.*

"How much do you think? Fifty thousand dollars?" Jim said aloud. It was a wild guess, a nice round sum that would give Neck the ability to set the reward at whatever amount he thought best.

Realistically, Jim knew he could not raise fifty thousand dollars without help.

Neck studied the distraught father.

"How about five thousand?" he countered. "We have to be careful here; too much of a reward could start a rash of kidnappings."

"That seems low to me," Jim said.

"Let's start with that, and we'll increase it as needed," Neck explained. "But I doubt we'll ever go past fifteen thousand dollars."

"Well, you're more familiar with what a reward should be," Jim acknowledged.

"I only have one problem with a reward. Anyone who has seen something bad shouldn't need a reward. They should report it because it is the right thing to do," Jim explained. "Rewards are too much like ransoms to me. If it's only the crooks who know what's happened to Mark, then it seems to me that we are rewarding the crooks."

"Maybe, but they're the ones who may know something," Neck countered before changing the subject. "We have to take you to the American Consulate. They want a family member to file a formal missing-person report.

"After that we'll go by the office of Juan Benitez Ayala, he's the comandante of the Mexican Federal Judicial Police," Neck explained as he outlined the schedule for the rest of the day. "We have to be at the sheriff's office by six o'clock for a meeting with all the agencies involved in the search."

Remembering his cold reception earlier that day at the American consulate, Neck added as they walked out the door, "Don't expect any help out of them; this is just a formality."

At first the receptionist would not let the men talk to the consulate commander, but finally she did call Don Wells.

After assuring Jim that all hospitals and jails were being checked, Wells warned Kilroy against trusting the Matamoros city police. But he promised to ask the Mexican police to look again.

"Matamoros city police make about $150 a month and many are corrupt," Neck said as they left the consulate. "We have found them to be unreliable."

It's hard to tell how serious Wells is about finding Mark, Kilroy thought as they walked out of the office.

MFJP Comandante Juan Benitez Ayala, the man who had cleaned up the corrupt federal police in Matamoros, was another matter.

Jim Kilroy was about to meet a modern-day legend, according to Neck. Only a month before, Benitez and his men came to Matamoros disguised as peasants, automatic weapons hidden under flowing serapes. Riding in on smoke-belching buses crowded with desperate peasants anxious to earn a few pesos in the big city, Benitez and his men went undetected. Quietly they surrounded the Mexican Federal Judicial Police office. Then, carrying search and arrest warrants that had been issued surreptitiously in Mexico City, they stormed the building. Guillermo Perez Rodriguez, the former comandante, escaped with approximately three million American dollars; but Benitez's men recovered 4.5 million dollars in cash and one million dollars in jewelry, according to Notimex, the Mexican government press agency. One million dollars was found in the trunk of an automobile and the rest was found packed in suitcases abandoned in the comandante's office. Perez's personal assets in Brownsville were also attached. Ten officers, including Juan Manuel Ibarra, assistant comandante, were accused of various crimes.

Then Benitez did the unthinkable—at least in Mexico: He sent all the millions of dollars in loot to the money-starved national treasury in Mexico City.

In less than a month his life was in such danger that he had come to live under close guard as he continued to shake up the border underworld. Corruption and narcotics were his special targets.

Jim Kilroy:

Benitez was eating when we were escorted in, but he immediately ordered the meal taken away, gesturing for us to be seated on couches in front of his desk.

"Look at all those automatic weapons," Eddie whispered to me. I was just as startled as he was to see them near every hand. We were in an armed encampment. It was like a war-time command post. Oran had explained that the life of an honest comandante is always at risk. He attracts enemies like flies to honey and seldom stays at one post more than eighteen months. When he arrives he brings his own men; when he leaves he takes the survivors with him.

Instead of presiding behind his desk, Benitez joined us at the couches, only he hunkered down in a farmer's squat to be near us, the better to communicate.

It was a simple gesture that filled me with respect. Here was one of the most powerful men in Matamoros, yet he was humble enough to take a lesser position and peer upward into his guests' eyes. I knew this man was going to help me.

Benitez listened intently as interpreters explained that Mark was missing. I wanted to encourage him to help me, so I kept an unswerving gaze on him and occasionally he would look at me and our eyes would lock.

Oran asked if there was anything I had to add. I sensed that any man would understand the special bond between father and son, so I pleaded with him in English:

"Tell him that I want my son. He's worth getting back. Please find him for me. Please!"

After the translation, the young comandante of the Mexican Federal Judicial Police looked straight into my eyes. We did not share a common language, but at that moment we shared an unspoken emotional bond that superseded mere words in any language:

"We will find your son. And you will come to this office to get him."

It was a plea and an answer that would be uttered whenever we met.

Neck and Jim Kilroy barely had time to get back for the six o'clock meeting that was attended by two representatives of the State Judicial Police, a representative of the Mexican Federal Judicial Police, four U.S. Customs agents, four Cameron County sheriff's deputies, Kilroy, de la Houssaye, Neck, Gavito, and Mark's three friends.

It was the first time Jim Kilroy had met George Gavito, whom he warmed to immediately.

Fresh pictures of Mark were distributed. Bradley, Brent, and Billy were questioned by the Mexican authorities.

"The state police don't seem to be making any commitment," Jim whispered to Eddie.

"I think the Mexican cops have Mark, anyway," Eddie whispered back.

It was decided to pass out fliers to spring breakers at the next day's free concert on South Padre Island.

"We've got to do something to reach the kids who are here now," Gavito stressed. "By Sunday they will go back to school and anyone who might have seen or heard anything will be gone. We've got to concentrate on the people who might have been with Mark. Every student is a potential witness."

As the group met, businessman Joe Rodriguez read the story about the missing youth in the evening newspaper. A father of four, his heart went out to the Kilroy family. "It's a disgrace that this kind of thing happens," he told his wife, Emma, a school teacher.

That night as Jim Kilroy joined the lawmen for an evening of investigation in Matamoros, Joe and Emma said a special prayer for the frightened family.

"Something has to be done to help the Kilroy family," Joe told his wife.

Jim Kilroy:

Even with my worries and grief, I couldn't help but reflect upon how bizarre everything seemed as my first day on the scene drew to a close and we returned to our motel in Port Isabel. I couldn't believe this was happening in our lives.

You don't realize, I mean *really* realize that Mexico is a different society until you come up against it. Nothing works the way it does in America, and I learned quickly not to expect it to work the same way.

I kept wondering how this is happening, that I'm trying to find my son in another country. We all had been jerked from our normal life. It was very bizarre.

For example, how often does an average citizen ride in a drug dealer's car? On the way over to meet Benitez, Oran told me that the Mercedes we were in had been taken from the Hernandez family, a gang of known drug dealers. He said that when Saul Hernandez Rivera had tried to smuggle fifty thousand dollars into the United States, the car, along with the money, had been seized. In time, there would be a special, bizarre irony in that knowledge.

But I did have positive feelings about the men who were involved in the search. I'm not convinced that it was simply fate that brought Benitez to the border only a few weeks before he would play such an important role in my life. Benitez had been impressive that afternoon. His humble attitude when he squatted to talk to us made him ten feet tall in my opinion. It was obvious that he was a man in a powerful position who still treated all men as equals. Not only Mexico, but the world needs more men like him.

Soft-spoken, intense Oran and aggressive George seemed a good team to balance gang-buster Benitez.

I didn't know it at the time, but my search for Mark would take several bizarre turns during the next few days.

While Eddie and I were passing out posters in Brownsville, a woman stopped, looked at a poster, and told me that she thought Mark was being held in a room above Garcia's in Matamoros. She promised to find out and let the police know.

Before I could react, she disappeared into the crowd.

"You should have grabbed her!" Eddie shouted when I told him about her.

By now I was really concerned. Had I let someone escape who might know about Mark or someone who might have seen him kidnapped?

Eddie and I went back into the streets. I was determined to find her, and I did. To my amazement, she didn't look anything like my description of her to Eddie although I recognized her when I saw her. My description was different from reality. For the first time I understood why Billy had so much trouble trying to recall the person he had seen talking to Mark.

I didn't want to scare her off, so I approached her carefully, thinking that possibly my son's life was on the line. Whatever I did could mean the difference between life and death.

I tried to talk to her, but she panicked. She ran to a taxicab and took off while I scribbled the license number down.

Eddie and I went to the police station to discover her already there complaining about the wild-eyed Anglo trying to attack her.

Understanding officers explained that her mind was not normal. She often gave false information.

On another occasion when the boys were helping us, Eddie was approached by a man who said he knew where Mark was. This time we decided to tail him. As the five of us peered from doorways and hid behind trees we were pathetically obvious. We lost him in a matter of minutes.

"Boy am I glad we're not policemen," I told them.

Bizarre is the best word for those weeks of searching.

Friday

The probing investigators began to uncover violence against spring breakers. On Friday a badly beaten student was discovered in a Brownsville medical center. He had been mugged in the same vicinity where Mark had disappeared and on the same night. A fellow spring breaker had helped the bleeding man across the border. Benitez was notified; maybe the same miscreant had attacked Mark.

That same day a report filtered into Gavito's office about another hapless student who had been raped by three men across the street from where Mark disappeared. She had been taken behind a house only one block off the main boulevard.

For the third time, agents from Customs and the sheriff's office fanned out across Matamoros, again checking hospitals and jails.

"There's another one," Eddie counted as Jim drove past a squad car, lights blinking. On the drive to Brownsville from Port Isabel that Friday morning, the group passed more than a dozen automobiles pulled over by alert policemen. Seven students had died in automobile accidents the year before. Sheriff Perez and other police officials were determined it would not happen again.

"I think we need to move to Brownsville, to be closer to the investigation," Jim told Eddie.

"I have relatives in Brownsville, and I'm sure we can stay with them for a few days," Eddie said. Luke and Rosie Fruia were to roll out the welcome mat for the weary searchers. Jim and Eddie would stay with them until the syndicated television series, "America's Most Wanted," would arrange hotel rooms for a few days as the series filmed a special report on Mark's disappearance the next week.

A television reporter was waiting for Jim as they pulled up to the sheriff's office. Letty Fernandez had read the newspaper article the day before, and she wanted an interview.

"Sure," Jim said, turning to Eddie as the cameraman prepared. "This is going to be very important," he told his friend. "It gives me an opportunity to beg to get my son back."

I've got to do a good job, Jim thought, summoning up all his courage for his first television interview. *I've got to keep my mind clear and say just the right thing.* But emotion overcame him the moment Letty began the interview.

Later that night, the Rio Grande Valley got its first look at Jim Kilroy, a father near tears whose voice broke as he pleaded with unknown antagonists, "I just want my son back. No questions asked!"

Gavito had decided to take one thousand dollars from a drug slush fund to help fuel interest by the Mexican state police.

"Sometimes they just aren't interested in helping unless there is money involved," he told Jim after the television interview.

He sent Jim Kilroy to the Lincoln Park School for the handicapped where workers were busy printing five hundred fliers to be distributed at the Joe King Carrasco concert that afternoon on South Padre Island. It was the most that could be done on such short notice. Before the search ended, these special workers would produce three thousand posters in Spanish and English, bearing Mark's picture. While Jim was awaiting delivery of the fliers, he telephoned the bishop of Brownsville to request prayers and a special announcement concerning Mark at the coming Sunday's Mass in area Catholic churches.

Sandra "Sandy" Cornelius's eyes were glued to the television screen. She had just learned that Mark Kilroy was missing and tuned in an all-news station for more information. She did not know the Kilroy family, but in the small community of Santa Fe, people joked that someone can barely sneeze without everyone knowing about it. She had knowledge of the Kilroy family, a vague awareness similar to what she had about hundreds of other families in the community.

Her life changed forever when she saw Jim Kilroy standing in front of the sheriff's office, his eyes brimming with tears.

"Help me find my son," he pleaded, the soul-searing distress leaping from the screen into thousands of homes. For that single moment, Jim Kilroy was the epitome of parental concern, his face racked with stress. The interviewer went on to explain that Mark had disappeared in the early hours of Tuesday morning.

There's no telling how long that family is going to have to be down there, Sandy thought, disregarding the rest of the newscast. She picked up the telephone and called Jackie Gates.

"Did you hear about the boy who disappeared?" she asked when Jackie answered the telephone. "The family's down there searching. And if they're searching, the father can't be working; so they need money to live on," she reasoned. "Can we use your shop to have an auction and garage sale?" Once the project started rolling, it would become a community-wide event.

By Sunday people in Santa Fe and all the surrounding communities had generously donated brand-new items that included lamps, diamond rings, racing bicycles, hats, T-shirts, furniture, and mirrors. One hotel donated a brunch, a florist added flowers, and another firm provided a limousine for a night on the town. Some of the most prized donations would come from individuals who brought in homemade dolls and handicrafts.

The benefit garage sale, baked-goods sale, and auction would be held April 7-9 at the Santa Fe Arts & Crafts Depot.

As the news broke about Mark's disappearance, Helen was flooded by requests for interviews. Her first reaction was to refuse them all.

"How can I open up my family and my home to public viewing?" she said to her dear friend Mary de la Houssaye, who had been her constant companion since Mark disappeared.

It was a personal dilemma for Helen. Decisive when working in life-and-death situations as an Emergency Medical Service (EMS) volunteer, Helen has a tendency to keep her opinions and her life private. She did not want to do anything that would endanger Mark or hamper the search for him. She knew she had to convince people to help her find her son. But she could not help but worry: *Will I say the right thing?*

Finally she turned to Mary.

"I have to do it, and I have to trust the media," she said. "Maybe someone will come forward with information." That night she watched herself on television in a story that also featured Jim's emotional plea.

A very private family had gone public.

On this day in Brownsville, Gavito asked his investigators to examine all impounded automobiles. "Check for blood," he instructed them.

It was a routine step in homicide cases, a step Gavito had been reluctant to take in the Kilroy case. Now he had to face reality. If hope began to dim at forty-eight hours, then it was virtually abandoned at seventy-two hours. That time had come and gone at two o'clock Friday morning. He telephoned Neck.

"Oran, I think we're going to have to conduct this as a homicide investigation," he began. "I believe Mark Kilroy is dead."

The suggestion came as no surprise. There had been no ransom call. Mark had not been found in a hospital, nor in a jail. He was not sleeping off a drunk or with a girl, or both. There were no known drug deals.

"I think we should start looking for a body," Gavito said, underscoring his thoughts.

Although it had been only briefly discussed, both had come to believe that Mark had been a victim of an unscrupulous Mexican police officer.

"He's probably the victim of a bad deal, something that went bad with a police officer," Gavito continued.

"We've had lots of calls from a lot of people with that theory," Neck added.

"I wouldn't believe that so strongly if it wasn't for the fact that we still don't have a body," Gavito said, thinking out loud. "If someone had knocked him in the head and thrown him in the brush or the river, his body would have been found. A robber would leave the body in an alley.

"But a police officer would know how to dispose of the body. He could take it into the interior. It would just disappear. The officer could have killed him by accident. He could have been too rough, or a gun might have gone off accidentally," Gavito continued, pausing to consider the situation.

"Let's make it a homicide investigation and ask Benitez to check the police for us," Neck agreed. "But let's break it easy to the Kilroy family."

"And while we're at it, we need to go ahead and search the brush," Gavito added, using the local term for known areas where bodies might be dropped.

From that moment on the two men were searching for Mark Kilroy's body. They would drop hints that Mark might be dead, but they never encouraged the family to give up hope. Like doctors diagnosing a fatal disease, they longed to be proven wrong.

That afternoon Mark's three friends joined Jim and Eddie in passing out fliers which offered a five-thousand-dollar reward for information leading to the return of Mark Kilroy. Hundreds of carloads of carousing spring breakers zoomed out of the parking area following the Joe King Carrasco concert on South Padre Island and the posters disappeared in less than an hour.

"I'm not sure they're taking these posters because the police announced that Mark is missing or if they think it's a freebie of some kind," Jim shouted to Eddie as automobiles roared by and students leaned out to snag a poster.

Jim Kilroy and his friend Eddie sent the three young men back to the hotel while they went back into Matamoros to tape up a few posters they had saved. The men carefully selected shop windows facing the street.

Later that night the Cameron County Sheriff's Office dispatcher received a disturbing call from a woman in Matamoros who said, "I know what happened to Mark Kilroy. He was killed by some really bad people. What they did was so terrible I had to call and report it."

She said she was afraid to discuss it on the telephone. But she promised to call back later.

Saturday

Gavito was jolted out of bed Saturday morning by a telephone call from Benitez. He had captured the assailant who had robbed the severely beaten and hospitalized spring breaker. Benitez assured Gavito that the mugger had nothing to do with Mark Kilroy's disappearance.

He found that guy in less than twenty-four hours, Gavito marveled.

The two continued by planning that morning's search of the Rio Grande. The lawmen knew that gases from a deteriorating body would cause it to rise to the surface after seventy-two hours. Gavito's men would walk along the river looking across to check the Mexican side of the river while ten of Benitez's men would peer across at the American side.

Also, they would be joined by more than thirty-two Border Patrol agents, ten Cameron County Sheriff's deputies, and ten U.S. Customs agents who had given up their day off to volunteer for the search. The Border Patrol's helicopter would even be used.

Jim Kilroy:

It was a scene right out of a motion picture, except I knew that this was real, not make-believe. George, Eddie, and I drove along in a four-wheel-drive pickup truck, our eyes riveted to the muddy Rio Grande as it sloshed along between two countries. Small dirt roads followed its winding path, weaving up and down arroyos, disappearing for a few feet behind scrub brush and then back into sight. The searchers fanned out in front of us, some on horseback, others on foot. Across the river I could see Benitez's men as they walked along.

Overhead a helicopter passed by, following the banks of the river. The chopper would eventually pull up when it reached the Gulf of Mexico and then head back our way.

At that moment I had such deep, mixed emotions that even a year later I still haven't sorted all of them out. I didn't want to be the guy to spot Mark if he was there. But I didn't want to be the guy who *didn't* see him if he was there and someone else didn't see him.

And, more importantly, I didn't want *anyone* to find him. I still had strong hopes that we would be reunited with our son.

It was an unbelievable clash of emotions.

Ever since I had started searching for Mark, I had had this urge to hold him just one more time, to put my arms around him and hold him. If we found him in the river I couldn't hold him again.

So I prayed. I prayed to find him. I prayed not to find him. I prayed that if he was found, it would be by someone else. And finally, I prayed that we would not find him here, but that I would be reunited with him.

The river was low, possibly the lowest it had ever been, George said as we bumped along. Muddy flats spread out on either side. Sometimes footprints could be traced coming from Mexico, disappearing into the river, emerging on the other side, and disappearing into the brush.

"Look over there," George said, pointing across the river. Crouched behind a bush, several naked aliens tried to shrink from sight. Their clothes were bundled beside them.

As soon as we pass they'll hold their clothes over their heads and forge the river. It's only about waist high here," George said.

I became concerned when I watched the searchers. Many of them appeared to be moving casually along, almost not looking. George laughed when I mentioned this to him.

"Don't worry. They'll spot anything that's there," he assured me. "I would bet that they've already radioed back for a greeting party for those aliens we saw back there."

No body was recovered on that long, hot day. But when the search was repeated Sunday, half a body was found. The officers suspected that the man had been killed six months before in a shootout with Mexican federal agents.

The Lincoln School and the sheriff's office are normally closed on weekends, but as the first week came to a close both remained open. The school was busy churning out posters with English and Spanish pleas printed side by side. The sheriff's office was filled with volunteer workers.

Before the river search Jim had suggested a change in the posters.

"Why not add one line telling people to contact their priest or minister?" he said. "Since Mexicans are afraid of the police, they might tell their minister and have him contact us. If *we* think the Mexican police are involved, what do you think the Mexican people are thinking?"

Kilroy had begun to understand the dynamics of the border. Mexican citizens are afraid of the police because corruption is common and torture is an accepted method of interrogation. Their fear could explain the lack of solid clues and the preponderance of anonymous telephone calls.

In Santa Fe the telephone began ringing nonstop early Saturday morning in the Cornelius home as hundreds of residents asked how they could help. Soon it became obvious that Sandy Cornelius and Jackie Gates were going to have to run companion events: An

auction of the new items and a garage sale of used items at Jackie's
art shop.

Before the day ended plans were being made for even more
events, including a dance that would also feature a smaller auction. It
would be held April 15.

Meanwhile, Keith Kilroy went into the backyard he had shared so
many times with his older brother. The trees, the fences, the animals, everything reminded him of Mark and the times they had
shared together as young boys. For the first time since Mark disappeared four days earlier, Keith wept.

"Mark, you've always been more than a brother to me," Keith said
aloud, looking at the familiar surroundings, each spot chock-full of
special memories. "You are my best friend. *Where are you?*"

Jim Kilroy watched in agony as students began to return home to
friends, family, and school. Spring break was coming to an end for
this group of students, and a surge of new faces began to fill up the
beaches and jam the streets. Also Bradley, Billy, and Brent would be
leaving. Their parents were anxious for them to return home. Because Billy was a potential witness he agreed to stay longer, but
Bradley and Brent would drive back home on Monday.

Eddie was disturbed to find that a number of the reward posters
that he and Jim had put up the night before had already been taken
off the windows. *Were bar owners uncooperative because they feared
it would hurt business?* he wondered. No. He soon discovered that
there was no sinister motive behind the missing fliers; well-meaning
citizens were taking them down to show to friends in their neigh-
borhoods.

Later that night George Gavito dropped by Oran Neck's office.

"Take a look at this," Oran said, tossing several color photographs
across the desk.

They showed a cement culvert covered with graffiti. Scrawled at
the bottom above a crude pentagram was the warning: "Mark Kilroy
was the first."

SECOND WEEK

"For the love of God, we have to help this family find its missing son. If you know anyone who may know anything, encourage them to contact the sheriff's office. Ask your relatives in Matamoros, your friends, anyone!

"Let us help them. The Kilroys have suffered enough.

"And pray for this family. Pray that they will find Mark."

The Rev. John Nicolau, pastor of Saint Luke's Catholic Church in Brownsville pleaded with his parishioners. It was not unusual for this passionate priest to submerge himself into current events, especially those affecting his adopted community. More than twenty-five years before, he had come to Brownsville from his native Spain. Now, the Rio Grande Valley was his home, and its dramatic tragedies are grist for his dynamic sermons. He had no idea that Jim Kilroy was in his Palm Sunday audience as he acknowledged the suffering of the present world while offering his congregation the joy of a resurrected Christ. He wanted only to touch the hearts of his flock as he prepared them for the Easter season.

"Jesus died, and He is alive. There is a life everlasting," he said in concluding his sermon.

"Mom," Keith called for his mother as he entered the house. "You'll never believe what happened to me just now."

Mary LeCompte had approached him at Mass that Sunday morning at the family's home parish of Our Lady of Lourdes, where Father John DeForke had put the message "Pray for the safe return of our Mark Kilroy" on the church marquee.

Everyone's concern caused Keith to experience a strange mixture

49

of comfort and depression. However, because many of his friends were as melancholy as he was, depression more than comfort was beginning to envelope this young man as Mary approached him.

"Keith, I have a suggestion for you," Mary had said. "I know your brother is missing and I know your pain. Make a promise to Our Lady and be prepared to keep it. Then pray that she will intercede with God so that your family will find Mark, whether he is dead or alive. No matter what, remember that Mark will always be alive because we have God's promise of everlasting life."

Keith told his mother that as Mary spoke, a peace began to surround him, a peace that seemed to make the noisy crowd distant, a peace that filled him with a serenity and happiness.

"And when you finish that prayer, add 'Thy will be done,'" Mary had told Keith, reaching out to touch his hand before turning to walk away.

"Mom, she told me to tell you and Dad to pray the same thing," he added.

But Helen just shook her head as her mind rejected the idea of finding Mark dead. *I'll pray for Mark to be protected and that we find him, but I can't even say the words "dead or alive,"* she thought to herself.

As the day progressed, she could not shake the image of a hurt and bleeding Mark lying under a dirty blanket in a filthy jail cell or of her son lying unconscious by the side of the road, his life slowly ebbing.

Finally, she had to call Jim at the sheriff's office.

"What if the people are afraid to come forward?" she asked her husband, reciting all her worries. "Tell everyone we just want our son back, no questions asked, no punishment. We just want him back."

By now she was crying, almost inconsolable at the thought of her suffering son.

"What if someone has him captive and they're giving him bad food?" she said. "He could be dying of dysentery."

Try as he could, Jim could not soothe her. George Gavito was seated nearby, so Jim handed him the telephone.

"Mrs. Kilroy, this is George Gavito," he said.

"Lt. Gavito, please don't give up. Nothing is impossible with the Lord. Mark is suffering and needs our help," Helen said, pouring her heart out to this man she had never met.

"We are doing everything we can," he said quietly, his normally booming voice filled with the soft tranquility of reassurance. "We're all praying, too."

I wish I could tell her everything will be all right, George thought to himself. *But all I can tell her is that we're doing everything possible.*

Helen realized that he cared. And in that realization came a bit of peace.

It was not the first time Gavito had to console a grieving parent. Police officers have to maintain a delicate balance. They have to develop the necessary hardness to deal with the criminal element, yet maintain a tenderhearted compassion for the suffering victim.

"You have a tough job," Jim said softly as Gavito hung up the telephone.

Early in the week, Mayor Jack Long and Thelma Webber, affectionately called Gramma by almost everybody, spearheaded a town meeting in Santa Fe. Also attending was Gwen Huddleston, Billy's mother, who would coordinate media information on hometown activities as well as the Kilroys' movements in Brownsville and Austin.

From that brainstorming session sprang plans to raise signatures on petitions to be sent to the presidents of both Mexico and the United States, to assemble packets of posters and petitions which would be sent to all the universities which had had spring break the week Mark disappeared, to organize groups to distribute posters throughout Southeast Texas, and to coordinate a letter-writing and telegram campaign aimed at politicians in both countries. Several Santa Fe women even sent telegrams to First Lady Barbara Bush in a mother-to-mother appeal for support.

It was a difficult time for Jim Kilroy. Sunday had marked the sixth day his son had been missing. Brent and Bradley would leave for home the next day. Billy would stay since he had seen the suspect. The students who could have been witness to Mark's disappearance had scattered to the four winds, returning to their college studies. Now the search seemed even more difficult.

As word of Mark's disappearance spread, the new media descended upon the small town of Santa Fe, seeking any information on the missing youth. Clusters of people talked in hushed tones speculating on what might have happened to one of their own.

One of the most sought-out men was James Bownds, Mark's high school principal. He told news media that Mark "never was in trouble. Oh, he might get called down by his teachers once in a while like all the kids, but he certainly was never in any serious trouble at all. Mark wasn't really a part of any clique. He played sports, but he wasn't a jock. He made good grades, but he wasn't a part of the brain group. You just don't think it will happen to one of your own people," he said.

When Mark was vice president of the student council, Frank L. Napoli, director of student activities, had worked closely with him.

He described the student as having had a winning smile that could melt a heart of stone.

"Even when you chewed him out, and he deserved it, and he knew he deserved it, he would just flash that smile," the teacher explained.

"He showed a lot of respect for his family. They were close, and the parents stayed in touch with his teachers," he continued. "He respected authority very much. He was one who would say, 'Yes, sir' and 'No, sir.' It was evident that respect was a family tradition. It was expected. Mark's just lost," Napoli told Bownds when they discussed the missing student. "He'll show up, flash that grin, and everything will be okay."

The news media began to paint a picture of a handsome, athletic, gentle young man, whose life was almost the American dream, in what many people picture as the near-perfect life of a middle-class family. It was easy for fellow Americans to identify with Mark; he was an earnest young man with a quick smile—the type parents would like to see their daughters marry.

Mark was a better-than-average athlete who played high school basketball, track, baseball, and golf for the Santa Fe Indians. The high school he attended with his three spring-break buddies was the only one in town, and it was located right next to the only elementary school and the only junior high.

According to his close friends, Mark did not have a steady girlfriend.

"He had lots and lots of friends," said Rico Garza, a high school chum who knew Mark well.

P. R. "Mike" Thomson says he is not a "church-going" man, but this philosophy teacher at the University of Texas in Austin led his students in a two-minute prayer at the start of class one day when publicity convinced him that Mark was not just missing but in danger. Mark Kilroy was his top student in "Contemporary Moral Problems," with a mid-term average of 93. Only a week before Mark disappeared, Mark, the professor, and another student had spent thirty minutes after class discussing "the meaning of life."

Thomson penned a letter to the Kilroy family. Included was a two-page essay entitled "Who Am I?" that Mark wrote only days before he disappeared.

Who Am I?

I believe that I am sometimes perceived differently than I really am. Take for instance if I would give some flowers to a girlfriend of mine and she would think that I have some ulterior motive in mind when really I was just being a nice guy. Of course all guys have some other motive at times when it comes to dealing with girls, but it is sometimes blown out of proportion with me. This also happens with guys sometimes.

I have trouble with people being able to trust me. It seems that everyone is suspicious of me from the start. I consider myself one of the most trustworthy people around. This is an attribute that I hold very high in others, also. After I get to know a person, they then trust me most of the time.

One thing I never try to do is hurt someone's feelings. I believe this is one of the worst things a person can do to another. I usually spare feelings of individuals I don't much care for, but I can't hold back on arrogant men and women. Confidence is a much needed thing if goals are to be reached, and even over confidence (funny at times) is bearable. Arrogance is something I can't stand, even if it is somewhat justified (usually not). I think in attacking an arrogant individual it isn't as cruel because it is really needed because it is a sad state of mind and also I am not perfect, I can't always be "Mr. Nice Guy."

In addition to Santa Fe residents and Mark's friends and acquaintances, total strangers began to call Helen to offer words of encouragement and prayer. Cards and letters began to arrive as concerned citizens reacted to the family's suffering. One was from Linda Ceyanes, who had met the Kilroys at Marriage Encounter. She wrote, "God knows where Mark is. God is in control of everything. Put your trust in Him. You cannot do it on your own."

It was so clearly, simply stated that it became Helen's strength.

The Kilroy story intrigued "America's Most Wanted" producer Ray Mize when he read an Associated Press dispatch Monday morning about the desperate search. Although the syndicated series had a longstanding policy against covering active cases or focusing on missing individuals more than sixteen years old, Mize believed this one was worth checking out.

Perhaps there was also a subconscious motivation. The syndicated series had been created with the help of John Walsh, the Florida businessman whose young son, Adam, had disappeared. After a frantic search, the child was discovered dead. A made-for-television movie in 1983 chronicled the event, and Walsh became a national crusader in the field of missing children.

"We never do stories on current cases," Mize warned Neck after a briefing. "But let me see what I can do."

Within twenty-four hours the series had committed to a segment on the Kilroys, hired a model to portray Mark in the reenactment, and had a film crew on the scene Thursday and Friday. Eddie de la

Houssaye returned home as Jim moved into a hotel provided by the syndicated series. Brent and Bradley flew in for the filming, as did Helen and Keith.

As Helen prepared for her first trip to the border she retrieved a complete set of clothing from Mark's room and carefully packed it into a corner of her suitcase. Logic may have told her otherwise, but her mother's heart knew that her son would be in need of clean clothing.

Jim Kilroy felt alone. He was in a strange town and fighting indifference in an effort to keep alive the search for his son. As he had often done in the past, he turned to his religious faith. "In times of trouble you turn to God," he frequently had told his family. It was also something he knew Mark would do, and he found great comfort in that thought.

Jim Kilroy:

I don't go to church every day, but in Brownsville I was going a lot. I was scared. I didn't know if I'd ever see my son in this world again. I wanted to know what had happened. Yet I was afraid of finding out. I wanted to find him, and I wanted to find him alive.

It seemed to me as if everything had failed. The circulars drew telephone calls, but most were empty leads. The police were flooded with tips that were helping to solve all kinds of crimes that had nothing to do with Mark. Television interviews had brought in more leads, but none had panned out.

We felt it was time to increase the reward and that fifteen thousand dollars would be the maximum because of ransom fears. But we had to be careful. If it appeared that I was putting up the money, then whoever had Mark might just wait for the reward to be increased again, or ask for more money because it might appear that I was wealthy. I needed some way to present the increase in the reward so that it appeared to come from others rather than myself.

I was asking God how to do this thing.

When you start to feel low, that's the time you need to pray the most.

I knew that I needed help—lots of help—from the Mexican government, from my government, from the police in both countries, from citizens in both countries, and especially, from God.

Standing at the back of Saint Luke's Catholic Church, a stranger watched Kilroy's silent anguish as he knelt in prayer. Joe Rodriguez had read newspaper accounts of the search and had seen Jim and Helen on television. But there was a special impact now that Kilroy was praying in Joe's home parish after a noon Mass they both had attended. Jim Kilroy was no longer a half-conceived image that sprang from a newspaper story, or a two-dimensional video impression from the nightly newscast. For the first time, Joe Rodriguez saw Jim Kilroy, the man—a flesh-and-blood father praying in anguish. Empathy drew tears to the corners of his eyes.

A former coach who was inducted into the Texas High School Coaches Hall of Fame in 1981, Rodriguez was now a businessman who stayed in touch with the city's youth.

What if something like that had happened to one of my children? the businessman silently asked himself. A father of four, two of them near Mark's age, he understood the high jinks of youth and the tolerance required in a father's love.

Mark's disappearance had stirred anxiety in the business community where merchants were well aware that some of the youngsters who come down on spring break drink too much, and maybe even end up in jail, or worse, in the hospital. But they always show up; they are always found. Several businessmen, including Joe Rodriguez, had held a meeting. Disturbed about what the Kilroy family was suffering, they decided it was time to do something.

When Rodriguez saw Jim praying in the church, he decided to approach him with the businessmen's offer of help.

As Jim continued to pray, asking for guidance and help, he prayed especially for assistance in presenting the additional ten thousand dollars he hoped would entice someone to come forward with news of Mark.

I don't know what else to do, he prayed, his troubled soul seeking comfort. Then his prayers were interrupted by the approach of a man he did not know.

"Mr. Kilroy, my name is Joe Rodriguez, and I want to help you," the stranger said. "A group of businessmen has discussed this, and we want to help you increase the reward. We have a pledge for another ten thousand dollars or whatever you need."

"Great!" was Jim's astonished reply.

"I'll meet you in an hour at the sheriff's office," Joe said, leaving Jim to finish his prayers.

Does he really mean it? Jim wondered, anticipation beginning to build as he watched Joe leave.

When Jim arrived at the sheriff's office he found Joe Rodriguez deep in negotiations with Neck and Gavito over the amount of the reward. Within a matter of minutes the Brownsville businessman had used the telephone to reaffirm various pledges that would raise the additional money.

Then a new worry surfaced. Since the Mexican economy is on

the brink of collapse, would a reward of fifteen thousand dollars—
valued in millions of Mexican pesos—cause a rash of spring break
kidnappings? All the Kilroy family needed was to be accused of
posting such a large reward that it loosed a reign of terror. Jim
shuddered to think of young men or women being snatched off the
streets of Mexico and held for ransom.

"We have to be careful," Rodriguez said, articulating the unthinkable. "We don't want to give someone any wrong ideas. If the reward
is too high, it could start a rash of kidnappings."

"From the very start, we agreed that fifteen thousand would be
our limit," Gavito added, equally concerned.

Jim certainly did not want to have to deal with extortion and the
trauma its promise of hope and threat of violence might bring.

The four considered the situation in silence.

"I don't think it's too much," Rodriguez finally said. "We have to
do something, and this could give us the break that we need. I agree
with Oran and George. I don't think we should go over fifteen
thousand dollars. That could be disastrous."

Jim noted that within a matter of minutes, Rodriguez had begun
to use the collective "we."

"I agree," Gavito added.

"Me, too," Neck nodded in agreement.

Joe and Emma Rodriguez had both been distressed that the Kilroy
family was separated. Joe had learned that Helen was staying in Santa
Fe to be near the telephone should anyone call with ransom demands or, their wildest dream come true, Mark should telephone.
So before the press conference to announce the increased reward,
Joe turned to Jim and said, "When we're through with this, we'll go
pick up your clothes. You're going to stay with us."

Jim was stunned.

"But . . ." he started, not so much in protest, but buying time to
consider the situation.

"No buts, no ifs, no nothings," Rodriguez said with a smile.
"We're your new family until this ordeal is over."

With that simple statement, the Rodriguez family home would
become home to the Kilroys as they continued their search for
Mark.

Although they never met him, Mark became a vivid addition to
the Rodriguez family's collective memory; soon they would be talking of him as if they had known him for years.

"This has got to be hard for him," Bradley whispered to Brent as
Mark's three buddies were joined by an actor from Plano, Texas.
They were back in Matamoros, recreating the fateful evening that

Mark disappeared for "America's Most Wanted." It was Thursday, and Mark had been missing for ten days.

"It helps that he's nice," Brent whispered back, nodding toward the actor.

Since the director demanded accuracy, filming took place at the exact hour the four students had walked into Matamoros on March 13. The crew recreated the evening, often stopping to confer with the men to determine the exact sequence of events that occurred that devastating night. It took the better part of two days to capture the short segment on film. That was an amazing feat, according to veteran producers, who said a segment usually takes six weeks to produce. The segment about Mark was put together in three days and would be broadcast on the fourth. A live tag at the end of the segment would feature Jim and Helen.

The Kilroy family declined to watch the reenactment being filmed. The camera captured them as they put up reward posters in Matamoros, but the family did not cross the border without three undercover police officers.

There was a problem, though. None of the television stations in the Rio Grande Valley carried the syndicated program, and this was the prime target area. When television station KVEO (Channel 23) learned of the snag, it committed to a one-time broadcast on Sunday. Executives at the station also used portions of the show to develop a public service announcement which ran six or seven times daily, asking the public for information concerning Mark.

Oran Neck, George Gavito, and Jim had fallen into a pattern of meeting early each morning. On this particular day the topic was the peculiar lack of support from state and city law-enforcement agencies in Mexico. The State Judicial Police were startlingly resistant, although the agency had sent two representatives to the first meeting. Since the Rio Grande had failed to yield Mark's body, it was decided to contact Texas Attorney General Jim Mattox for help. Perhaps Mattox could solicit support from the attorney general in Tamaulipas, the Mexican state in which Matamoros is located. Meanwhile, the federal police, as represented by Benitez, continued to give total support to the search.

The same day of the request, Mattox dispatched Francisco Castillo to Brownsville on a fact-finding mission. The attorney general's aide was amazed by the uninhibited party attitude of the students on spring break in the border cities.

"You won't believe this," Gavito told him as he pulled his unmarked automobile to a curb in Matamoros. Then, leaning out, he yelled at a student, "Hey, let's party!"

"Let's par . . . ty," the student replied, making two words out of one.

"Get in! I know where there's plenty of action," Gavito shot back, leaning across to open the door. As the student started to get in, Gavito slammed the door in his face with the stern warning, "Don't ever get in the car with just anyone!"

Castillo was incredulous at what he had just seen.

"They're here for a good time," Gavito explained after several more demonstrations. "Maybe they're a little too drunk, or maybe they're not too drunk, but their inhibitions are lower than normal. Besides, this is spring break. It's a time to be friendly. Everyone knows everyone else. Everyone talks to everyone else. As you can see, the trust is unbelievable."

Castillo was briefed on the case as Gavito drove to the Hard Rock Cafe (London Pub) where the four friends had spent the last hours of the evening Mark disappeared. The owner had spent ninety minutes with Benitez's men the day before and had nothing new to tell them. Castillo ended the day by walking the streets with Gavito, talking to vendors and partying students. He returned to Austin the next morning.

Later that week Joe and Emma Rodriguez made the first of several trips into the Matamoros tourist district where Joe would conduct intense one-on-one interviews with the *valadores*, the men who park and protect automobiles at the clubs.

"I want to know about Mark Kilroy," he would say to them in Spanish.

Without exception, each one would reply: "I don't know anything."

"Look, we are offering fifteen thousand dollars. That's more than you can make in two, maybe three years," Rodriguez said to stress the enormous value of the American dollars in the Mexican marketplace.

"Hey, man, I wish I knew. That's a lot of money, but I don't know anything. I really wish I did." Joe heard the same answer over and over as he walked from club to club, Emma patiently waiting in the car. Each night ended the same.

"You would think that someone would know something," a frustrated Rodriguez said as he got into the car. "You would think that one of these men would have seen something that night."

Billy studied mug books in Mexico. After hours of searching, he pointed out one picture that seemed to resemble the man he saw talking to Mark. It was decided to bring the man in for questioning and let Billy look at him in a Mexican lineup.

The same night Mark disappeared, four men had shot and killed a truck driver in a robbery in the plaza across from Garcia's where

Bradley and Brent had stood looking back for Mark. Suspects had been captured and Billy was to look at them as well.

Since Billy had seen a suspect, the lawmen feared for the student's life and the young man was by now a virtual prisoner, escorted everywhere by armed officers. Before Billy left for Matamoros to attend the lineup, Jim pulled Billy aside.

"Whatever you do, don't identify anyone unless you are pretty sure of it," he warned. "Otherwise, forget it; we don't want to accuse an innocent man."

The lineup turned into a nightmare for Billy, who was escorted into Mexico by Cameron County Deputy Sheriff Ernesto Flores. In the United States the victim or witness stands behind a two-way mirror while looking at the suspects, who face the reflective glass. In privacy, the witness can talk to officers or take his time. In Mexico, the witness is thrust under the very nose of the suspect in an eye-to-eye confrontation. Billy found himself standing only inches away from the four suspects who were as nervous and scared as the college student. And only minutes later the shifty eyes from the face in the mugshot glared into Billy's eyes.

None of the men matched his memory of the person he glimpsed talking to Mark.

After concentrating on students the first week, Federal Comandante Benitez decided the second week to turn Matamoros's underworld upside down. By the end of the week he had questioned eighty people and arrested or detained twenty-five known criminals for harassing, assaulting, or selling drugs to spring breakers. Also, he had brought in every street vendor for questioning.

The publicity had generated attention on both sides of the border. More than twenty calls a day were coming into the sheriff's office. Each lead had to be evaluated, but very few held promise. Most promoted a familiar theory: Look into the ranks of the Mexican police.

Most of the responses were crank calls, psychic visions, and lonely people just wanting to talk to someone. But there was one intriguing message from a woman who had dated a Matamoros police officer. The man had bragged to her that he had been taking Mark into custody when the student bolted. In an attempt to stop him, the woman said she was told, the officer fired a shot intended to fly harmlessly over his head, but had instead struck him, accidentally killing Mark.

It was the American law officers' first real lead with promise, and they immediately called Benitez. The woman's story was a perfect match to the prevailing theory: a Matamoros city police officer, extortion, an accidental death.

Neck and Gavito arrived at the Mexican Federal Judicial Police office in Matamoros to find the officer the woman had described seated in a chair in the middle of an interrogation room, his pistol still strapped to his hip. Benitez had ordered him yanked out of his patrol car; the vehicle had been left standing in the street. It was an unsettling experience for the two Americans to see another lawman, still armed, in the seat of accusation.

Careful to observe proper protocol, Neck and Gavito only observed the interrogation. The officer was a good friend of an underworld businessman. He threw out his name several times but to no avail. He repeatedly denied knowing anything about Mark Kilroy, turning suspicion toward his partner.

When the woman's name was brought up, the officer suggested, "Maybe I was drunk."

The two American officers could see the third degree was about to get out of hand. It would be a federal offense if they were present during an investigation in which torture was used.

Gavito signaled Benitez's attention.

"Let's put this guy on a polygraph," he recommended. "We can bring one over tomorrow."

Instead of two men, Benitez had three waiting to take the sophisticated test the next day, the suspect and his partner, plus another unidentified man.

"Who's the other guy?" Neck questioned.

"I want him on that machine," was all Benitez would reply.

A polygraph takes sensitive measurements of blood pressure, pulse, and heart rate. An experienced operator tracks the needles as they glide across the paper. Any stressful rise in the physiological feedback is noted on the graph. Substantial needle movement often indicates the subject is under stress and probably lying.

As the operator prepared for the tests, Benitez kept walking around the room warily eying the process.

"Something looks wrong," he said to no one in particular as the officer was hooked up to the machine.

"Something just doesn't look right," he turned to Gavito and Neck. "It just doesn't look right."

Wheeling around, he exclaimed, "That's it!"

Benitez dashed to a cabinet, grabbed a seltzer bottle, and put it on the polygraph machine as the needles begin to jump off the graph paper.

"That's better," he said as Neck and Gavito barely concealed their amusement.

A shaken seltzer bottle filled with chile peppers and the burning sensation the foaming concoction initiates when discharged up a suspect's nose has elicited more "truth" in Mexico than all the polygraphs in the United States. It sometimes wins false confessions as well—but the three suspects got the message.

It took more than twenty minutes before the suspects' overstressed systems returned to normal and the polygraph tests began. The first suspect did admit to extortion of students, but he was cleared of suspicion in Mark Kilroy's disappearance. The other two also passed the Kilroy test. Neck and Gavito never found out why the third suspect was tested.

For the first time Helen Kilroy took a handful of posters and walked between the moving cars and trucks at the International Bridge. Normally shy, always quiet, this was her most unusual undertaking. There was a unique sense of assuagement now that she was on the scene. After spending so many days waiting by the telephone, she found release in handing a flier to each driver. She was comforted by the empathy of strangers.

Many of the drivers rolled down their automobile windows and a gust of cool air often brushed her face. Some talked to her.

"This is my son. He's missing," she would tell them, always appreciative of the compassion that swept across most faces.

"I'm so sorry," one woman told her. "I know how you feel, I lost a son."

The Kilroys' close friends, Joe and JoAnn Luna, had made the long drive from Santa Fe the previous night to bring them ten thousand posters that had been donated by a printing company. That Saturday the Lunas joined Jim, Helen, and Keith in distributing the posters. Before the search would end, every one of those posters would be distributed.

"This is amazing," Helen told Jim during a break. "Everyone takes a flier and keeps it."

Helen wished to communicate with more of the commuters, and struggled to learn how to say "my son is missing" in Spanish. The best she could muster was *"Mi hijo"*—my son.

Jim was amazed at Helen's ability to handle the job requiring contact with hundreds of strangers. Shyness was replaced by determination. She would do whatever it took to find Mark.

Many months later Helen would have the chilling thought that as she had distributed the posters she might have come face to face with someone who knew of Mark's whereabouts.

Neck and Gavito flew to Washington, D.C., Saturday to field telephone calls on Easter Sunday, the night that "America's Most Wanted" would feature the Kilroys.

ABOVE LEFT: Keith and Mark practice Dad's shaving technique. ABOVE RIGHT: Mark in a family wedding, 1971.

RIGHT: 1978 Pinewood Derby race-car winners—Mark, first place best design; Keith, speed trophy.

BELOW LEFT: Keith and Mark show off Mark's big catch.

RIGHT: Family dog Benji, Charlotte (foster child in the Kilroy home), and Mark, 1982.

Helen, Mark, and Jim Kilroy, 1986 when Mark graduated from high school.

Mark, baseball all-star, 1983.

LEFT CENTER: Jim and Mark Kilroy in Australia, 1987.

ABOVE: Mark, Christmas Eve, 1987.

LEFT: Mark (left) and brother Keith with Uncle Ken Kilroy (center) at grandparents' 50th wedding anniversary, 1987.

Keith and Mark surfing in Australia, 1987.

RIGHT: Eddie de la Houssaye, Mark Kilroy, Mary de la Houssaye, Keith Kilroy, Jim Kilroy, and Helen Steier (grandmother) at Keith's high school graduation 1988.

BELOW: Mark, his mother, and Keith on a family outing to celebrate Mark's 20th birthday.

THIRD WEEK

Easter Sunday.

A time to glory in death. A time for rebirth, for rededication. A time for jubilation.

"He *is* alive!"

Father Nicolau shouted the words in joy that Easter morning as believers celebrated the resurrection of Jesus Christ at Saint Luke's Catholic Church.

Helen clutched Jim's hand, fighting back the tears.

"He is alive," she whispered to herself, "Mark is alive."

It was something she wanted to believe with all her heart as the search entered its third week. Seated in church among members of like faith, it was easier to have hope, although the police officers were beginning to offer hints of discouragement. Her faith offered her the belief in eternal life, of a resurrected life in a spiritual world. But she lived within the prevailing reality of flesh and blood, and it was within this reality that she hoped to clutch her son to her breast. She remembered the admonition Mary LeCompte had given to Keith on Palm Sunday. "Pray 'Thy will be done,'" she had said. She had also suggested that the family pray to find Mark dead or alive. Helen wondered if she ever could pray that about Mark. Would she ever reach that point in spiritual growth? How could she ever let go of Mark?

Only a few weeks before she had spent Mark's birthday flooded with a mother's memories. His twenty-first birthday had been more of a milestone to her than to him. She sat in church, releasing one precious memory after another, memories that could only be stored in a mother's heart.

One special moment kept shining through. She was fascinated that it did because it was a fleeting instant of emotional joy without historic importance to her family. She could have thought of a high school triumph, or a first job, or some other milestone that marked Mark's passage through life. Instead, this special memory filled her with a bittersweet serenity.

She found her mind wandering back twenty-one years to a small bedroom where sunlight filtered through curtained windows before playing across a baby's bed. She remembered standing there, a young woman who had experienced the miracle of birth, the miracle of what two people's love had created, and whispering to her young son, "You are such a treasure." She remembered lifting him from his bed and holding him close, thinking at the time that she could not hold him tight enough.

"I don't think I can ever love you enough," she remembered saying to the cooing infant.

Mark had constantly amazed her. When he was five years old, he came home from kindergarten with a note he had carefully printed. It promised his parents a special gift. After dinner he seated them in the living room, then fetched a school book. He stood in the center of the room and in an unfaltering voice read a page out of the text.

"It's amazing," she beamed to Jim. "He's not even in school and he's reading."

But her pride went beyond achievement; her first born had demonstrated a child's natural sensitivity which eventually evolved into a more mature perception of human nature. It was a trait that his mother cherished. Helen believed it was an attribute that culminated in his decision to become a doctor.

As a ten-year-old Cub Scout, Mark earned a religious award that required him to keep a journal and perform an act of service. Helen's father was hospitalized and struggling for breath due to a respiratory illness.

The child made his grandfather a nativity scene out of ice cream sticks. But it was his journal entry that she would cherish in her heart.

"I pray that my grandfather will not be lonely," he had written in childish scroll.

It was a heart-warming, yet peculiar entry. Helen had expected Mark to pray that his grandfather's health would improve, which would have been a normal prayer for a child. Instead, the perceptive little boy, who sensed the lonely hours which grew into months of hospital confinement, had sought an emotional succor for his grandparent.

Only a few years ago his strong perception of family ties demanded the sacrifice of a teen-age dream. The Kilroys had gone on a vacation to Australia in 1987. The long trip back would require a break in the journey at either Hawaii or California. The family could spend a few extra days before resuming the trip. Mark and Keith eagerly chose Hawaii with its promise of surf and sand, a perfect conclusion to the vacation and most teen-agers' dream of paradise.

Meanwhile, Jim Kilroy's parents' fiftieth wedding anniversary celebration coincided with the family's trip. For Mark there was no decision when the anniversary plans in California were revealed.

"We have to change the stopover to Los Angeles and go to the anniversary party in San Diego," he told the three other family members. "We just can't miss it.

"How many people do you know who have been married that long," he said, before adding. "Besides, this is a once in a lifetime event."

Another special memory also filled her mind: Mark was in his room studying. Helen had assumed that he was deep in his sociology books, preparing for a crucial test the next day. But when she walked by, she found him reading his Bible.

That's wonderful, she remembered thinking. An hour later, she passed by and he was still reading the Bible. Now she faced a real dilemma. Mark needed to study for his big test the next day.

"What do you do? Do you go in and tell your son to quit reading the Bible?" Helen laughed when she told Jim.

Easter Sunday services were ending. Helen tucked her memories safely back into her mother's heart as the congregation rose as one. The joy, the hope of resurrection had refreshed her spirit. As the choir brought "He Is Alive" to its conclusion, Helen knew she would have the strength to fight on, no matter how long it took to find Mark.

She appreciated the irony that Easter Sunday would end with her live appeal on "America's Most Wanted." She could only hope that it would move someone to help them find her son.

In Washington, D.C., Neck and Gavito watched with millions of other viewers that night as Helen nervously described a mole on Mark's chin, an identifying mark that had been partially removed in childhood.

In Santa Fe, Sandy Cornelius watched the show from her sick bed. Although she had developed double pneumonia, the auction/bake sale/garage sale remained on schedule.

Eddie de la Houssaye, who had returned to Santa Fe several days before, turned on the video recorder as he and Mary watched their friends on national television.

Shortly before the broadcast, Jim had received a telephone call from the host of the show, John Walsh, who could truly understand the Kilroys' emotional suffering. Walsh's son Adam had been kidnapped and killed. He understood the agony of the search and the subsequent grief should the search end with death.

Walsh offered hard-earned advice to Jim and Helen: "You have to be very, very careful of your marriage," he said. "Most parents of kidnapped or murdered children get divorced. Sometimes, all they have is their grief."

"Because many parents will not give up the search, they run into trouble at their place of employment, and many lose their jobs," he explained.

"After six months, people begin to forget your problems," Walsh continued. "I pushed hard. I was very intense and people would say, 'Oh, no, here he comes again.' Be careful not to press people too hard," he advised.

The couple barely had time to reflect on Walsh's advice before the segment was broadcast. It seemed to Jim and Helen that the live appearance was over almost as soon as it started; both had wanted to ask the nation to pray for their son, but there was not enough time.

As the camera faded, the switchboard lighted up. Hundreds of calls came in that night; over the next few days, more than eight hundred calls were logged. Savvy operators shielded the lawmen from the regular crank callers while feeding potential leads into their extensions. All calls from Northern Mexico received special attention.

The men were stunned by the power of the broadcast. Helpful tips placed Mark all over the country—from an eighteen-wheel tractor-trailer outside Charleston, South Carolina, to a truckstop in Arizona where one man swore he saw Mark eating a snowcone. A few minutes later another caller insisted he had seen Mark Kilroy surfing off the coast of Seattle, Washington, while still another caller had seen him in Los Angeles. Every call was logged. The men spent hours on the telephone as the show followed the time zones across the country, each hour bringing a new flood of calls. By the end of the evening, Gavito turned to Neck and said, "I believe we've had him reported in all fifty states."

Over the next few days Neck and Gavito methodically checked with state police on each reported sighting only to come up empty.

One story did draw their interest. A woman who called from Denton, Texas, told the officers the same night Mark disappeared a group of men in a black Chevrolet had tried to pick up a group of girls in Matamoros. Her boyfriend had fled in terror as the men in the black automobile pulled up next to them, jumped from their black car, and tried to force the girls into the sinister vehicle. The women escaped without harm.

And then came what they thought might be their biggest break.

An anonymous telephone call found Neck and Gavito in the sheriff's office. Gavito flicked on his telephone tape recorder as the tipster provided the name and address of a man in Las Sprinetas, the toughest neighborhood in Brownsville.

"He's bragging that he killed Mark Kilroy," the caller said, providing enough gory details to convince the lawmen to check it out. Five cars were dispatched to the home, which was quickly surrounded. Neck's men covered the back while Gavito's deputies went though the front door. The suspect bolted out the back, over a fence, and into the waiting arms of Customs agents.

"We've got the goods on him," Oran said when he saw marijuana and stolen items in plain sight.

What happened next occurred in a matter of a few seconds, but it played out like a comedy worthy of the Keystone Kops. The lawmen found themselves surrounded by angry neighbors who had begun to pour out of nearby homes.

Even more irate was the mother of the nineteen-year-old suspect. She stormed up to the nearest officer, fearlessly peered up into his face, grabbed his tie, and began to jerk it. The towering officer stared at her in disbelief. Undaunted, she began to yank on his badge as neighbors yelled encouragement. Unable to move the officer, she doubled up a fist and walloped him in the stomach.

"That's enough, ma'am," Deputy Tony Lopez said politely as he picked the woman up to set her aside. But the rest of the pack attacked, and the officers soon found themselves in the middle of a riot.

"Get everyone out of here," Neck commanded, pushing the suspect into his car. The officers scattered in a mad dash to the safety of patrol cars. As Neck slammed the gas pedal to the floorboard and the car began to pick up steam, he was aware of a pounding on the window.

Somebody's about to break in, he thought as he looked over to see a frantic George Gavito running alongside.

"Let me in!" he yelled. "Don't leave me here!"

Oran hit the door release and George piled in laughing.

"I locked my keys in my car," he exclaimed. "Let's get out of here; I'll send a wrecker back for it."

"You're some cop," Oran grinned back.

It was an exhilarating moment as they exchanged looks.

Did they have the person who knew what happened to Mark Kilroy?

"I think so," Neck said in answer to the unspoken question.

The teen-age suspect proved tough to crack. He readily admitted to marijuana use—and both officers suspected he was high when arrested. He confessed to burglary, but he steadfastly denied any knowledge of Mark Kilroy's disappearance. Gavito's instincts told him there was something still untold, and he suspected it concerned Mark.

"You're not going to talk to me?" Gavito asked.

"No," was the only reply.

A Mexican national, the suspect had successfully applied for citizenship under the alien-amnesty program in which the government had offered amnesty to any illegal alien who would declare himself and apply for citizenship.

"I think I know how to break him," Gavito said privately.

Without warning, the smug suspect found himself hustled back into Gavito's car and driven to the International Bridge. Gavito parked facing the bridge and quietly waited, occasionally leaning out the window to peer into Mexico.

"What are you doing?" the suspect finally asked.

"I'm looking for Benitez. You won't talk to me, so I'm going to turn you over to him. In forty-five minutes you're going to be telling me everything you know about Mark Kilroy," Gavito replied.

"You can't do that. I can't go over there," the suspect broke into tears, heaving great sobs.

Gavito was amazed at the display.

"Why not?"

The weeping boy told a tale of vengeful murder. A few months before a Mexican police officer had slapped him. The youth had returned later with a carbine and pumped seven bullets into the officer, then calmly walked across the border into the United States.

Further interrogation convinced the Americans that he did not know anything about Mark, so Gavito turned him over to the U.S. Immigration Service. Since there is no extradition treaty with Mexico, since the American charges against him were minor, and since he had been approved under the amnesty program, he was released within a matter of weeks.

It would be the most trying week of the investigation as Neck and Gavito bounced from one lead to another.

A high-ranking city official in Matamoros called to say he knew where Mark was buried. Agents were dispatched. After spending the better part of a day digging at various sites, the official suggested that the officers come back another day.

"Maybe the voices will be more specific when they come to me tonight," he said.

Neck and Gavito were contacted when a young man arrested in nearby Mission, Texas, confessed to Mark's murder. He claimed to have killed Mark Kilroy as a human sacrifice near a big rock during a satanic ritual at Boca Chica Beach. He also claimed to be one of the leaders of more than four hundred satanists in the Valley. A polygraph test revealed it to be a false confession but his estimate of the number of satanists in the Valley bore elements of truth.

A Hispanic friend of the Kilroys contacted her kinsmen in Matamoros to check on street rumors and discovered that common gossip pointed a finger at San Salvadorian refugees. Because many of them had fled political repression only to be stopped at the American border, they were desperate, had no money, and had no place to stay.

"The [Mexican] people are afraid of them," the Kilroys' friend said.

She had also discovered a puzzling report concerning local ranches. "Tell the Kilroys to check all the ranches around here. Something might be going on at them," she was told. "Also, there are slaughterhouses. They should be checked."

Jim and Helen realized that they had been concentrating on the twin cities at the border. The ranches might be worth investigating. But the reference to slaughterhouses puzzled them. Did the rumor mean that police should check commercial slaughterhouses where cattle are processed for consumption, or did the gossip have a darker, more sinister meaning?

For the rest of the week, Jim concentrated on getting the word to the ranches through Spanish radio stations. It was a daily battle to keep the search for Mark on the air. Each time the radio stations publicized his search for Mark it would be erroneously reported that the youth had been found and the radio spots would stop. Coupled with the language barrier, it was a frustrating task.

An English-language newspaper published in Mexico City reported on March 24 that Mark had been found in a Brownsville hospital, the victim of a drug overdose. It quoted Jose Antonio Solis, president of the Matamoros Chamber of Commerce, as the source of information.

Jim once again got the radio stations straightened out. But it lasted only a few days before another similar report brought publicity to a screeching halt.

Neck was surprised to hear Don Wells, head of the U.S. Consulate in Matamoros, on the other end of the line when he answered one late-night telephone call.

"We have a lead to Mark Kilroy," Wells began without preliminary.
That woke Neck up.

"You have?" both question and statement.

"A fisherman has been brought in to us. He says he picked up a
gringo several weeks ago," Wells remembers telling Neck.

"We'll deliver the fisherman to you in the morning."

"No. Right now. In the morning is too late. Right now, and we'll
get Mark's parents."

"I said we'll do it in the morning. You have agents over here in the
morning."

He may have seen him, or know where he is, Neck thought after
Wells hung up. Now he was too excited to sleep, the adrenaline
revitalizing his tired body.

It was a restless night. He visualized the Kilroys reunited with
Mark, the family joy and the huge celebration that followed, everyone involved in the investigation congratulating each other. Jim had
told the lawman that he wanted to march through the streets of the
two cities, his son by his side.

Then realism enveloped his reprieve, dashing his hopes against
the cold, hard rocks of fact. This long after his disappearance, the
odds of finding Mark alive were virtually nil. And from information
two weeks old. Neck knew he was grasping at straws.

News media from both sides of the border had been called to the
8:00 A.M. meeting. A somewhat bewildered fisherman was paraded
out. Yes, he had seen Mark Kilroy, he said. He had given him a drink
of water.

So where is Mark?

"The last I saw him, he was walking along the beach in a daze," he
replied.

"When?"

"Two, maybe three weeks ago."

Neck and Gavito bleakly exchanged looks.

"He wanted the reward," Neck said, as Gavito nodded.

Once again Jim Kilroy had to inform the radio stations that Mark
had not been found. Once again he had to plead for air time to
promote the search.

The Kilroys decided to solicit the support of Texas politicians with
a quick trip to Austin that had two goals. First, they hoped to keep
publicity alive in their search for Mark; second, they wanted to bring
pressure to bear on the State Judicial Police in Matamoros, the Mexican agency with investigative jurisdiction that had refused to cooperate. Perhaps American elected officials could persuade their Mexican
counterparts to help.

In a whirlwind twenty-four-hour trip, with the press dogging their every move, the Kilroys visited Lloyd Criss, their home-town state representative; Rider Scott, the governor's general counsel; and Mike Toomey, chief administrative assistant to Governor Bill Clements. They also spoke with Gay Erwin, state director for U.S. Senator Lloyd Bentsen; Commander Joe Murphy of the Texas Department of Public Safety; and Texas Attorney General Jim Mattox, who had already dispatched Francisco Castillo, his special administrative assistant, to Ciudad Victoria to talk to Mattox's Mexican counterpart.

Even President George Bush had become the object of a telegram campaign by Santa Fe townsmen. Jim and Helen's trip to Austin had proven successful. Publicity concerning the case was at its height. The heat was being turned up through a variety of political pressures, but still there was no break in the case.

Neck and Gavito knew that in Mexico any body that was discovered would be reported immediately. People who found a corpse would run, not walk to the nearest police station as a means of self-protection. If a body was discovered and it was later learned that someone was seen near it or in its general vicinity, that person would be subjected to Mexican "interrogation" techniques.

"If this were a normal case and Mark were dead—which we both suspect—you would think we'd get the body," Neck said early one morning. "We've got the pressure turned up so high that it would be better for whoever did it to go, dig up the body, and throw it in the street."

It was not wishful thinking. He knew that criminals often did that to help shut down an investigation. Often when a body was found, the family gained relief, buried its dead, and tried to reassemble its life.

The pressure was also beginning to backfire on the lawmen as the third week drew to a close. Neck and Gavito were increasingly coming under criticism from officers in other law-enforcement agencies who had tired of the high profile generated by the publicity. Several felt that the two men were foolishly following a case that would never be closed. After all, they said, the investigation was in its third week without even one substantial lead. Even Sheriff Perez was beginning to hint to Gavito that the homicide detective had other responsibilities. On Saturday, April 1, Mark would have been missing nineteen days.

Neck was given a freer rein; but he offered to take his vacation time to continue the search.

The men began to work less and less on the case during office hours, but they made up the difference by devoting every spare hour of their personal time to the investigation.

"We need to set a deadline on this," Gavito said one evening as the two men relaxed. "We have to look at it like cops."

"Maybe we *are* getting personally obsessed with this," Neck agreed. "But how do you let go? How do you put this on the back burner? It's not like any other case we've ever investigated."

"I'm running out of ideas. I don't know what to do next to keep the media interested," Gavito said gloomily.

The officers even considered boosting the reward past fifteen thousand dollars—but decided it was too risky.

Jim Kilroy:

It was a difficult time for Oran and George. The men had not taken a day off from work since the investigation began March 14. The concept of an eight-hour day had evaporated under the press of work. A ten-hour day was short. Twelve or more hours a day was more likely—even an eighty-hour week had become normal, not only for them, but for their men, too.

It didn't make any difference what time of the day or night I showed up, one or the other would be in his office. Every Sunday I went to the sheriff's office after Mass, and every Sunday I found George there. It was his day off, but I knew he would be working on the case, following up one more lead.

These men were walking a tight rope that no one had considered, even fellow officers: They investigated without jurisdiction since Mark had disappeared in Mexico.

Technically, there was no case.

"There is no violation of U.S. law in Mark's disappearance," Oran told me early on. "We don't have the jurisdiction to investigate."

But that didn't stop them from pressing forward.

George would laugh: "I've investigated without jurisdiction in Matamoros for fifteen years. Don't worry about it."

Without the goodwill of Juan Benitez Ayala, the two had nothing. Benitez never told Gavito and Neck that he didn't have time to follow every lead. That courageous and honest officer has yet to receive the full recognition he deserves for pioneering the type of cooperation between our countries that could shut down the drug lords.

A technicality protected the investigation.

"Until we find out what happened to Mark, we don't know if there has been a violation of U.S. law and we will not know until we learn something," George explained.

The case will stay open, George promised. But I held my breath, because I feared that the investigation could be shut down at any minute or relegated to secondary status.

Every day I thanked God for these three men and asked that He would use His divine providence to protect and keep them on the job.

Texas Attorney General Mattox's aide Castillo was successful in his conference with the attorney general in Ciudad Victoria, the capital city of Tamaulipas. The Mexican official pledged renewed interest by the Mexican state police after nearly three weeks of neglect. But Matamoros State Judicial Police Comandante Silvio Brusolo claimed to have received no official report when he telephoned to talk to Gavito. It was an angry confrontation.

"Hey man, you had two representatives at the original meeting we had three weeks ago," Gavito replied, anger building in his voice. "Since then, all they do is tell us they know nothing and that's when we're lucky enough for them to return our calls."

When he hung up, Gavito grinned at Neck.

"The heat's beginning to build," he said.

The SJP's original lack of cooperation had puzzled the American detectives. Doors were closed that had been opened for years. When the doors were reopened after the Mexican governor expressed interest in the case, Jim and Helen were dispatched by the U.S. Consulate to make an official report with the State Judicial Police in Matamoros where they received a chilly reception that was almost threatening. No consulate official accompanied the parents, but Sheriff Perez sent Sheriff's Deputy Ernesto Flores as translator and escort for the Kilroys.

The interview was interrupted by a dour-faced man who said something in Spanish to the SJP official conducting the interview. As the Kilroys started to leave, Jim turned to Ernesto. "Don't you think I should meet the comandante and encourage him to help us search for Mark?" he asked.

Ernesto just shook his head. "Jim, that was the comandante who just came in here," he said, explaining that Brusolo had instructed the interrogator to be sure and get a comprehensive statement from the parents. "I don't think he wants to be encouraged; I don't think he wants to talk to you!"

When Ernesto returned to the sheriff's office he told Gavito, "I'm not going back over to that SJP office. There's a feeling in the air of bad trouble."

The SJP demanded to interview Mark's companions, but they wanted the interview to be in Mexico. Fearful that the young men would be tortured, Neck and Gavito refused the request.

The heat ignited a new brushfire a few hours later.

Not only were Mexican nationals haranguing the U.S. Consulate in Matamoros, but U.S. congressmen and senators kept up a steady barrage of telephone calls seeking information on the case which was becoming a political hot potato through national and international publicity. The politicians wanted to know what was going on. Were officials any closer to finding the Kilroy boy? What was the United States doing to help the Mexican police?

Don Wells of the U.S. Consulate called Gavito to discuss the progress of the case. Gavito recalls saying to Wells in frustration, "Your job is to protect the citizens of the United States of America, not to defend the Mexican police. If they're mad, let them be mad."

Gavito's and Neck's frustration was eased, however, by an outpouring of support from the whole spectrum of society.

One tipster identified himself as a man Neck had sent to prison. Out on parole, he had overheard three people discussing the Kilroy case at a bar.

"You might want to talk to them," he told Neck. "They're capable of doing this. I know. They're my friends. And, you can tell them I told you about them."

Neck marveled. "You'd think this guy would hate me," he told Jim Kilroy. "But instead he's trying to help."

The three men were picked up. Yes, they were discussing the missing gringo. But wasn't everyone in Brownsville and Matamoros?

Early on, the lawmen had considered turning to the Mexican Mafia for help. Now was the time.

"The Mexican Mafia isn't the same as the Mafia in the United States," Neck explained to Jim. "In Mexico, a Mafia leader can be defined as a businessman who has contact with the underworld."

"And some of them have high profiles," Gavito added. "Some of them have their names in the society columns of newspapers all the time."

The two explained that Mafia leaders traffic in smuggled goods feeding the demand for electronics and staples in the struggling country.

"One of our major concerns right from the start was that Mark had been so beaten up that whoever did it won't give him back to us until he looks better," Gavito explained.

"We can't get into some of the rooms in the hospitals," he said, listing intensive care, operating, critical-care heart units, and other inaccessible areas where Mark could be hidden. "So we don't know for sure that he's not in one."

"And the hospitals will only let registered nurses into all the rooms," Neck added.

The next day two registered nurses were hired by a Mafia leader after he met with the law officers.

"By every room, I mean the restrooms and storage rooms and closets, anywhere he could be hidden in a hospital," the Mafia leader instructed the nurses when he sent them out that Friday.

At the close of the day, two weary nurses had surreptitiously checked every room in every hospital in Matamoros. They both agreed when they reported back that Mark was not in any hospital in Matamoros.

The lawmen convinced Jim and Helen to go home. They needed a rest, and they needed to attend to neglected business. Jim had been on the scene for sixteen exhausting days.

Helen looked worriedly at the two men just before leaving.

"I promise. We won't let up," Neck told her.

"We'll continue to do everything possible," Gavito added.

Jim and Helen distributed fliers one more time at the International Bridge on their way out of town. Late that afternoon, the parents reluctantly drove to the city limits. Jim stopped on the side of the road. He stood by the car, looking back into the city, overcome with emotion.

"I never wanted to leave this place unless we would be bringing Mark home," he said.

"I know," Helen said as the two shared their grief. "But we'll be back in a few days."

The woman identified herself as a psychic. The dispatcher at the Santa Fe Police Department was skeptical, but took the report anyway.

The woman claimed to have had a vision the night before. She saw a young man trembling in fear under a tree. She also saw a large piece of yellow plastic lying on the ground with a few leaves blowing across it.

The dispatcher passed the report on to Chief Mike Barry, who sent it on to the Cameron County Sheriff's Office.

Everyone noted that it was April 1, April Fool's Day.

FOURTH WEEK

Jim Kilroy suggested that maybe he should try to contact San Antonio Mayor Henry Cisneros.

"He is a good friend of the president of Mexico," Mark Whitworth, a friend of the Rodriguez family, had explained when offering to help the Kilroys contact the mayor.

George Gavito jumped at the idea when Jim telephoned him from Santa Fe.

"And all the people down here, in the Valley and in northern Mexico, are his fans. I think he can do us some good because he is so well liked," George added.

"Who knows? He might appeal to that one person who might know something. You figure for every murder there's always at least two people who know about it. It would take more than one person to do something to someone the size of Mark."

"Cisneros would sure be encouraging to the Mexican police, especially a man like Benitez," Jim agreed.

"And Cisneros could hold a press conference. It would be a good human interest story that would keep this in the news," Neck suggested later.

The days of the fourth week dragged slowly into each other. Every day, as they had for three weeks, agents checked new leads. They kept tabs on jails, hospitals, and the automobile impound lots in Matamoros. Every day, as it had been for three weeks, they found nothing to lead them any closer to Mark Kilroy.

Meanwhile, Santa Fe had become a beehive of activity as a chance remark by Helen sparked a new round of publicity.

"I'd like to tie a yellow ribbon on the tree in front of the house,"

Helen said to Billy's mother, Gwen Huddleston. "It would show that Mark is missing, but he is not forgotten."

Gwen swung into action, recognizing another good way to keep Mark's name before the public. Soon yellow ribbons fluttered throughout Santa Fe, showing the nation that Mark was not forgotten.

On April 6, twenty-four days after Mark disappeared, Santa Fe Mayor Jack L. Long declared a portion of the next week, April 12-16, as Mark Kilroy Awareness Days. Elementary school children would open the observance on April 12 by tacking yellow ribbons to an old oak tree in front of Our Lady of Lourdes Catholic Church.

"(We) ask everyone in the community, surrounding communities, and in our nation to become involved by wearing yellow ribbons to display their support to Mark Kilroy, the Kilroy family, and all those searching for Mark. Our prayers are with you!" the proclamation read in part.

Supporters immediately began wearing bright yellow ribbons; some bore the legend, "Miss You Mark."

"Will you accept a collect call from Danny Lopez?" the operator asked when the call came in at 7:30 Tuesday night.

Since Jim Kilroy did not know anyone named Danny Lopez his first inclination was to refuse; but in a heartbeat he realized this person could be calling about Mark.

"Yes, I will," Jim said, routinely turning on the tape recorder attached to the telephone.

The voice on the other end of the line asked to speak to Helen. Jim picked up an extension in the bedroom after handing the telephone to Helen.

"I know where Mark is," the voice said.

The parents listened intently as he continued, saying Mark was being held captive in a notoriously tough neighborhood in Houston, only three blocks from a juvenile detention center.

"Did you see Mark?" Helen held her breath, thinking that this could be the break they sought.

"Yes." He went on to explain that he had made a trip to a residence in the ghetto to purchase marijuana ten days ago. Then, suddenly cautious, the caller was ready to end the conversation.

"I'll call back at midnight," he said, before adding. "These guys who have Mark are very dangerous. Don't involve the police."

"What do you want? Do you want the fifteen thousand dollars reward money?" Helen asked.

"How much?"

"Fifteen thousand."

"I hadn't heard about that," he said as Helen noted the surprise in his voice.

"Do you want money?"

"Yes I do. I'll call back. Let me find out what the men who are holding Mark want to do."

Helen was staring at the telephone when Jim came in the room.

"Do you think . . . ?" she left the thought unfinished.

"I don't know, but we should call the police," was his immediate reaction. "I'm glad Ken told us to put the tape recorder on the telephone."

Santa Fe Police Chief Mike Barry was home when Jim called.

"I'll be right there," he said.

He had never met the Kilroys, or Mark; but like thousands of others, he agonized with them in their present tribulation. A thirty-five-year-old father of two, with another on the way, Barry could easily understand a parent's anguish. It was a desire to be of service to good people like the Kilroys that had inspired him to become a law officer.

Barry is a no-nonsense policeman who worked undercover narcotics for seven years before being named Santa Fe police chief in early March, only a few days before Mark disappeared. On the way to the Kilroys he considered the situation. The telephone call sounded like extortion. But there is no extortion law in Texas; extortion is a federal offense. If the caller tried to extort money from the Kilroys, Barry would have to work the case as either theft by felony or, if a threat of bodily harm should occur, he could then investigate it as attempted aggravated robbery.

I'll have to treat it as if it were a true kidnapping, he thought, keying his radio microphone. "Call the FBI for me and ask them to meet me at the Kilroys."

After hearing the tape, Barry arranged to have a trace put on the Kilroys' telephone, hoping it would pinpoint the house Danny Lopez would call from. Barry suspected, however, that Danny would be using a pay telephone. As the evening wore on, Danny did not call. The officers left. As the weary lawmen were eating an early-hours breakfast, the telephone rang in the Kilroy home at 2:12 A.M. It was a different man who tried to pass himself off as Danny. He talked briefly, then promised to call back in thirty minutes.

The lawmen returned to the Kilroys, where Barry used the telephone to check the trace, which turned out to have been ineffective.

They began another nerve-jangling wait until the telephone rang.

"Who were you talking to?" Danny sounded angry.

Helen refused to comment.

"I know that the cops are involved. So do the people who have Mark," he added.

"No, everything's fine," Helen said. Her calm voice belied her trembling spirit as she tried to soothe the man who could hold her son's life in his hands.

"We're going to test you to see if you are going to do what we say," he said.

"Did you find out anything?" Helen asked.

"We want two thousand dollars at 5:00 P.M.," he said, going on to describe a fast-food restaurant in Galveston as the meeting place.

"Give the money to the woman in the restroom. Then look on the paper towels—the tenth one—and you will find a telephone number and a time to call Mark," he said. "You can talk to Mark for five minutes. Then you will get eight thousand dollars more, pay that, and you'll get your son back," he finished his instructions.

"Why are you doing this?" Helen asked.

"To help you get Mark; so he can come home," he said. Then he added that the person Helen was to meet would be dressed in black.

"I'll do anything—if you're telling the truth—to get my son back," Helen said.

"I'll call back at 2:00 P.M.," he said before hanging up.

Again the telephone traces were ineffectual due to late-night delays. In the middle of the night, a call from nearby Galveston might be routed through Houston.

It was a sleepless night for the Kilroys.

"There's nothing I can do to help you," Jim said.

"I know," Helen replied. "But, Jim, this could mean that Mark is alive."

Both felt the stirring of hope, an emotion that had begun to sag during the past few days.

As they waited for the telephone to ring again, Helen recalled a conversation she had had with Jim a week earlier when she and Keith had noticed that Jim had begun to refer to Mark in the past tense.

"Don't do that," Helen had urged. "We don't know that Mark is dead. He could be alive. And it bothers Keith and me when you talk about Mark in the past tense."

"I didn't realize I was doing it," Jim answered. "When I first put out the posters for Mark I felt very sad, very lonely, and depressed. Each time I put one up I would ask God, 'Why me? Why my son? Why my family?'

"I tried to not look at his picture—just keep myself busy and not dwell on it," Jim tried to explain.

"But on about the fifth or maybe the sixth day, I found myself looking at the posters. I remember exactly what I was doing. I was putting one on a telephone pole. I looked at Mark's picture and, Helen, I felt happy for him," Jim said, incredulous at his changing emotions. "Ever since then whenever I think of Mark, I feel happy for him."

Helen listened in silence.

"At first I thought it was weird, but now I believe that God gave me this as a sign that Mark is with Him in heaven," Jim continued.

"But how do we know that Mark is not still alive?" Helen asked again. "And I know that Mark knows that we will never stop looking for him."

"Don't worry. I'm not telling anyone but you about the way I feel," Jim reassured her. "If I did that, people would quit looking for Mark and I will not allow that to happen. I will never give up."

Helen told Jim about the woman who told Keith to pray for Mark, to pray that he be found either dead or alive.

"I just can't pray that," Helen said. "I want him back alive."

"But Helen, if Mark is dead, then he would be all right," Jim said, leaning on the beliefs of his Catholic faith. "This feeling that I have, I know that God gave it to me as a sign that Mark is with Him in heaven. No one is deserving of heaven, and it is only God's mercy and love that can get you there," he added. "I think all of the prayers for Mark had much to do with what I'm feeling."

"I know that Mark will be fine if he is dead. I know that he will be with our Lord, but I just can't think of him in the past tense . . . in this life. At least not until we find out what's happened," Helen said, tears forming.

Jim gently took his suffering wife into his arms. He was living within the reality of the situation and within the emotional release he had found through his religious faith. He had discovered a peace that surpasses understanding. But he could not allow the search for his son to abate because of his emotional reaction to the thought that Mark might be dead.

And I'm not ready to give up all hope that he will be found alive, he thought within himself.

"We'll find our son," he reassured her. "I won't stop until we do. We'll keep the heat on."

"I know," she said.

But will Mark be alive, or dead? she thought.

She was still thinking about the conversation, wondering if the search was just about to come to an end with these mysterious telephone calls, when the telephone rang again at 1:45 P.M., fifteen minutes early. The caller said that plans had been changed. Helen was to go to an apartment complex by a service station in Galveston and wait at a pay telephone at 5:00 P.M. She would be watched. A Spanish female would approach her. Helen was to give her the two thousand dollars, and she would give Helen the telephone number which she could use to call Mark.

"I want proof that you have Mark," she insisted.

"I'll call you right back," he said.

In twenty minutes a new voice was heard.

"Do as you are told. You are not dealing with dumb people," the man said, his voice exuding a chilling, demanding authority.

I can't believe this is happening, Helen thought as she went through the pre-meeting checklist with the tense team members from the Galveston County Organized Crime Task Force.

Experts had concealed a shortwave microphone in her purse. Only moments before she had rejected the use of a bulletproof vest.

"It weighs too much," she told the concerned officers.

Chief Barry had stood reassuringly by as she was given two thousand dollars in marked bills.

"We'll do everything we can to keep you from getting hurt," an officer said.

"What do you mean?" Jim interjected.

"You never know what will happen."

Jim turned to his wife.

"You don't have to do this, Helen," he said.

"Oh, but I do. If they have Mark, we have to get him back."

Before they left for Galveston, the telephone company pin-pointed the origin of the mysterious telephone calls. The police were puzzled to discover that both telephone calls that afternoon had been made from the county jail—the first from the holding tank and the other from the booking and receiving cell.

For Jim Kilroy, it was an unreal experience, almost like watching a docu-drama unfold on television, only this time his wife's life was in jeopardy.

The meeting was carefully timed:

At 4:48 P.M. plain-clothes officers surrounded the meeting spot.

At 4:50 Helen arrived ten minutes early, got out of the car, and walked to the telephones. Unsure what to do—should she pretend to be using the telephone?—she decided to be as obvious as possible so she could be easily spotted. She waited, occasionally whispering a license-plate number of a suspicious vehicle into the hidden microphone. Curiously a strange calm began to settle over her. If there was danger, it would be worth the risk to find her son.

At 5:13 a beige stationwagon driven by a Hispanic female passed by Helen and then left. "I guess that's not her," Helen said into the mike.

At 5:18, Helen whispered, "Here comes another, and it looks like she's stopping." A blue stationwagon driven by a Hispanic female pulled up to the pay telephones; a toddler was strapped in a car seat. The woman walked past Helen to use the telephone. Helen tried to ease close to her without being obvious, hoping the microphone in her purse would pick up the conversation. *Is this for real?* Helen wondered. *The woman certainly does not look like an extortionist.* But weeks of searching for her son had prepared Helen to expect almost anything.

At 5:22 P.M. a pickup truck carrying two Hispanic men parked behind a fence that ran along the back of the nearby service station. Helen watched as one man got out and went into the restroom in the service station. Wearing blue jeans and a white Corona T-shirt, he seemed suspicious, Helen thought. *I'd better watch him.*

At 5:23 P.M. the pickup truck left. *Why would he just leave the man in the restroom?* she wondered. Her question was answered in a few seconds.

At 5:24 P.M. Corona shirt left the restroom, walked to the woman at the telephone, and they both got into the stationwagon and left. Helen continued to maintain her post as frustration mounted. No one returned, no one new appeared.

At 5:30 the surveillance was terminated.

After playing the pivotal role in a real-life drama, Helen was exhausted.

"I don't think I can take much more of this," she told Jim. "I must have felt every emotion under the sun—and a few new ones. Each time I looked at someone, each time someone drove by, I couldn't help but wonder if we were about to get Mark back," she told him on the drive home.

"Maybe it's over," he said, reaching across to touch her hand. "Maybe it was all a hoax."

"I don't know. We're just not sure if they have Mark or not," Helen answered.

The two had been home several hours when the telephone rang shortly before midnight. A new voice told Helen that he had watched her at the service station, but he also said he had spotted an undercover police officer.

"Really?" Helen said, hoping her voice showed the proper amount of surprise. "I don't know anything about the police being there."

"I believe you are trying to be cooperative," he said. "Now, we'll set up another meet."

This time they were to meet in a cemetery in the middle of Galveston.

"And if you don't cooperate, if you involve the cops, we'll send you one of the fingers of your son," he threatened, sending a shudder of fear through Helen. "There will be four people watching you."

When he tried to set up the new meet in the middle of the next week, Helen coolly suggested that the meeting occur the next day. Again she demanded proof that they had Mark.

"I'll let you talk to Mark," he said, then hung up before elaborating.

"I've had it," she said. "I'm going to find out if they have Mark or not."

At 12:56 A.M., April 6, a little more than an hour later, the Kilroys were again called collect.

"Miss Helen, everything is set for 6:00 P.M. today," the man said.

"What happened to me talking to Mark?" she shot back. "I want to see something before I leave any money."

She had made a decision to spar with the criminal.

"What kind of proof? I could have Mark write something."

"How about a picture?"

"Okay, I'll take a picture."

"A current picture?" she asked, her emotions ranging between hope and despair as she thought, *If he's willing to send a picture they may have Mark.*

"Yeah, I'll get you a picture," he said.

"Why can't I talk to Mark?" she pressed the point, praying that the culprit would not break the connection.

The question was ignored.

"Do you have Mark's driver's license?" she asked, holding her breath as she slipped her hand into her apron pocket.

"Yes. I have everything," he answered.

"What else?"

"I have his social security card, his wallet, his clothes, and his watch," he answered.

Helen could feel a dread and a relief beginning to flood her body.

"What kind of watch is it?" she probed.

"I can't tell the brand name," he replied.

"Will you bring some of this?" Helen asked.

"Yes. I'll bring a picture and his social security card."

"I'll meet you there."

When Helen hung up, she had her answer.

"They don't have Mark," she said, her voice a bit flat from the emotional drain.

"How do you know?" the police chief asked.

Helen pulled a wallet from her apron.

"Here's Mark's wallet. It has his social security card," she explained. "He left it behind at the hotel when the boys went into Matamoros. He took his driver's license for identification."

Once again Helen was given a microphone and the same two thousand dollars in marked bills. The law officers would have understood had she declined to keep the appointment. But she had accepted the risk, saying "They should not be allowed to do this to anyone else," and bravely drove toward the cemetery.

Helen eased her car onto a Galveston street leading into the historic cemetery. More than thirty undercover agents were sprinkled throughout the graveyard, posing as grounds keepers, mourners, or visiting families.

She stopped the car in the middle of the burial ground and turned off the engine so the agents could pick up sound on the hidden microphone. Within a matter of seconds, perspiration covered her as temperatures in the automobile soared. She could only crack the windows a few inches for fear someone might jump into her parked automobile.

"Look at him," the two-wave radios crackled.

A seedy-looking individual wearing a nylon stocking for a hat had entered the cemetery. He appeared to be wandering aimlessly around, perhaps a mugger looking for a grieving victim.

"He's going to be surprised if he tries to mug her," one agent chuckled over the radio.

However, the suspect was only using the cemetery as a shortcut.

"False alarm," the radio crackled again.

In a few minutes, three people drove by the cemetery in the same stationwagon that the woman with the baby had driven during the previous attempt to meet; but they never turned in.

Helen was never contacted as she sat sweltering in the automobile.

"If you get another telephone call, just blow it off," Barry advised the Kilroys. "It's just a hoax."

But Barry would not drop the investigation. On April 27 warrants were issued for the arrest of five suspects in the attempted aggravated robbery of the Kilroys, a charge selected because one suspect had threatened to cut off Mark's finger and send it to the family. Two of the suspects had used pay telephones inside the jail to coordinate the outside movements of three others. The two in jail were found guilty of aggravated robbery. The other three were charged with possession of cocaine since four to five ounces of the drug were discovered when arrest warrants were served. Officers also found ten thousand dollars in cash in a shoebox in the home.

"You can never understand greed," Barry mused.

Mayor Cisneros of San Antonio agreed to help, but he could not come to Brownsville until Sunday. Jim and Helen would drive down late on Friday. They wanted to stay in Santa Fe for two special events to be held earlier that day: A group of hometown school children planned to release clusters of yellow balloons bearing messages concerning the search for Mark, and the auction/bake/garage sale was set to begin.

Since Sandy Cornelius was still confined to bed, her husband, Eddie, had taken a week's vacation to help her with the weekend events. The bake and garage sale would be held Friday and Saturday, and the auction of new items would be on Sunday.

Baked goods poured into the Cornelius home. One five-year-old girl baked five dozen cookies that would be sold at auction for forty-five dollars, then redonated and sold again for the same amount.

By Friday Sandy was on the job, a bit woozy, but ready to see the project to completion. As the garage sale progressed, customers began telling volunteer salesclerks to "keep the change," adding just a tad more to the growing fund.

"I know we've never met, but it's like I've known you for years," Sandy said when Jim and Helen dropped by.

By the end of the auction Sunday night, seven thousand dollars would be raised.

The Santa Fe High School senior class of 1986 would also raise nine hundred dollars at a benefit car wash on Saturday at the Alta Loma Volunteer Fire Department.

The Kilroys spoke briefly to the youngsters gathered at the high school stadium Friday morning. When the yellow balloons were released during the ceremony, Helen watched them waft heavenward, thinking *each one is like a little prayer from an innocent child. I pray that one of those prayers will bring my son home to me.*

When the ceremony ended, the Kilroys began the long drive to Brownsville. In Helen's suitcase was a fresh set of clothing for Mark, and tucked to one side of the automobile trunk were a pillow and a blanket. He had been missing for twenty-five days—surely as a captive or he would have contacted them. After nearly four weeks of captivity and brutality and without proper nourishment, Mark would need special care when Helen brought him home.

As the week came to a close, Joe Rodriguez arranged a private meeting in Matamoros with another Mafia leader, someone he had known for years.

"Nobody's blaming anyone," Joe began the meeting. "The Kilroys just want to get their kid back. Jim Kilroy has told me that he wants his boy back, even if it is a body," Joe said, pausing to let the meaning soak in before emphasizing. "We just want a body if that's what they have to accept."

"Joe, there's something different about this," the businessman said in frustration. He had already been looking for Mark. "You'd think that I would know something, or hear something. But it's quiet on the streets. It's not the police. It's not an accidental death, if he's dead. And that's what's frustrating. We can't get a handle on this. It's not a normal missing-person case," he said.

"There's something very peculiar about this."

FIFTH WEEK

Driving into Brownsville Friday night, Helen and Jim had tuned in a radio preacher whose sermon topic was the power of prayer. Helen had been so fascinated with what he had to say that she stayed in the automobile to hear the end of the sermon after the couple parked in the driveway at the Rodriguez home.

"Sometimes people wonder why God doesn't answer their prayers," the minister had said. "Maybe He has been answering, but you weren't listening. Maybe your prayers have been answered already in a much better way than you could possibly ask for.

"Could it be that God has something much better in mind than what you have in mind?" he had said. "God may be preparing you for His answer to your prayers."

The minister concluded by challenging his listeners to demonstrate their faith in God by putting their lives—and their future—in His hands.

"Is your faith lacking?" he asked. "Have you turned everything over to God?"

It was a pair of questions that Helen pondered all weekend. So she was not surprised to find herself once again thinking on that sermon as she knelt in prayer at Saint Luke's Sunday morning. She let her mind wander over the events of the last four weeks. She remembered her trembling fear when Billy had told her that Mark had disappeared, and the warmth that flooded over her when the Rodriguez family opened its heart and home to them. She thought of the daily frustrations of keeping the search alive, and her stark fright when forced to deal with extortionists, a terror tinctured with the faint hope that Mark was alive. Her heart filled with gratitude for men such as Chief Mike Barry, Oran Neck, George Gavito, Juan Benitez Ayala, and hundreds of others who were searching for her son. And there was a special appreciation for Jim. Often, he had been the family's source of strength during this ordeal.

All these people have held my future in their hands at one time or the other during the past few weeks, Helen mused. *All these events have shaped my future.*

She realized it was time to do something she now believed she should have done the day Mark disappeared.

"Heavenly Father," she prayed, her heart about to burst with emotion. "I want Mark back."

She hesitated before continuing.

"I want Mark back. I want him back *alive*," she stressed the word *alive*.

"I want him back alive," she repeated, then paused before she continued, "but if he is dead, I want his body back so that our search for him can end. I pray that you return him to us," she paused before adding, "dead or alive."

She had said it. And instantly she was amazed at the stirring of inner peace. Helen looked at the crucifix hanging over the altar.

"Thy will be done," she said softly, her head bowed in submission.

As San Antonio Mayor Henry Cisneros met with Mayor Fernando Montemayor Lozano of Matamoros and Mayor Ignacio "Nacho" Garza of Brownsville early that afternoon, Serafin Hernandez Garcia, Jr., eased his pickup truck onto the highway leading to Ciudad Victoria.

Unknown to Serafin, he had been spotted by Juan Benitez Ayala's men, who pulled in behind him. Serafin was a member of a family of known drug dealers that Benitez had under surveillance. The comandante's intelligence network had revealed that a ton of marijuana was to be transported into the United States that day from the Hernandez family ranch, Santa Elena. Until now, however, Benitez had not been able to find the location of the Santa Elena ranch.

It was a routine workday for Benitez, whose federal department is responsible for curtailing drug traffic in Mexico. The young, charismatic comandante of the Mexican Federal Judicial Police (MFJP), had already distinguished himself with a series of high profile drug busts. He had stepped into a tumultuous post. Benitez's predecessor and his predecessor's top men had milked the office of millions of dollars in bribes and confiscations. He knew that his job, and his reputation as a tough, honest cop, was on the line. It was an assignment he tackled with relish.

The MFJP agents followed Serafin to the outskirts of Rancho Santa Elena, about twenty miles due west of Matamoros; but the lawmen's hopes of a big drug bust were dashed when Serafin was arrested. Most of the marijuana had been moved across the river the night before, and only a little more than fifty pounds remained in a shed on the ranch. Serafin was taken into custody after a .357 magnum pistol and a small amount of marijuana were found in his pickup.

As so often happens, the Kilroy mystery began to unravel by happenstance.

While searching the ranch, Benitez's men discovered Domingo Reyes Bustamante, a twenty-nine-year-old caretaker who had been aged beyond his years by hard physical labor. They decided to take him in, too.

One of the federal officers found a small, tightly locked shack near a corral. A nauseating smell oozed from the building. Holding his breath, he pried a window shutter open only a fraction of an inch. Flickering candles illuminated irregular patterns along the back wall.

"*Brujeria,*" he whispered under his breath. The comandante would want to know about this.

"I would like to bring you up to date on our investigation," Matamoros Mayor Fernando Montemayor was telling Cisneros.

Gavito and Neck were amazed at what they were hearing. They had no knowledge of an investigation by the Matamoros City Police. For weeks they had been begging for help with no response, and now Montemayor was reassuring Cisneros that an investigation had been conducted.

Gavito could feel the tension between the two mayors. It was a tautness that had carried over from introductions in the hotel restaurant between Cisneros and the Mexican contingent composed of State Prosecutor Octavio Javier Singlaterry, City Manager Roberto Solis, Chief of Police Jesus Urquiza, and Mayor Montemayor. Kilroy had offered a batch of posters to Urquiza who had shown a noticeable lack of interest.

"We just want to help this family get their boy back," Cisneros had said at his eloquent best when the men retired to a meeting room at the restaurant. Montemayor had listened coldly to Cisneros's plea for cooperation between the two cities.

These guys are going to stonewall us, Gavito thought as Montemayor began to speak, revealing his tack. Neck's eyes reflected the same surprise.

"They must have had a meeting before they got here," he whispered to Neck.

"Our investigation shows that Mark Kilroy made it back across the bridge into the United States," Montemayor said. "So, it's your investigation and your problem. We don't have a problem."

"What are you talking about?" Cisneros shot back, anger flashing in his voice. "He was with three boys who will swear he didn't come back."

"Mark crossed back into Brownsville on the old bridge," Montemayor answered, describing an older bridge at the southern end of Avenida Alvaro Obregon. "That's why no one saw him. They were waiting at the new bridge. That's the way the investigation is," he said matter-of-factly. "The man went back to the United States and they're saying we have him over here. They're ruining the tourism in Matamoros," he added.

Gavito had to fight to maintain control. He was already angry at the men across the table because he believed they were blocking the investigation.

Ruining tourism, he fumed to himself. *Now, instead of a boy's life, we're talking about ruining tourism.*

Gavito tried to channel the conversation back to its original purpose: "Comandante Benitez is cooperating with us 100 percent," he said, looking around the table.

The Mexican state prosecutor seized the opportunity to demand American cooperation.

"We want to talk to the three boys that were with Mark," he said. "And we want to do it in Matamoros."

"No," Gavito replied. It was a gut instinct honed by years of law enforcement. Something in the prosecutor's voice, something in the subsequent persistent requests, sounded an alarm.

"These boys are at the university; they've already taken too much time off. They've already missed too much school; they just can't come down," Gavito quickly added.

"That's the only way we can continue the investigation. We need their statements and I have to do it in Matamoros," the prosecutor insisted, hammering home the request.

Gavito leaned over to Cisneros.

"There's no way I'm going to take these boys to Matamoros," he said in a stage whisper. Cisneros looked at Neck, who nodded agreement.

"Look," Cisneros countered. "These boys don't want to come to Matamoros. They fear Matamoros. How about neutral ground, the Mexican consulate in Brownsville?" he continued. "That way you can take the statement; you'll be on Mexican soil."

The compromise accepted, Gavito agreed to contact Mark's buddies and ask them to be in Brownsville on Friday.

Jim and Helen had felt that their presence would hinder free exchange between the mayors, so they elected to wait in the restaurant with Joe Rodriguez and his son, Tony, until they were invited to join the group.

"We didn't come here to blame anyone. I just want to find my son," Jim said as Cisneros translated. Kilroy was surprised when Cisneros began translating. Jim had been told that Montemayor spoke English and that he would speak directly to the man.

"We just want your help," Cisneros stressed for Jim.

Montemayor told Jim the same thing that he had just told Cisneros, that Mark had reentered the United States at the old bridge. The cool reception from the mayor also shocked Jim. He had been told that Mayor Montemayor had lost a son about Mark's age. Jim had hoped that the mayor's loss would trigger a sympathetic reaction; but the meeting deteriorated rapidly until it ended with Cisneros suggesting a joint press conference.

It was a strained meeting with the press. Publicly, Montemayor pledged the cooperation he dodged in the private meeting. And afterward, the Mexican officials scattered, although Cisneros asked them to accompany him on a walking tour to where Mark disappeared in Matamoros.

Finally Cisneros asked Jim if he could do anything else to help.

"I would like for you to meet Benitez," Jim said. "I want you to encourage him to continue his good work."

"I've been hearing a lot about this Benitez guy," Cisneros said.

As Gavito headed for the nearest telephone, Neck escorted the group over the International Bridge and past an open park, dense with trees, a favorite spot for vendors.

"Benitez has questioned all these people," Neck said, encompassing all the vendors with a wave of his hand.

Gavito rejoined them with word that Benitez was not at his office. "He's raiding a ranch," he said. "I think it's something to do with drugs. They said he'll be back in a little bit."

The men walked the length of the Mexican block, roughly equivalent to two in the United States. On their way back, Neck pulled up just short of Garcia's, the curio shop which dominates the large intersection.

"This is about where Billy saw the man talking to Mark," Neck said, standing in front of a white building.

Cisneros nodded, quietly looking up and down the street. He slowly examined the area, almost as if soaking up the atmosphere.

It's as if he's reaching out to grab any memory of Mark which might be floating around, Gavito thought as he watched the politician.

"Let's go," Cisneros said abruptly, striding north to the International Bridge.

The comandante had just begun questioning Serafin when the interrogation was interrupted. Benitez had a visitor. Mayor Henry Cisneros, the charismatic Hispanic mayor of San Antonio, Texas, had come to plead the Kilroys' case. Benitez recognized Cisneros, one of the few Hispanics to make an impact on national politics. His relationship with Mexico had always been good, but now that a close friend and former roommate at Harvard University, Carlos Salinas de Gortari, had become president of Mexico, his international clout along the border was considerable.

Jim Kilroy was surprised at the changes he found when they arrived at Benitez's office. The once-empty parking lot was now filled with vehicles, some of them dotted with bullet holes. Inside, the men passed an eighteen-foot sailboat packed with marijuana. It had been seized on the main highway.

"Benitez has been busy," Jim said.

"He sure has," Neck replied.

Benitez put Serafin in the hallway and Cisneros brushed by the ordinary-looking suspect on his way into the comandante's office.

Serafin had his back to the group, reading something tacked to the wall, but Gavito recognized him from a kidnapping case he had worked the previous year.

"¿Qué pasa, Hernandez?" the lawman said, stopping to talk to the baby-faced suspect.

"Nada. They have me in for questioning on a little marijuana case," Serafin said, coolly dismissing his present situation. "Nothing serious."

With very few exceptions, people do not recognize extraordinary evil when in its presence. The modern tendency is to accept theatrical evil rather than the insidious malevolence found in reality. A crescendo of music, a pregnant pause, a sly look captured only by the camera, these warn an audience in the world of make-believe. But in the theater of reality, a Henry Cisneros can brush by an average-looking suspect in the hallway without thought of evil.

To look at him, Serafin appeared to be what everyone assumed him to be that night, a baby-faced man facing drug charges. Nothing serious, as he had told Gavito. There was no clash of cymbals nor closeup of shifty eyes to betray his secret thoughts. The face of evil would be a recurring theme over the next few days as law-enforcement officers sought to correlate this average-looking man with the insane activities they soon would uncover.

Former classmates at Nimitz High School in Houston's Aldine School District describe Serafin as normal, quiet, and eager to please. His yearbook photo shows the 1986 graduate as a clean-shaven, chubby-faced student dressed in a neat dark suit accented by a bow tie and a ruffled shirt. His passion was baseball, and although he only made the junior varsity team, that did not keep him from serving as the manager for the varsity team.

"He seemed real normal, just an average kid," baseball coach Del Hinze would remember a few days after the news broke.

Nimitz Principal Jack Welch only has a vague memory of Serafin, who was born in Weslaco but was reared in Houston. Serafin's grades were average and discipline was for minor infractions, just like the majority of his fellow students.

No one could come up with any weird behavior that would foreshadow his involvement in a drug cult that practiced human sacrifice.

Perhaps the irony of ironies is that Serafin was majoring in law enforcement at Texas Southmost College in Brownsville when he was arrested. He had enrolled in 1987 after his family moved to the Rio Grande Valley. In a college class assignment he had written that he wanted to be a highway patrolman with the Texas Department of Public Safety.

"Who was that?" Neck asked as Gavito joined them in the comandante's office.

"It's a guy with the Hernandez family. I met him about a year ago when his uncle was kidnapped in a bad drug deal," Gavito said, dismissing the chance meeting.

There was no indication that Serafin had recognized Jim Kilroy, who by then had developed a high profile in the twin-cities area.

As soon as Cisneros was introduced to Benitez, he got straight to the point.

"People say that I am a friend of the president of Mexico," he began. "I am going to tell you something. I am a good friend of the president. I just visited him in Mexico City."

It was a statement of fact.

"And when I get back to San Antonio, I am going to write him a letter to tell him that you are the only one who has cooperated with these men in trying to find Mark Kilroy," he quickly added.

Cisneros understood the dynamics of Mexico. What could he give a comandante?

Money?

Power?

With his loyal following, and political support in Mexico City, a comandante has everything he could want or command, including the power of life or death. In dealing with a comandante who is both honest and professional, Cisneros realized that appreciation, coupled with the pledge of recognition, was his most powerful tool. In that session with Benitez, he gave and used it freely.

It was a wide-ranging discussion. If Benitez suspected that Serafin was tied to Mark Kilroy's disappearance, he never let on. The officers discussed surveillance of a small curio shop near Garcia's. The owner had become a suspect only a few days after Mark's disappearance because of an anonymous telephone call. Officers discovered that he had dropped out of sight on the same day Mark disappeared.

The MFJP had finally located his home in a small *colonia* outside Matamoros, and Benitez had two men watching the house. The man had a reputation of using his powers as an auxiliary police officer to shake down spring breakers. As soon as the suspect showed up, he would be brought in for questioning. Neck and Gavito believed it to be a solid lead, a rarity among the thousands of wispy clues that had already vanished like puffs of smoke.

"I raided a ranch today and picked up a member of the Hernandez family," Benitez said, changing the subject.

"I saw him outside," Gavito said. "I had dealings with him a year ago."

"We got a little marijuana. I had heard that a metric ton was being transported today, but it went last night," the comandante continued.

"At least I caught him with a little marijuana, though," he said, gesturing to the evidence piled in his office. "I was just beginning to interrogate him when you came.

"And there was something else. Some of my men found a *brujeria* shack.

"We also picked up another guy," Benitez said of Reyes, the caretaker. "We have some babies missing and he might be the guy who took them. We've had two babies kidnapped in the past six months."

Neck looked at Cisneros, explaining, "Babies are also big sellers on the black market in the States."

"You know, it's possible that this *brujeria*, maybe even the missing babies, could have something to do with the disappearance of Mark Kilroy," Benitez suggested, almost as an afterthought.

Neck and Gavito nodded in agreement. It could be devil worshipers. Jim Kilroy felt a vague uneasiness at the discussion.

Still, on this particular day, the baby-faced drug smuggler in the hallway was the last person the American lawmen considered a suspect in Mark's case.

Benitez took a notepad and wrote a name on it, handing it to Oran. "There's a Cuban involved with the dope case. He's staying at the Holiday Inn in Brownsville. You might want to pick him up for questioning," he said.

Neck looked at the one-word note: Constanzo. He slipped the paper into his pocket. Jim Kilroy paused when the men rose to leave Benitez's office.

"Please find my son," he said in English. "I want him back."

"You will come here to get him," Benitez replied in Spanish. "I will find him for you."

It was an untranslated ritual. Although Gavito had to translate the first time, the two men had come to exchange the pledge in parting, by now speaking more to the heart than to the ear.

As the men left, Gavito looked up to see Serafin staring at the group. He appeared to be glowering in defiance for some reason.

"Look at the wall!" Gavito yelled at him in Spanish, upset by the stare. "What are you looking at us for?"

As they walked toward the automobile Neck patted his breast pocket containing the note and told Gavito, "I'll have one of my men check this out."

Serafin proved to be taciturn when Benitez returned to the interrogation. Always polite, always soft-spoken, Serafin evaded the questions in a soft, whining voice.

There was time for other methods later on. Maybe the caretaker would crack easily, Benitez decided. He could confess to something, or give him information to use on Serafin.

"Take him out," Benitez ordered, "and bring me the caretaker."

In the past four weeks Benitez had questioned more than a hundred people about the disappearance of Mark Kilroy, so it was almost second nature to show the caretaker a picture of Mark.

"Have you seen him?"

"*Sí, jefe*. He was at the ranch," Reyes replied. "I cooked him a meal of eggs."

"What?" Benitez was flabbergasted.

Reyes did not say anything, a baleful look on his face as he considered the ramifications of what he had already said, and what he was about to reveal.

"When?" Benitez shot back when he regained his composure, adrenaline pumping.

"Three, maybe four weeks ago."

"What day?" Benitez could not believe his luck.

"Maybe a Tuesday."

"What was he doing there?"

The caretaker hedged: "I don't know. I was told to feed him and then I was told to go tend to my goats. He was gone when I got back," he said.

"Were any other people there?"

The caretaker named three men. Agents were sent to roundup David Serna Valdez, Sergio Martinez Salinas, and Elio Hernandez Rivera for questioning. Elio was Serafin's uncle and was believed to be the current ringleader of the Hernandez gang.

Reyes had nothing else to tell. Unsure of the caretaker's role in the drug-smuggling operation, Benitez had him placed under protective custody.

So, Mark Kilroy had been seen alive, and it was only a few hours after he had disappeared, Benitez thought. Somehow, he knew the man was telling the truth. Benitez had seen the spark of recognition when Reyes had identified the picture.

For the first time, Benitez began to realize the enormity of this particular case. Perhaps it went beyond his wildest expectations. It might even deliver the Hernandez family to him.

Taking control of the Matamoros comandancia put him at a disadvantage when dealing with certain elements of the underworld. Because he had been there less than two months he had not had time to develop informants. Sometimes the lifeblood of investigation is the men who are willing to snitch on their fellow criminals for a few extra dollars.

Since arriving in Matamoros, the thirty-five-year-old comandante had been trying to put the Hernandez family out of business. It was an old battle. In 1986, Benitez had led a raid on a 250-acre marijuana plantation owned by Saul Hernandez in Tuxtepec, Oaxaca. The comandante, then a nine-year veteran of the drug wars, knew that the Hernandez family was involved in drug traffic in Matamoros, Oaxaca, and Michoacan.

Saul Hernandez Rivera, Elio's older brother, had been the brains behind the gang until he was murdered in January 1987, along with another drug figure. Saul had been machine-gunned down as he entered the Piedras Negras restaurant and bar in Matamoros. Also assassinated was Tomas Morlet, who was one of the first individuals picked up in the investigation into the death of Enrique "Kiki" Camarena, an American Drug Enforcement Agency officer who had been tortured and murdered in Guadalajara in February 1985. Morlet had been questioned, and for a time was considered the "mastermind" of Camarena's kidnapping and subsequent murder. Then for some unknown reason he was released, according to the book *Desperados* by Elaine Shannon.

If the Hernandez gang had anything to do with Mark's kidnapping—and possibly they had murdered him—it would be the beginning of the end. With Elio in custody, Benitez would have key members of the Hernandez hierarchy in jail, and what's more, he might have legal reason to charge them with kidnapping, even murder. He suspected that Mark was dead since he had been seen with the gang members. Also, he suspected that Mark had been kidnapped, but the caretaker had said that Mark's hands were untied. If that proved to be so, then was Mark a visitor by choice? And one thought was even more disturbing: maybe Mark had had drug dealings with them.

Benitez now knew one thing for certain. The gang would soon be destroyed.

The Mexican lawman intensified his interrogation, suspecting that of the four suspects, Serafin would be the weak link. And until the other three were arrested, Serafin was his only lead.

On the drive back across the border, Gavito told the men about his strange meeting with Serafin Hernandez Garcia in August 1988.

It had been a convoluted drug deal in which a Cuban named Adolfo de Jesus Constanzo had ripped off $800,000 from *gringo* drug dealers and then fled to Mexico City. In retaliation, Ovidio Hernandez Rivera, Serafin's uncle, had been kidnapped. Also kidnapped was Ovidio's infant son. The kidnappers wanted the money or the marijuana. The family reported only the kidnapping and for two sleepless days, Gavito had sought the return of Ovidio and his son while the Hernandez family wept in his office, bemoaning the threat to their brother and nephew. George recognized them as being members of the Hernandez family of drug dealers in Matamoros.

"Why would they kidnap our little nephew?" Gavito quoted the family members as asking. It was then that Gavito had first met Serafin Hernandez Rivera (Serafin's father) and Elio, Ovidio's brother.

The kidnapping resolved itself when Ovidio and his son were released, and the family declined to press charges. Gavito figured the drug dealers had reached some secret agreement with the family.

"They certainly live a different life than we do," Jim said.

The ringing telephone jarred Gavito out of a deep sleep. It had been a rare early night. Cisneros had been safely sent on his way back to San Antonio and Jim Kilroy was planning to return to Santa Fe the first thing in the morning.

Now a caller was saying the remains of a young Anglo had been discovered near Monterrey.

"Tell me more," Gavito said, sleep fading from his mind.

"Anglo, blond, about the same height," the caller, a pathologist, told him. "He had a wedding ring."

"Everything fits but the wedding ring," Gavito said, wondering if some devious murderer had slipped a ring on Mark's finger to throw off investigators.

"Did you find a woman?" he asked.

If a man was missing, then logic would place a wife at the scene, especially if honeymooners had been waylaid.

"We didn't find a woman," the pathologist reported. "We could give positive identification with dental records."

"What have you got?"

"He's got a cap on one front tooth and quite a bit of dental work," he said.

"It's not Mark," Gavito said. "According to his parents, Mark had little dental work done."

"Why don't we look anyway?" the pathologist pushed.

"It won't do any good," Gavito said, closing the conversation.

But the pathologist would not be denied. The next morning he telephoned again, insisting that Gavito obtain dental records for him.

To help his colleague, Gavito put a missing-person report on a national network. Within minutes he started receiving calls.

"Did you see that report?" one caller asked. "Someone's found a body outside Monterrey. That could be Mark Kilroy."

The calls continued. Erstwhile investigators saw the description and called immediately, failing to check and discover that the Cameron County Sheriff's Office had filed the report.

"That's great," Neck told a disgusted Gavito. "It means that people are thinking of us. We've still got a high profile out there."

Reluctantly, Gavito called the Kilroys that afternoon. They had just returned home. He hated to disturb their break away from the intensity of the search on the border.

"Jim, I need Mark's dental records. They have a body in Monterrey and the pathologist believes it could be Mark," Gavito explained, before adding, "I told him it wasn't Mark, but he insisted. I told him Mark didn't have much dental work; he didn't, did he?"

"Not that I know of," Jim said. "But you can call his dentist."

When Jim hung up he turned to Helen, and said, "I believe they've found Mark and don't want to tell us until they are absolutely sure."

He wondered if it had anything to do with the devil worshipers Benitez had discovered.

Gavito spent most of the afternoon with a telephone at each ear, trying to describe Mark's dental records to the pathologist in Monterrey. It was difficult enough trying to translate between the two, but Gavito had to search his memory for the correct Spanish translation of medical terms. Often he had to circle the word with a series of layman's descriptions until the pathologist could understand.

To his surprise Mark had had extensive dental work, including a cap on one front tooth that appeared to match the body in Monterrey. A number of cavity amalgams also appeared to match.

"Look guys, I think we've gone as far as we can on the telephone," Gavito said, his shirt stained with sweat from the extraordinary concentration required to allow the men to communicate. "Send the records down here. We'll send them on to Monterrey."

Oran made special arrangements for a U.S. Customs car to be passed through Mexican Customs to deliver the charts to Monterrey. Tied up with television interviews, the Kilroys asked Gwen Huddleston to fetch the dental charts and put them on a 10:30 P.M. Southwest Airlines flight to the Valley.

"Who knows?" Gavito told Neck. "It looks like a good lead."

"Who knows?" his friend agreed. "Maybe we'll know something tomorrow."

The men were exhausted by almost four weeks of constant pressure.

Later that Monday night, after thirty-six hours of questioning, Serafin confessed. Although he was considered the weakest link, it had taken a day and a half to break through a stubborn resistance that law officers found puzzling. Armed with Serafin's confession, Benitez was able to elicit confessions from the other three to various kidnappings, murders, and drug trafficking.

Although he would not admit to participating in the college student's murder, Serafin knew where Mark was buried at the ranch, and he agreed to take them to the spot. He hinted that he might even know where one other body was buried.

"Two?"

"*Sí, dos.*"

Once again, Benitez heard the name of Constanzo, only this time he heard of him as the drug-gang leader. For the first time, he heard of Sara Maria Aldrete Villarreal, a Mexican national who attended classes at Texas Southmost College in Brownsville.

Benitez knew he would have difficulty persuading his men to search the ranch, especially the area around the voodoo shack, until it was cleansed of evil spirits. It only took a few seconds outside the foul-smelling shack for his men to become convinced that it was a place of unspeakable evil. Was that blood that was barely discernible in the yellow shadows the flickering candles cast on the wall of the shack? Benitez ordered a trusted aide to find a *curandero* to expunge the evil from the diabolic shed and grounds as soon as possible. For good measure, Benitez suggested that the police station be exorcised as well.

With those tasks safely ordered, he decided to contact the Cameron County Sheriff's Office and the U.S. Customs Service, and then he would grab a few hours sleep. He had been up nearly two days and he wanted to be at the ranch at first light. The young comandante knew that it was going to be another long day, possibly one with international repercussions.

"I believe that Mark Kilroy's body has been found," Benitez told a groggy George Gavito when he called shortly after 1:00 A.M. Tuesday morning. "A boy named Serafin Hernandez has confessed to the kidnapping of Mark Kilroy."

My God, it's Hernandez, Gavito thought. It had only been a matter of hours since he had seen him in the comandante's office.

"He told me that he had buried Mark at the Santa Elena ranch," Benitez continued. "There's another body there. Hernandez said they had killed two people. It has something to do with that brujeria shack.

"Let's meet in the morning to go to the ranch," Benitez suggested.

Gavito called Neck.

"Are you sure it's Mark?" was Neck's first question.

"Well, you know they kinda caught me asleep," Gavito said.

The men had had their hopes dashed by so many false leads that they had begun to be skeptical of almost everything.

"I'm more awake now; let me call him back and then I'll call you back in a little bit," Gavito said.

Benitez was glad to supply more detail. He sketched the events of the past thirty-six hours, including the identification of Mark's picture by the caretaker, Domingo Reyes Bustamante, and the subsequent investigation.

"He definitely was the boy sitting out there, according to Reyes. He told me that the boy had been left in the back of a Suburban, tied up overnight," he said.

"Do you feel good about this confession?" Gavito asked.

"I do. Serafin's talking freely about this. It's not something we made him tell us about Mark Kilroy," he explained, letting Gavito know that a minimum of force had been used. "We picked him up on the drug investigation, and he came up with the Mark Kilroy deal on his own. He's pretty well gone into detail," Benitez said.

"It sounds good to me," Gavito said, pausing before hanging up. "Thanks for everything you've done," he added.

"De nada."

Gavito and Neck agreed to meet at the sheriff's office at 6:00 A.M. to drive over to Rancho Santa Elena. Each would spend the next few hours alerting men who would pick up their video cameras and prepare for the events of the day.

"But before we go over, I'd like to get those dental charts that Jim Kilroy is sending us," Gavito said. "If this is what we expect, then we'll need the dental records to help identify Mark."

It was another twist of fate that would put the charts in their hands at the moment of greatest need. The records were due early that morning.

In one of those ironies of life, Oran Neck noted that Gavito had called him at 1:30 A.M. that Tuesday morning. It was virtually the same hour of the same day of the week that Mark Kilroy had disappeared twenty-eight days earlier.

BOOK THREE

THE DISCOVERY

RANCHO SANTA ELENA

George Gavito called the Kilroy family early Tuesday morning. "Stay near the telephone. We think we may have found Mark," he said.

Jim turned to Helen.

"It doesn't look good. He said they have something on Mark, but he couldn't tell if he was alive or not. I believe they've found his body and wanted the dental charts to identify him," he said as he gently took his weeping wife into his arms.

The cries of the tortured could have been heard only by their tormenters as extraordinary death occurred on this ordinary but lonely ranch about twenty miles west of Matamoros.

Except for the muffled voices of the lawmen, shocked at each new grisly discovery, the ranch was silent as it gave up its horrible secrets. Who had been there to hear the cries? It was a rhetorical question Gavito and Neck would find themselves asking over and over that day as they worked amid the unearthing of unbelievable butchery.

Cameron County Sheriff's Deputy Ernesto Flores accompanied the first wave of officers at 6:00 A.M. that morning. The drive out the Reynosa Highway to the turnoff was unremarkable. Cows and horses grazed peaceably on either side of the bumpy, wavy road that Mark Kilroy had traveled on the way to his death. Crosses decorated with flowers dotted the area, tradition marking the site of deaths that occurred on the roadway. A goat and cow herder armed with a machete patiently walked behind a mixed herd on the side of the road. An occasional shanty came into sight, the family wash hung

out to dry. The land there is fertile, alluvial farm country, with
workers toiling in corn fields, patiently hoeing.

The dirt road twists and nearly doubles back on itself at the
turnoff where automobiles leave the pavement to ease down the
rugged lane, barely wide enough to accommodate approaching vehicles. The MFJP caravan passed a large barn. Behind it, in a small
grove of trees, stood the caretaker's shack where Reyes lived. The
lawmen's destination lay several hundred yards beyond that, where
the dirt road ended. Two piles of hay behind the shack and a
wooden corral completed the layout, which was located only a few
hundred yards from the Rio Grande. The home site was surrounded
by corn fields where young stalks were just beginning to thrust
above the very land that hid hideous secrets in a paradox of new
growth and death.

Serafin said Mark Kilroy's body was buried near the southwest-
ern, outside corner of the corral. He walked directly to a mysterious
wire sticking from the ground, nudged it with his foot, and simply
said, "Here."

"Start digging," Benitez said, handing him a shovel.

As Serafin bent to the task, Benitez assigned men to dig at other
possible burial sites. Chicken feathers came up with the first shovel-
fuls; but until Oran Neck arrived on the scene, they went unnoticed.

Benitez turned his attention to the smelly tarpaper shack.
Wooden doors on the south and west sides were tightly closed, and
windows in front and back had been shuttered. Every entrance had
been secured with locks. It took the men more than thirty minutes
to wrench the south door from its hinges. Cautiously, they looked in
to see candles flickering in the semi-darkness.

No one entered the shack until the other door had also been
ripped from its hinges. Sunlight filtered into the room to reveal a
place of pagan worship—an altar with four candles burning at its
bloody corners.

A Hispanic *curandero* was on hand to purge the area of evil
spirits. Dressed in an MFJP jacket, he fired a machine gun into the
air as part of the ritual to drive away the diabolic spirits. He was
the first person to enter the shack; sounds of broken glass could be
heard as he performed rites of purification. Finally, he announced it
was safe for the officers to enter.

Stepping into the foreboding building, the men did not realize
they had unlocked a Pandora's box of evil which sustained itself
through human sacrifice. Then they saw the black cauldron of death
standing against the center of the blood-splattered north wall. It was
heaped with what appeared to be human brains and hearts. Four

smaller black pots contained animal parts; chicken feet protruded from one of them.

On the floor lay paraphernalia used by the occult-worshiping drug smugglers who believed that rituals involving these putrid pots would make them invincible to the police, to bullets, or to bad luck. Leaning against the wall behind the large cauldron was an ordinary machete with a few rust spots on the blade. Chile peppers, half-smoked cigars, and boxes of white votive candles were scattered about the floor. Nestled on an inside window ledge was a delicate bird's nest constructed of human hair and tissue paper.

The stench compelled the disgusted officers to dismantle the altar and take it outside, where reporters later found the items along one end of the shack.

After they arrived with the dental charts, Benitez escorted Neck and Gavito straight past the hut to the corner of the corral where Serafin was digging.

"We're pretty sure we've got him," Benitez said as they walked across the corral. "There's an Anglo body that's starting to be uncovered."

They found Serafin waist deep in the grave, carefully digging. A shovelful of the rich soil brought up more chicken feathers.

Neck has seen feathers in similar ritualistic burials while stationed in Miami, Florida, the main port of entry into the United States for a variety of Afro-Caribbean sects. The Customs agent thought he knew what the chicken feathers meant; but there is an old tenet in law enforcement which says it is better to ask than to assume.

"What is this?" Neck asked, waving several chicken feathers at Serafin.

"Have you even seen the movie *The Believers?*" Serafin said, pausing in his work.

The Believers is a motion picture starring Martin Sheen as a police psychiatrist who investigates first *Santería*, a Caribbean blend of perverted Catholic traditions and African paganism, which practices animal sacrifice, and finally *Palo Mayombe*, that dark side of *Santería* which believes in evil for evil's sake and sometimes practices human sacrifice. In the movie, Sheen's character must protect his son from evil spells and ultimately, human sacrifice. It is filled with Hollywood's version of horror, including preposterous *Santería* spells that cause one character to grow snakes in his stomach and a festering sore on the heroine's face to turn into a black boil that produces thousands of spiders.

The two American lawmen took Serafin from the grave.

"Tell us about it," Neck said as they walked away from Mark's

grave into the corral for privacy, a lawman on either side of the
suspect.

The three had only taken a few steps when Serafin stopped. He
looked across the sixty-foot-square corral.

"I think if you should dig over there," he said, pointing to a
corner inside the corral which was nearest to where Mark was
buried on the other side. "I think you might find someone else."

"What?" Neck and Gavito exploded in unison.

"What do you mean?" Neck said, quickly regaining his composure.

"You might find three bodies," Serafin said, a slight, almost be-
mused smile on his face.

Then Serafin pointed toward the inside southeast corner of the
corral. "You might find two bodies over there," he added.

"What have we stumbled on?" Neck asked Gavito. He already
thought he knew, but he just wanted to see George's reaction.

"Serial killers, maybe?" Gavito answered.

"I'm afraid it's worse than that," Neck said.

"What?"

"It looks to me like we've got an Afro-Caribbean cult," Neck
explained, holding up a chicken feather. "This tipped me off. When
I was in Miami we would find chicken feathers. It's *Santería*; that's
what they called it. People from Cuba who practice black magic
sacrifice chickens and goats and animals like that. I've never heard of
human sacrifice though," he said. "Maybe this is something new."

Neck soon discovered that the cult practiced not only *Santería*
but also *Palo Mayombe*, the dark, fiendish religion that required the
use of human body parts and human blood. Experts from Miami
would help define each of the items that had been discovered surrounding the pagan altar in the tarpaper temple. Each candle, each
pot, each grisly item in the large cauldron was ascribed a particular
magic trait in the practice of the Afro-Caribbean rituals.

The nefarious cauldron was typical of *Palo Mayombe* practitioners.
Black and large, it had the look of the well-known witch's cauldron;
an appearance which drew immediate speculation that the odious
concoction inside the pot had been boiled over a blazing fire. But the
lawmen would later learn it had not been. Satanism was the first
thought in many minds, but the rituals practiced here were not
satanism in the purest sense, because Satan had not been directly
worshiped. Instead, these believers had worshiped pagan gods.

Large sticks protruding from the top of the cauldron, and an inky
black goo inside the pot was composed of blood and brains from
the victims. A turtle shell and a horseshoe could also be seen in the
mysterious kettle. Coiled in the center was a white, waxen object

that had not soaked up the bloody residue. Protruding rounded bones gave it the appearance of a spine, an object important to these drug smugglers because they believed a necklace made from a human spine would bring good luck.

That's what the cult members had intended for Mark Kilroy's spine. After his death, the suspects had cut the backbone from his body, threaded the bones with a wire, and buried the spine several feet above the body, leaving the wire sticking several inches above the ground. The drug smugglers planned to use the wire to pull the spine from its burial place after the flesh had loosened from the bones. The abrasive action of pulling the bones through the earth would clean them. The drug smugglers would then fashion a necklace from the spinal column to wear during ceremonies. Serafin had been guided to Mark's grave by the wire protruding above the ground.

The cultists believed a human spine would protect them from spinal injury, according to Felix Jiminez, a Miami homicide detective.

Two of the four pots in the shack contained decaying goats' heads, while a third held a number of small gold beads. A fourth pot, and one of the few items taken into protective custody by the police, was half-full of American pennies.

White candles in glass containers, cigars, corn cobs, red peppers, and garlic were scattered on the floor.

Neck surveyed the wrecked altars before turning his attention back to Serafin.

"Is that what *The Believers* is all about, black magic and human sacrifice?" he asked.

"That's where we got some of the ideas for what we're doing," Serafin added.

To their horror, Serafin went on to explain that Adolfo Constanzo was *El Padrino*, godfather of the group. He was the chief executioner, the man who had sacrificed Mark Kilroy.

Constanzo!

Benitez had given the lawmen Constanzo's name on Sunday; but then he had only been linked to a drug case. Neck used a radio to immediately dispatch a team to the Holiday Inn to capture the ringleader.

Mark Kilroy!

Their search had ended, but in a way so horrifying that it defied and defiled human sensibilities.

Human sacrifice!

It took time for the hardened officers to adjust to the thought of such desecration of human life. The idea is repugnant; but there seemed to be a special profanity in the knowledge that Mark Kilroy

had met his death at the hands of men who killed him in the name
of worship.

"My God in heaven," Gavito whispered, making the sign of the
cross.

"A human sacrifice?" Neck questioned, his mind trying to reject
the implications of the atrocities that had been performed on the
very ground where he stood.

"Are there any other graves here? How many are out here?"
Gavito demanded.

"I'm not sure, but if you look over there," Serafin said, pointing
to a spot outside the corral near one of the haystacks, "you might
find someone there."

For the remainder of the day, Serafin would dig for a while, then
be pulled from the grave to walk with Neck and Gavito. As Serafin
talked, Neck and Gavito heard the name Sara Maria Aldrete Villarreal for the first time. She was the group's Godmother or *La Bruja*,
the witch, Serafin said. She recruited men for the gang and made
them watch *The Believers* over and over. On other occasions Serafin
would beg Flores to take him to the U.S., saying that there he would
plead guilty to any crime.

By the time the stunned lawmen were through that day, nine
graves would be pinpointed; a total of twelve bodies would be
recovered.

Benitez, too, was thunderstruck by what they had found.

"We need to seal this area," Gavito suggested. "I don't think we
want anyone to know what's going on out here. We know Constanzo is in Brownsville, and we don't want him to get word or he'll
escape," he said.

"And I think you might want to consider bringing the three other
suspects out here," Neck added. He wanted Elio Hernandez, David
Serna, and Sergio Martinez on site. "There's no telling what else
we're going to find out."

Gavito used his police radio to call for additional supplies, order-
ing them out of the Cameron County Sheriff's Office in an attempt
to keep the discovery confidential.

"We need gloves. And round up all the body bags you can find in
the funeral homes in Brownsville; make sure you have at least fifteen
body bags, because we don't know how many we're going to find out
here. The gloves are in our office. Don't tell anyone at the funeral
homes what's happening, just get that stuff out here as soon as you
can," he said, wondering if fifteen body bags would be enough.

"And these men haven't had anything to eat or drink since
they started this morning. Send someone to the jail kitchen and
have them make up sandwiches, some coffee, and some of those

cinnamon rolls. Add some soft drinks and lots of water; it's hot as hell out here," he continued.

Benitez would clear the way for the food trucks to roll across the bridge.

"Oh, yes," Gavito said as an afterthought. "Bring some filters—those face masks like they use in surgery. And get us some of those sample bottles of cologne."

The masks and the cologne would be the only way the men would survive that stinking day on the ranch. Neck and Gavito even reached the point of putting cologne on their fingertips and wiping it on the inside of their noses to kill the stench.

Unfortunately, it did not matter how tightly the area was sealed. The word had gone out Sunday night after the drug raid at the ranch. The suspects had moved to the Holiday Inn in McAllen, and Sara had booked Constanzo, Martin Quintana, and Alvaro de Leon Valdez (nicknamed *El Dubi*, a Spanish slang term for a marijuana cigarette) on a 9:30 flight Monday morning to Mexico City. She had followed at 8:45 that night, after spending the day settling her affairs in Brownsville and Matamoros. As the gruesome revelations began to unfold on the ranch outside Matamoros, the Godfather was more than a thousand miles away watching the story on television.

During questioning, Elio Hernandez Rivera also fondly referred to Constánzo as *El Padrino*.

"I thought you were the leader of the Hernandez gang," Benitez countered.

"No. I'm his assistant," Elio said proudly. "He even gave me the right to sacrifice."

"To what?" Benitez thought he understood what Elio had said, but he wanted to make sure, to be absolutely clear—because a new element was entering the picture and it froze a piece of his heart.

"To sacrifice. To kill."

"Animals?"

"*Sí*, and people," Elio grinned.

Although he already knew it, Benitez was stunned.

"And Mark Kilroy?"

"*Padrino* said he would bring us good luck," Elio replied, his calm demeanor belying the atrocity he discussed.

My God in heaven—human sacrifice, Benitez thought, startled anew by the admission. He had heard of these cults; but they were usually found in Central America or the Caribbean, seldom in Mexico.

Elio took his shirt off to proudly display crude crosses that had been seared across his chest, back, and shoulders.

"This is my authority to sacrifice," he added, explaining that Constanzo had performed the searing initiation with a white-hot knife blade.

Benitez studied the scarred back with revulsion building in his soul. With superhuman effort he kept his personal feelings under control.

"Did you sacrifice?"

"*Sí, jefe.*" It was a proud admission, even though one of the victims had been a fourteen-year-old boy, Elio's distant relative.

Not only had he sacrificed, but Elio bragged that he could keep a victim alive long enough to split the chest and rip the beating heart out, just as his forefathers, the ancient Aztecs, had done.

The group had practiced an eclectic religion that appeared to use elements of *Aztecia, Santería*, and especially *Palo Mayombe*. But with the exception of Elio, the suspects claimed to be willing lackeys, not murderers.

"I smuggled drugs and kidnapped five people, but nothing else," Serafin maintained during hours of interrogation at the site and back in jail. All five of the people he kidnapped were later slain and mutilated.

The method of death depended on the victim. The lawmen learned that only four of the victims were sacrifices who were selected at random. The rest were either killed over bad drug deals or for revenge. These had died by knife or gun; sometimes they were tortured to death. One man, a former policeman, had been tortured by having his breast sliced off and hot boiling water poured over him.

Sometimes the beating heart was ripped from a victim's body and placed in the *nganga* as a gift to the warrior spirit. The fourteen-year-old boy had been decapitated and his body had been turned upside down over the *nganga* to catch every drop of blood.

During one of their walks around the killing grounds, Gavito and Neck learned that Serafin had been initiated into the cult when his family settled in Brownsville after he graduated from high school in Houston.

"Do you want to join?" Elio, Serafin's uncle, had asked him. He told Serafin that he believed it was a good religion that offered protection and good luck "in school and things."

"I have to think about it," Serafin had replied.

"We were family. I trusted him. So after a while I told him I would join," Serafin said, continuing his tale. "It took me awhile because I'm nervous about this sort of thing. I'm one of those scared-type persons. They just gave me a necklace with gold beads on it," he said, denying any bizarre initiation into the cult.

But no matter what form of interrogation was used, Serafin would never admit to killing anyone or taking an active part in the human sacrifices, although he admitted being present when ten people died, mainly from knife wounds.

"I picked up Kilroy, and four others; but I never killed anyone. That's the truth," he insisted. He also admitted being active in drug smuggling.

Serafin's jobs with the cult had been specific.

"I dug some graves," he added. "But mainly, I helped pick up guys."

Several days after his capture, Serafin would tell a reporter that he had wanted to quit the cult, but feared Constanzo.

"I was scared that he might do something to me. He didn't threaten us; but we knew that if we didn't do what he said, he'd do something to us," Serafin said.

The authorities learned that two more people had been killed during the four-week search for Mark Kilroy.

Benitez was astounded. The men discussed the atrocities as if talking about a plot on the latest *novella*, a Mexican soap opera. There was no remorse, there was no fear—except of Constanzo—and there was no contrition, no sign of repentance for what they had done.

Instead, each man exhibited a cavalier attitude toward the situation. Serafin even bragged about his connections with the Matamoros police. The prisoners acted as if *El Padrino* would descend from on high to free his followers.

Without fear of physical or spiritual retribution, there can be no regret. Without regret, rarely is there a confession.

That's why Serafin was so hard to break, Neck thought. *These people don't seem to know right from wrong. They're convinced that anything they do is right. No wonder it took hours to break him!*

Neck was told about ritualistic cigar smoking. The men would come out nearly every day and put the pot of pennies in the underbrush. Then they would light cigars, believing the smoke was a form of incense that would be pleasing to the gods. The worshipers believed the ritual would make them richer.

Reyes said that Sara Aldrete was a regular visitor to the ranch. The caretaker said that she usually wore a black, tight-fitting bodysuit during her visits. Fellow students at Texas Southmost College would eventually recall her passion for black.

Throughout the day the suspects were interrogated, and a picture of Mark's last hours began to evolve.

After Mark was grabbed, Serafin had eased the truck north, and turned right at the large intersection, driving past the front entrance to Garcia's. Across the street was the vendor's park where Bradley and Brent stood staring down the street searching for Mark in the swarm of students. There was nothing to cause the men to look inside any of the passing vehicles for a struggling student. A captive Mark Kilroy passed within only a few feet of his friends. He may have already been handcuffed.

Another quick right onto Las Rosas and Serafin was headed south on the dark side street. There was little traffic. Most of the students were one street over, driving and walking north on Avenida Alvaro Obregon, intent on reentering the United States at the end of the night of fun and frolic.

After hours of drinking beer while watching for the right victim, and then the extended search when he missed his first two intended victims, Serafin needed to relieve himself.

He picked up speed until he passed Margaritas Street, stopping at a parking lot near Sergeant Pepper's, the bar that Mark and his friends had patronized the previous night.

As Serafin and his accomplice, Malio Ponce Torres, urinated, Mark kicked open the door of the pickup and jumped free. He dashed onto Las Rosas, running north with all his might. It was a desperate race for his life and his young, athletic body responded. By the time Serafin and Malio reacted, Mark had a substantial lead. The two gunned the pickup out of the parking lot in hot pursuit. For Mark, it was only a short block to Margaritas Street, then a quick left to humanity-filled Obregon and freedom.

Sergio Martinez Salinas, Ovidio Hernandez Rivera, and David Serna Valdez had been trailing Serafin in a Mercury Grand Marquis. They had seen Serafin and Malio grab Mark.

They followed Serafin around Garcia's and onto Las Rosas. As they neared the Margaritas intersection, the automobile headlights picked up the fleeing student. As Mark attempted to dash around them, the car squealed to a stop and all three jumped out, pistols at the ready.

"Freeze!" one of them shouted.

"Police!" another joined in.

"Freeze!" the third called out.

Only a few yards from freedom, Mark Kilroy stopped his flight on the darkened street.

"What does *freeze* mean?" Benitez asked Neck. "Why would he stop when someone yelled '*freeze*'?"

"It's a term commonly used by American police," Neck explained. "*Freeze* means to stop whatever you are doing."

He tried to find a proper illustration.

"Water runs until it freezes. It turns to ice and then it is still. In America the police use the term to tell someone to quit running," Oran continued. "When they yelled out both 'Freeze' and 'Police,' Mark stopped."

Neck then turned to Gavito, "there is indication that they also used handcuffs when they captured him," he said, trying to analyze what happened. "That could have led him to believe he was dealing with the police."

The suspects were reluctant to talk about impersonating police officers. Sometimes they admitted to using handcuffs; sometimes they changed their story.

"Also, they were dealing with a boy who had been taught respect for authority," Neck added.

"And, perhaps he thought help had arrived," Gavito said, bitter at the profanity done in the name of his beloved profession.

The four suspects stood laughing, each eager to lay the credit for shouting "Freeze!" on the other.

Gavito's glower brought them under control.

Their attitude is incredible, Neck thought. *They really do believe they are invincible.*

On the way to the ranch, Mark had not been given another chance to escape.

"What's going on, man?" he repeatedly asked Serafin. "Why are you doing this?"

"It's okay; everything's going to be all right," Serafin reassured the frightened student.

When they reached the barn at Rancho Santa Elena, the cult worshipers tied his hands and feet, put tape over his mouth and eyes, and put him on the back seat of a Suburban. The four stood guard to make sure the trussed-up captive would not escape again. Throughout the night they checked on him and offered reassurances.

"We're going to let you go here in a little while," or "Don't worry, everything's fine," were typical comments in English aimed at the distraught student. Frustration and fear released itself in tears as the student wept until he dropped off into a fitful sleep. At sunrise Mark was moved into the barn, where he stayed until noon when other members of the cult arrived at the ranch. Out of Mark's sight, only a few hundred yards away, Sergio Martinez Salinas began digging a grave near the corral behind the small shack.

"Mark studied Spanish two years in high school, and a year in college," Jim Kilroy later told the officers. "I would suspect that he didn't let them know he spoke Spanish."

The American law officers were never sure if Mark knew what fate awaited him because his captors kept promising to release him. The hostage could have been led to believe that he was being held for ransom by unscrupulous policemen. If so, he would be confident that his parents would pay any ransom to retrieve him.

"I told Mark at different times that you had to be very careful in Mexico," Jim told Neck and Gavito. "If you did anything that was wrong or thought to be wrong, the police would grab you for any reason and hold you for a big ransom. I had said that police often work undercover in Mexico," Jim said. "They don't always wear a uniform. They try to entrap you."

The cultists appeared to have always communicated with him in English. But Mark could have picked up additional information when the men conversed in Spanish among themselves.

Shortly before 1:00 P.M., Mark was untied and his blindfold removed. He was escorted to a small grove of trees about one hundred feet in front of the barn.

"Sit down," one of the heavily armed captors told him, indicating a hammock.

By now either a calm or a depression or a sense of hope that a ransom was about to be paid had enveloped the young man. With his hands and feet unshackled, he calmly held his peace, occasionally asking the men to explain his abduction.

The caretaker was summoned from his shack.

"Cook him some eggs and bring him something to drink," he was told. Within a matter of minutes Reyes reappeared with two fried eggs and a glass of water.

Famished, Mark ate the meal in silence, still sitting in the hammock under the trees.

"Now, leave, and go tend to your goats," Reyes was told. He was used to strange activity at the ranch, so he left immediately, heading for the most remote area of the ranch.

The cult worshipers wrapped Mark's head with silver duct tape, sealing his mouth and covering his eyes. He was again tied up, put in the Suburban, and driven the short distance to the cult's tarpaper-covered temple, where Sara Aldrete stood by the door. There the struggling student was stripped of his clothing and led into the occult temple.

Neck believes that the cultists may have also been nude because subsequent investigation failed to reveal any blood in the vehicles that were confiscated—not one bloodstain, and more than seventy vehicles were searched.

"It is almost impossible to wash out bloodstains from automobile upholstery or floor carpet," Neck would say. "And if they took off their bloody clothes and threw them into the vehicle, then some of the blood would soak into the carpet or upholstery."

It is believed that the cultists shed their clothes before the sacrifice and then washed up afterward.

In the center of the small shack, the college student stood naked on a sheet of orange plastic, his head sheathed in silver duct tape, his hands tied.

It was 2:00 P.M. Mark had been in custody for twelve hours and the superstitious cult members did not want to deliver the sacrifice to the evil god, *Kadiempembe*, during the thirteenth hour. That would have been bad luck. So they quickly proceeded with their work.

Constanzo sacrificed Mark Kilroy with a series of machete blows to the top of the head. The high priest then scooped the brains from the college student's split skull and added them to the black kettle.

As El Dubi watched the sacrifice, he began to tremble violently, shaking so fiercely that he almost went into convulsions. De Leon would later tell the police it was the first time he had ever had such a reaction during a sacrifice.

Quickly, blood was drained from Mark's body into the cast-iron pot.

It was finished.

Now, according to the tradition of *Palo Mayombe*, the *nganga* had been refreshed with the sacrifice of human blood, even a human life. The group would have power and good luck. The men would have intelligence. The sagging spirit of the *nganga* would be more vital than ever because he had been fed with the brain of a college student. They petitioned the sinister spirit for strength, riches, and protection from police while smuggling drugs.

It was an exhilarating moment for this group which had sold its collective soul to a fiendish set of beliefs that promised wealth and power.

After death, Mark's body was mutilated. The spine was cut free so the sect could use it as a necklace. Before the men buried the victim, Constanzo ordered El Dubi to cut the legs off above the knee.

"He told me that each time you do this, you lose a little of your fear until you aren't afraid of anything anymore," de Leon said.

The legs were placed on the torso, which was lowered into the grave face down. Their bloodlust quenched, the men took turns standing watch over the grave for the next five hours.

As stunned law-enforcement officers began to understand the magnitude of what they had discovered, they were further jolted by the strange, mocking, devil-may-care attitude of the four suspects. The men continued to show no remorse, discussing their actions in a calm, rational demeanor that belied their deeds.

"You scum," Gavito yelled at Serafin at one point. "You were in my office just a year ago because your uncle and his son had been kidnapped, and all of you cried like little babies. 'Get my kinsman back,' you pleaded. 'These people are hurting our family. Help us keep our family together.'" Gavito's anguish exploded into vocal, mocking fury.

"And all the time you were destroying families," he roared. "All the time you were doing this!"

Neck stepped up to put a hand on Gavito as the officer struggled to bring his temper under control.

Because the carnage at the site was unimaginable, the acts of sacrifice unbelievable, the depths of human degradation unthinkable, veteran lawmen were outraged by the suspects' lack of contrition. The four men still seemed to believe they were protected by their cult charms. Although they had spent the night in jail; although they were under arrest for drug smuggling, and now murder; and although their hands were shackled, each still appeared to believe that no harm would come to him. They believed they were guarded by cheap whiskey, cigar smoke, small sacred stones—and human sacrifice.

They actually believe this stuff, Neck marveled to himself, unable to keep his amazement in check as he watched the suspects open the graves. *They thought they would get rich and powerful and not be touched by anything.*

He also was astonished to find the face of evil to be so benign. *These men don't look like killers*, he thought to himself.

"What did you do with the stuff you stole off the bodies?" he asked, returning to the present business.

"We didn't steal anything," Elio said, stepping forward, his voice bristling with indignity.

After what they had already confessed to, Neck was surprised to find the man offended at this latest charge.

"We wouldn't take anything from these people," Elio repeated.

Neck surmised this incensed reaction had something to do with a strange mixture of reverence and awe for the victims, a process of mind and religion that defied normal rationale—a process that would lead these men to stand watch over someone they had just brutally murdered and mutilated. It was beyond understanding, much less true comprehension, because it flew in the face of conventional reasoning.

The Customs agent also picked up on another undercurrent that ran counter to the kidnappers' public, mocking persona.

"They are talking about these bodies in almost reverent tones," he said, noting that the cultists had said over and over that none of the victims had suffered. He would discover later that that was only true of sacrifice victims. Others were brutally tortured and killed over bad drug deals or for revenge.

One cultist had been killed because he defied the godfather's ban on drug use.

"You can drink, but you can't use drugs," Serafin told them, explaining the cult rules.

"What about personal effects?" Neck pressed on. "Where are they?" Mark had had a gold watch given to him by his grandfather, a family heirloom that Neck would like to recover for the Kilroys.

All clothing and personal effects were scattered across Matamoros and the surrounding countryside, Serafin said. Nothing was burned or kept. The men said they had spent hours driving around the city, throwing out a watch here, a shoe there, a shirt somewhere else. Neck realized that it would be impossible to mount a search for personal belongings that were strewn miles apart. Anyone finding anything of value in that poverty-stricken country would keep it, thankful for the extra pesos it would bring.

Although he had been a homicide detective for fifteen years and had handled hundreds of cases, nothing had ever prepared George Gavito for what was happening around him.

He was near exhaustion from one of the most concentrated efforts of his career. When he came to Rancho Santa Elena that morning he had believed that authorities might recover one body, maybe two. But his blood ran cold when searchers started pulling body after body out of the ground. The smell and the cold-blooded way the smugglers acted would also be an indescribable memory. No matter how hard he would try in the future to erase those memories, he would fail. And no matter how vividly he would describe the scene so that others could understand the horror of it, his words would seem inadequate.

He had only seen a photograph of Mark Kilroy, but Gavito recognized the young man when his mutilated body was uncovered and the silver duct tape was removed.

"I actually recognize him," Gavito marveled to Neck as the two saw Mark's face.

The pathologist took the dental records from Gavito to confirm identification.

"I can be 90 percent sure right here, but I need to have my equipment at the lab to be positive," the pathologist said.

"I'm sure," Gavito said softly.

"The family needs to know," Neck added.

"It was something neither of us ever imagined could have happened. All of us—you, me, the Kilroys—we knew that Mark might be found dead; but this goes beyond belief. I don't know any easy way to tell them," Gavito shouted above the din of backhoes and bulldozers that were digging and scraping nearby.

Gavito looked up to see Benitez signaling for them to join him. The comandante had been talking with Deputy Ernesto Flores.

"Trouble," he said as he began walking across the pasture, his Uzi machine gun tucked under his arm.

"I understand that the State Judicial Police are on their way, Benitez explained as he climbed into his vehicle. "There's a whole convoy of them.

"They're coming to take over the investigation," he said. Suddenly the very organization that had appeared to be the one that kept a lid on the investigation, doing nothing, was ready to take over. Apparently they had been stung by Mattox's emissary's visit to the governor in Ciudad Victoria. Also, murder cases are the domain of the state police. Federal police handle drug cases. For Benitez to continue to investigate would be highly unusual.

Benitez had already anticipated this trouble and had received permission from federal prosecutor Licensiado Silva Arroyo to continue the investigation under the MFJP banner after he had flown the prosecutor to the site by helicopter. Arroyo had inspected the scene and ruled that there was enough drug involvement for Benitez to continue to head the investigation, although murder was now an integral part of the case.

The federal comandante had his men block the main entrance to Rancho Santa Elena where the dirt road runs off Mexican Highway 2.

Cameron County Deputy Sheriff Ernesto Flores watched a convoy of about thirty cars bearing roughly fifty agents come to a stop. Flustered, State Judicial Police Comandante Silvio Brusolo told Benitez that he had come to take over the investigation.

"You tell your men to get back into their cars, turn them around and head back into town," Benitez told him, getting out of his vehicle and squaring off.

"You don't understand," Brusolo said.

"Yes I do understand," Benitez told him levelly. "We've already checked with our attorney. There is enough of a drug connection for us to continue this investigation. We have been running this investigation from the start," he continued. Then he added the zinger: "We have one of your nephews in custody," he said of Sergio Martinez Salinas, who would drop a little bombshell of his own later that night.

"Your nephew is one of the killers. They used red lights and handcuffs like the police. I might be investigating you, and as far as I am concerned, you are one of the suspects!" By now Benitez was nearly shouting at Brusolo. "So leave!"

It was a tense situation.

Benitez cocked his weapon, and his men followed suit.

"Leave," Benitez said again, this time so softly that the word took on a deadly meaning.

We're about to get into the middle of a gun battle, George thought, looking for some place to hide should the automatic weapons cut loose.

The SJP comandante considered the situation, appraising Benitez's solemn-faced men, battle wise from combating crime in Matamoros, and weary from the tension of the day. He looked at Benitez, swallowed up in his large MFJP vest worn over a T-shirt, blue jeans, and tennis shoes. His automatic weapon was still at the ready.

Without another word, Brusolo waved his men back into their vehicles. It was several seconds after they left before Gavito, Neck, and Flores could feel the tension easing.

"That's one of the reasons we've been having a problem. One of the suspects—Sergio Martinez—is Brusolo's nephew," Gavito told Neck. "That nephew has been telling everyone that Mark was involved in drugs and that the search for him was nothing."

"Well, they found out differently," Gavito added grimly.

The first rule a detective learns is to keep his emotions in check when working a case. It is a rule that, for George Gavito, has no exceptions.

"You don't want to get emotionally involved," Gavito had often warned Neck, who had immediately befriended the Kilroys.

During the four weeks Gavito had worked on the case, he had tried to avoid social amenities with the Kilroys. He declined lunches, and tried to keep to himself, even when Jim Kilroy showed up regularly with coffee and biscuits for everyone on duty. Gavito had never wanted to befriend the family because of what he faced at that particular moment.

As he considered the aching task of informing the family that Mark had been found, the dedicated search by Jim, the insolent attitude of the suspects, the fragile state of the family, all came crashing down on Gavito.

"Are you all right?" Neck asked, noticing the peculiar look on his friend's face.

"Sure," Gavito said, somberly turning to Neck.

"You know what just happened?"

Neck shook his head.

"I just became a friend to the Kilroy family," Gavito said.

"What?" Neck began.

"Every rule has an exception," Gavito said to his uncomprehending colleague.

As George stood at the edge of the makeshift grave looking back at the shed where the altar had been dismantled, a plan began to form. He looked around the corral at men busily digging at other sites as the mocking suspects stood nearby. Something had to be done to alert the world to this atrocity—people had a right to know. And at the same time something had to be done to protect the Kilroy family from the ever-prying media which would demand even the most minute detail.

He knew that the shock of learning what had happened to Mark would be indescribable for the family. They knew Mark might not return alive, but no one in even their wildest imagination had anticipated the horror story being revealed that day.

Gavito did not want the family to suffer yet another emotional shock when it met the news media with its prying, often-personal questions. The media can become unruly as each reporter strives to find that one little-known fact that would make his or her story just a little bit better than the others. It is the nature of the highly competitive business and sometimes it brings even more grief to the families of victims.

If there was anything George hated, it was to see a reporter rush up to a grieving loved one and ask, "How do you feel?"

If Benitez would go along with him, Gavito believed he could defuse the tense situation and ease the family into the public eye. His idea would prove to be a stroke of genius that focused attention on the suspects while wrapping a protective cloak of empathy around the family.

Gavito's plan was simple. He would introduce the awaiting media to the suspects before they met the family.

"I want them to see what we saw," he told Neck and Benitez when he outlined his strategy a few minutes later. "I want them to visit the ranch, to interview these men, to see their attitude and then, I want them to meet the Kilroy family. We could even arrange a press conference with the police before we bring the press to the ranch."

Since the suspects were in the custody of Mexican police, it would mean taking more than a hundred reporters, photographers, and film-crew members into a foreign country. In the spirit of new-found cooperation, Benitez readily agreed.

"The people need to know," he said simply.

Now that that was settled, Gavito keyed his radio microphone.

"Tell [Carlos] Tapia to call the Kilroys and tell them to come down," he said. "Tell them to keep it quiet that they are coming."

He, Neck, and Sheriff Perez wanted to personally tell the Kilroys about what they had found. Then he had to set the stage for the family to meet the press.

Benitez said, "Tell the Kilroy family that I'm sorry the search ended this way. I wanted Jim to get his son back, but not like this."

The Kilroys were waiting by the telephone when Deputy Tapia called.

"Lieutenant Gavito asked that you come on down," he said.

"Have they found Mark?" Jim asked.

"I believe so," he said, then quickly added, "but I don't know for sure. The lieutenant will tell you everything when you get here."

"We'll be on the next flight down; I'll have someone call and tell you what flight number," Jim said.

"George asks that you keep this quiet. He doesn't want anyone to know that you're coming down," Tapia added.

"Okay," Jim said. Then he asked, "Does it have anything to do with devil worshipers?"

"I'm not sure exactly, Mr. Kilroy," Tapia hesitated. "But come down as soon as you can."

Helen was coordinating activities for Mark Kilroy Awareness Days when the telephone call came in. She walked into the living room.

"They think they've found Mark and I think devil worshipers are involved," Jim told her.

It was as if the very essence of their existence had been invaded.

"How would Mark have become involved with devil worshipers?" she whispered.

"I suspect it's that same group Benitez was telling us about," Jim said, not really knowing how to answer.

While Helen packed, Jim picked up Gwen Huddleston and Keith. But first he called Father John DeForke.

"We've just gotten a call that maybe they've found Mark. Devil worshipers are involved somehow," he told the priest. "Pray for us. We're going to need all the strength we can get."

After Jim left, Helen went to their bedroom, opened a suitcase and put it on the bed. Then she went to Mark's room and selected a fresh set of clothing for her son.

She stood in his room, her heart aching as she looked at his awards, his baseball caps hanging on the wall, the mementos of a happy life. Then she began to weep, the tears streaming down her face as she sobbed uncontrollably, overcome with sorrow.

It's okay, Mom. It was one of the last things Mark had told her just before walking out the door a few weeks before.

The thought of that special phrase made her feel as if Mark was reassuring her in the caring way he used to comfort her when he did not want her to worry or be sad. With that thought came a feeling of peace.

Her emotions now under control, Helen packed Mark's clothes into the suitcase—just in case. Next to them she tenderly placed a batch of yellow ribbons.

Jim Kilroy:

I believe that Helen and I both knew that Mark was dead. Keith refused to accept the possibility that Mark wouldn't be found alive until he was confronted with the reality of Mark's death.

I felt that George would not have us come down unless he was pretty sure that Mark had been found. All along he had been very careful about checking everything out before telling us anything.

On the flight to Harlingen I suggested that we all write something about Mark. We each wrote a few loving sentences and some of them were eventually used on Mark's tombstone.

We did a lot of praying during that flight, too.

We were almost in shock—shock that our son was probably dead, shock that Mark's disappearance was somehow involved with devil worshipers, shock that our search was nearing an end without the hoped-for conclusion.

We knew that the next few days would be among the most difficult in our life.

I remember thinking that if Mark was dead, I would never get to hold him one more time like I had longed to do during the long days of the search.

Deputy Tapia was waiting for the family. Helen spotted a camera crew recording their arrival. Once in the patrol car she asked, "What are they doing here?"

"They're reporters from a Mexican television station," Tapia said.

"Word is starting to get out?" Jim said, a half-question.

"Yes, they're already starting to broadcast this on Mexican radio," he said.

"George, Oran, and Sheriff Perez want to tell you personally what has happened. They don't want you to have any misunderstanding," he added.

It was a quiet ride to the sheriff's office where the family saw the press beginning to assemble. The sheriff's deputy did explain that drug smugglers who worship the devil were involved, but he revealed nothing else.

Tapia whisked them into a private office. They heard Gavito's voice on the police radio saying that the three lawmen were on the way to the sheriff's office.

The family waited alone. Occasionally a solicitous Tapia would ask if they wanted anything.

If the Kilroys had doubts, if they had false hope, these were quickly erased when Sheriff Perez, Gavito, and Neck came striding solemnly into the room. Jim, Helen, and Keith sensed that they had reached the end of their search.

The three men looked troubled, not really knowing what to say as the family looked at them with anticipation.

"It is Mark," Gavito said gently, a statement of fact.

"Are you sure?" Helen asked.

They all waited. Finally Gavito broke the awkward silence.

"Mark is dead," he said gently.

"I'm sorry," Sheriff Perez added.

"We don't have any doubt," Neck added. "We have proof. We have a statement from the suspects. We have pictures."

"The dental records match," Gavito added. "There is no doubt that it is Mark."

"Mark is dead," Neck reaffirmed.

The three Kilroys stared at him. Keith began to cry. Helen and Jim took their youngest son into their arms to comfort him. They had tried to prepare themselves mentally in case Mark was found dead. But it was the first time that Keith had accepted that his brother was dead.

After a long pause, Jim looked up, eyes watering: "Did he suffer?"

"No," Neck said. "He didn't suffer. He wasn't tortured or anything like that."

"How did it happen?" Keith wanted to know. He finally had a chance to learn the truth after weeks of replaying Mark's disappearance in his mind.

"Mark had been kidnapped and held for twelve hours," George began. "It's some kind of a drug-smuggling outfit that worships the devil. Oran knows more about that than I do."

"He was held for twelve hours. He wasn't killed right away?" Jim seemed almost relieved at this information.

"No. They held him for twelve hours," Oran took his cue. "Then he was killed by a machete blow to the back of his head because the devil worshipers did not want to hold him for thirteen hours. They believed it would bring them bad luck to kill him in the thirteenth hour."

Neck continued. The difficult part was past—or was it? How did he tell these good, religious people that their son had been a blood sacrifice on the altar of pagan gods? Straightforward, simple statements of facts were probably easier to understand in these emotional situations.

"He was a human sacrifice," Neck added in hushed tones.

"Are you sure he lived twelve hours?" Jim asked again.

Puzzled, Neck reassured him.

"That's good. Because if he lived that long, he had time to cry out to God, to make his peace with God," Jim explained. "And when one of God's children cries out, God listens."

It would be a rallying point for the Kilroys. Their belief in life after death offered them the hope of resurrection and reunion in heaven, a promise of a future eternity with their son.

"Did you get the people who did this?" Keith asked.

"We have four of them. We're looking for the others," Gavito said. "The ringleader escaped, a man named Adolfo de Jesus Constanzo. We're looking for him, and a woman named Sara Maria Aldrete Villarreal. She was the sect's witch."

"Would you like to see pictures of the four men?" George said, reaching into his pocket to bring out a set of Polaroid pictures.

Keith was the first to look at the photographs. He handed them to his mother. "I just can't picture those four guys doing something like this. They don't look like they could do that. They look like they are near Mark's age," Keith said. "They're so young."

Indignation at the injustice of what had happened to Mark began to build as Keith added, "Mark didn't deserve this. Out of all the people in the world he was the least likely to cause anyone trouble. Everyone who knew him loved him."

"How could anyone do this?" Helen asked. It was a rhetorical question that went unanswered.

"I think you should know that eleven other bodies were found," George said.

The family let that information soak in. Up to now they had been dealing solely in their own grief.

"You mean there were other killings?" Jim asked incredulously.

"They had been doing it for more than a year. They killed two others after Mark," George said. "We expect to find even more bodies. We believe that Mark was the only American."

Neck went on to explain that Mark had escaped briefly but was recaptured and taken to the ranch.

"I'm sorry we have to tell you this," Gavito said, tears brimming in his eyes.

"I don't know what to say," Neck added. He had been silently mourning for the Kilroys, tears trickling down his cheeks.

All of them, the lawmen and the Kilroys, had walked the long journey together through the valley of the shadow of death, and now it was time to mourn. So, as the Kilroys grieved over their loss, these tough law-enforcement officers wept unashamedly with them. The culmination of the search and the mourning together sealed a bond they would share forever.

After a time they composed themselves.

"We have to consider the press," Gavito said. "I have a plan."

"You do whatever you think is best," Jim said. "Then you and Oran tell us what we should do."

"There are papers that need to be handled to get Mark back," Gavito continued. "I'll take care of them. Right now, I think you should go home with Coach; he's waiting outside for you," George added. Joe Rodriguez had been notified that the Kilroys had arrived.

The family was taken out the back door to avoid the press.

Gavito, Neck, and Perez looked at each other, reached deep down into their emotional reservoirs, and walked into the maelstrom of questioning reporters.

Holy smokes, Neck thought to himself. He had been prepared for interest in the case, but he was caught off guard by the immediate impact of the story.

He was totally amazed. Although they had tried to keep the discovery quiet, he and Gavito walked into an office packed with reporters from Mexico and the Rio Grande Valley, and even members of the national press had begun to arrive.

"I didn't realize how important this was to the rest of the world," he whispered to Gavito, who gladly left most of the press relations to Neck. Within a matter of hours, Neck became the unofficial spokesman for a law-enforcement task force composed of agents from the Federal Bureau of Investigation, the Drug Enforcement Agency, U.S. Customs, the U.S. Attorney General's Office, and the Cameron County Sheriff's Office. These organizations would work together to pursue the cult gang members.

"We'll try to have more information for you at a press conference we've planned in the morning; at that time we'll be available for questions. Then we'll take you to Mexico to visit Rancho Santa Elena and then we'll have another press conference with the suspects that will be arranged by Comandante Juan Benitez Ayala,"

Neck told the clamoring reporters before escaping to the safety of Gavito's office.

Now that Mark had been found, their primary goal had been achieved. Since Mark had been kidnapped and murdered in Mexico, they had no case. In reality they had no investigation. Anything they would do from this point forward would be without portfolio, either to help the family, to help Mexican authorities, or keep the press informed.

A massive manhunt was already under way for Constanzo and Aldrete. Mexican authorities had raided Aldrete's Matamoros home and discovered an altar covered with fruit, and *Santería* paraphernalia in front of a blood-splashed wall. Nearby lay children's clothing splattered with blood.

It was decided to call Raphael Martinez and Dr. Charles Wetli. While stationed in Miami, Neck had learned that the men were authorities on Afro-Caribbean religions.

Back at the scene of the slaughter, twelve bodies lay beside the shack, nine of them encased in the body bags brought from Brownsville, all that could be found; the other three were covered with sheets.

Benitez surveyed the grim sight and considered what a black day it was for his proud country, and for the good people of Matamoros. He knew that the events uncovered this day would live for years, a black spot on this pleasant countryside.

With a sign he nodded at the bodies.

"Take them to the morgue," he said. Then, turning to the suspects, he walked up to Serafin, holding a pistol in each hand.

"Do you think your gods still protect you, Hernandez?" he asked. "Are they still all-powerful?"

He started firing the pistols, bullets whizzing on either side of Serafin, the guns' concussion buffeting him.

"Are you still invincible to bullets?" he asked. "Are you still protected from the police?"

Benitez looked at the quivering man.

"Take all of them back to jail," he said, making no effort to hide the utter contempt in his voice.

Jim called his brother, Ken, who began a series of sad telephone calls to the Kilroy family. Helen called her family. They scarcely had time to contact their relatives before the networks began interrupting scheduled programming with news bulletins.

Bradley Moore was unlocking the door to his room when the telephone started ringing.

"Mark is dead. They've found his body," his mother told him.

Bradley dropped the telephone in shock.

"Bradley! Bradley! Bradley! Talk to me."

It was his dad's voice this time. Bradley picked up the telephone again, to his parents' relief. His dad struggled to reassure his son. The student kept asking what happened, but he was unable to comprehend his parents. Bits and pieces would lodge in his mind. Later he would remember phrases like "mass grave" and "drug cult."

"Don't turn on the television," his dad urged.

After hanging up, Bradley telephoned a girl friend, and she came over to handle the endlessly ringing telephone.

Gwen Huddleston telephoned Brent Martin. She had other responsibilities to help the Kilroys, so the conversation was brief and to the point, with no details.

It was several hours later when Brent went to a video store that he chanced to see Mark's picture on a television screen. Shocked, he stood in front of the television set learning the gruesome details, tears trickling down his cheeks.

Within hours the news media had surrounded the Huddleston home. Billy left, seeking privacy.

Joe and Emma Rodriguez withdrew to allow the family a period of private grief. Once they were alone, the three Kilroys mourned anew, surprised that the revelations of the past hour had not generated bitterness.

"I just have too much sorrow to be angry," Keith told his parents.

It was at that moment, during their most intense grief, that the family began to discern the true meaning of the scripture, "Vengeance is mine, . . . saith the Lord." It was also the early stirring of an acceptance that would amaze the world after the press conference the next day.

"Those men will have to go before God's court and answer for what they did," Keith said, trying to articulate his innermost thoughts. "It's up to them if they want to be forgiven. If we try to do anything evil to them, then we're just going to stoop to their level."

Jim and Helen looked at their son, pride rising to top their churning emotions.

"I know, Keith" Jim said. "I'm like you. I have too much sorrow to be angry."

"It's been so long, and we've been through so much; hate won't help us now," Helen said.

The three joined hands and prayed. They prayed for strength, for guidance, and especially, they prayed for the soul of Mark Kilroy.

"I think we should have a Mass here at Saint Luke's," Jim suggested. "Maybe we could do it Thursday."

"It will be a Mass of Resurrection," Helen said, thinking of the joyous "He Is Alive" she had heard Easter Sunday at Saint Luke's.

Attorney General Mattox visited the family later that evening to express his condolences, and to ask permission to establish a memorial scholarship fund in Brownsville in Mark's name. Joe Rodriguez and George Gavito would administer the fund.

"It would be nice if it went to someone who wanted to enter the medical field," Helen suggested.

"Also, I think we should offer some of it to families in Mexico who might not have the money to bury their dead," Jim added.

Sheriff's Deputy Ernesto Flores came home from Rancho Santa Elena a disturbed man. He had helped kick in the door to the tarpaper temple. He had watched Benitez face down the State Judicial Police. And he had helped remove Mark Kilroy's body from the profane grave.

The stench had been so bad that when he arrived home he took off his clothing, bundled them around his shoes, and threw the whole package into the garbage, telling his wife, "I don't want the smell of that place on me or my clothes. As far as I'm concerned, those clothes are useless."

Next, he took a long, cleansing shower.

When Lt. George Gavito went home late that night, he too stripped off his clothes and threw them into the trash, after wrapping them in a plastic bag to seal the odor.

U.S. Customs agent-in-charge Oran Neck drove into the driveway of his home and sat there silently, thinking about the emotional pandemonium he had just endured. It was time for his weary body to rest. The lake behind his house reflected moonbeams, and the stars were brilliant pinpoints against the inky black night. Surrounded by peace and tranquility, his mind still screamed, Why? It had been twenty-four hours since he had had any sleep. Wearily he got out of the car, stripped the stinking clothes from his body, wrapped them in newspaper, and put them in a trashcan.

I wish it would be that easy to strip the stench out of my mind, he thought.

Helen Kilroy tossed and turned that night. The finality of the loss of her son was not all that kept her awake. She realized that she had gradually grown to accept the fact that Mark would be found dead. Although the actual confrontation with the reality of Mark's death had still been an emotional blow, the weeks of searching, and wondering, had dulled the sharp edges of her grief.

She was trying to understand what could happen to a human mind that could turn it to human sacrifice, especially in these modern times. When she was first told about Mark's death she had refused to think about what it really meant. But that night, Helen Kilroy looked at the ceiling and asked herself: *What does a human sacrifice mean?*

Jim had encouraged his whole family to pray when they learned about the devil worshipers, and they had prayed together that afternoon when they reached the safety of the Rodriguez home.

Now, alone with her thoughts, Helen asked herself again, *What does a human sacrifice mean?*

The tears welled up as the answer came back in the darkness.

Nothing. It is meaningless. It has no redeeming value, her subconscious shrieked at her. *Your son is dead, and his death was a sacrifice on a pagan altar.*

"But there has to be more," she whispered back.

How could a person come to do what was done to Mark? she wondered.

They had to be possessed by the devil, she decided, continuing to sort out her feelings. *How else could one human do something like this to another?*

They are just like any of us, her mind suggested.

They can't be like us, her logic argued. *Look what they did. You would never do that.*

They have a soul, Helen's heart answered.

She remembered what Keith had said when the three of them had mourned their loss in private.

"*Those men will have to go before God's court and answer for what they did,*" she recalled his words. "*It's up to them if they want to be forgiven. If we try to do anything evil to them, then we're just going to stoop to their level.*"

It had been wisdom born of suffering and loss.

The situation became a bit clearer. God would not turn away from these heartless killers, but they would have to be the ones to turn to Him, to repent and to ask for His forgiveness. The truth of the matter was that her forgiveness would have no bearing on their souls' salvation; only God's forgiveness would matter. Bitterness on the family's part would serve no purpose but to harm the Kilroys.

If not bitterness, then what?

The answer came back, strong and bold: *Love.*

"For God so loved the world, that he gave his only begotten Son, that whosoever believeth in him should not perish, but have everlasting life," she said, reciting John 3:16.

The cornerstone of Christianity is love: God's love for man; man's love for God.

God would not turn away from anyone, no matter how vile the sin. Out of love, God had ordered that a divine human sacrifice be offered for the sins of the world through the death of Jesus Christ, the world's Lord and Savior.

Just as it had been in the case of Jesus Christ, Mark's death had been the direct work of the devil. While Christ's sacrificial death had served the noble cause of salvation, Mark's death served only the trials and tribulations of this world. With the exception of Christ, no human sacrifice ever served any honorable purpose.

"Somehow, we have to find an honorable purpose," Helen whispered in the darkness.

If God can love these killers, then certainly we should, she thought. *Is it possible that these men did not know, or understand, what they were doing?*

She remembered a conversation on capital punishment—more of a debate, as she recalled—she had had with Mark the year before. Helen had stoutly defended a victim's right to anger and the desire for justice—even to the use of the death penalty—basing much of her argument on the mass murder of eight nursing students in Chicago in 1966. Convicted murderer Richard Speck had invaded the women's living quarters for a night of death.

Helen had even gotten a little perturbed at Mark because he took such a strong stance against capital punishment.

"Mark, you don't understand how those parents would feel. They see their child killed," she said, "and they would seek punishment. That person had taken someone's life and capital punishment is the punishment for doing something like that. It is the law of the land."

"A life is a life, Mom," he argued. "You shouldn't take a life. Life is a gift from God."

As she remembered that exchange, Helen did what only a few months before she would have sworn was impossible. She opened her eyes, attempting to peer above the ceiling, into God's very heavens; perhaps if she followed the example of a crucified Christ. . . .

"Father," she prayed, "forgive them. . . ."

Mark's body would be cremated. To the family it seemed a logical decision after learning of the atrocities which had occurred a month ago at Rancho Santa Elena.

"There's a funeral home in San Antonio that has offered its services," George Gavito told Jim early the next morning. "We can have the body brought across the border and sent there."

"Check them out. Make sure they are who they say they are," Jim urged. The family was apprehensive. After finding Mark's body, they were hesitant to turn it over to someone unknown to them. Some unscrupulous person might make unauthorized photographs. And as preposterous as it might seem, they were fearful that the body could disappear—by accident or design—and they would have to search again. It was logical paranoia considering their fragile state of mind.

The Kilroys decided to hold a public Mass of Resurrection on Saturday in Santa Fe followed by a private burial Monday in a Catholic cemetery.

Before he hung up, George reminded Jim that a four o'clock press conference had been scheduled that Wednesday afternoon for the Kilroys. He was preparing to leave for a morning press conference hosted by law-enforcement officers.

Jim's brother Ken joined Jim and Helen in Brownsville. As the three discussed the service there with Father Nicolau, a group of more than a hundred school children in Hitchcock pinned yellow ribbons on the big oak tree in front of Our Lady of Lourdes Catholic Church. It was the first day of "Mark Kilroy Awareness Days."

Brent, Bradley, and Billy were joined by Gwen Huddleston and Sandy Cornelius at the ceremony. Then the horror-struck friends spent the day secluded in the Huddleston home where they read newspaper accounts and watched developing television reports with growing revulsion. The end of the search brought a bittersweet measure of relief to the young men.

"I was kinda afraid we'd never know," Bradley told Brent. "I was afraid all my life I'd wonder what happened to Mark. Man, I don't know how I could have lived with that."

"I understand. It's a relief in the sense that you finally know what happened," Brent said. "The other thought is one that we'll all live with, and that is that any one of us could have been picked up."

Neighbors began to round up all the yellow ribbons they could find and began tying them to trees, fence posts, mail boxes—everything. Merchants began to put out yellow ribbons at their places of business. Before the day ended the city of Santa Fe was ablaze with yellow—a colorful memorial to one of its citizens.

Sandy Cornelius called band leader Pee Wee Bowen to let him know the fund-raiser dance they had planned would have to be postponed. The date they had set now turned out to be the same day as a Mass of Resurrection for Mark, she told him.

Meanwhile, Gavito and Neck were joined by Texas Attorney General Jim Mattox for the morning press conference. Neck remembers that only moments before the press conference began, Don Wells of the U.S. Consulate in Matamoros told him, "I just want you to know that my office will cooperate fully with you in this investigation. You just let me know what you need, and I'll see that it is done."

Neck looked at the man.

"It's too late. We found Mark Kilroy; we don't need anything from you now," he said, turning back to pressing matters.

Nevertheless, Wells stood behind Neck during the press conference. Wells later denied knowledge of the conversation. "I was just stunned. I was walking around in a daze. But I do believe this case represents a tremendous amount of cooperation between all agencies," he added.

The press conference went smoothly and within an hour, a caravan of cars crossed the border. For many veteran reporters, the first shock came when they arrived at Rancho Santa Elena. The site was unguarded; evidence was strewn about.

"Where's the pot of pennies I heard about?" one reporter asked.

"It was the only item confiscated by police," he was told.

A few reporters saw the human-hair-and-tissue bird's nest— before it disappeared.

Laying against the outside wall near the *nganga* was the rust-spotted machete that had been used to kill Mark.

Mattox joined Neck, Gavito, and Benitez in the media tour. After an hour, the caravan reassembled for the trip to the Mexican Federal Judicial Police building.

"Be sure you follow someone who knows where they are going," Neck urged the media. He had visions of reporters and photographers wandering all over the city.

The press conference at the MFJP building was the second shock for the reporters. Never had North American news people had such access to criminal suspects. The handcuffed men each took turns standing on a box perched a scant few inches from the edge of a balcony.

Before the press conference began, Benitez turned to Gavito.

"The Hernandez family is finished now," he said.

As the session progressed, the press came face to face with:

• Elio Hernandez Rivera, twenty-two, of Matamoros but an American citizen according to the U.S. Consulate. He was Constanzo's second-in-command and Sara's lover. She had introduced him to Constanzo. "We killed them for protection," he said of the sacrifice victims. Elio admitted shooting one victim and decapitating another.

- Sergio Martinez Salinas, twenty-three, of Matamoros. Known as *La Mariposa* or "the Butterfly" he was one of the men who had kidnapped Mark. He also dug the grave where Mark was buried. "I'm guilty," he said. "It was the thing to do."

- Serafin Hernandez Garcia, Jr., twenty-two, the other American citizen in the group. He was the man who had selected Mark Kilroy out of the thousands of students in Matamoros. "I was ordered to dig the graves and bury them," he said. "I'm guilty."

- David Serna Valdez, twenty-two, of Matamoros. He is also known as *El Coqueto* or "the Showoff." He, too, helped kidnap Mark Kilroy.

Within a matter of seconds the press from each nation was at each other's throats. When American reporters asked questions in English, irate Hispanic reporters protested.

"This is Mexico; speak only in Spanish," a few said loudly each time a question was asked in English.

"This is my press conference, and I'll decide what language is used and if these men want, they can ask questions in English," Benitez defied the native press.

The suspects wove a story of drugs and sacrifice.

Palo Mayombe had been practiced for the past nine months. Sara Aldrete would recruit men to join the cult by showing them videos of *The Believers*, the suspects revealed. They also said she lured some victims to their death.

The cult had a rigid leadership. Constanzo was the warlord and high priest, and Elio Hernandez Rivera was his second-in-command. They were the only two empowered to sacrifice humans. A grinning Elio proudly displayed his marks of authority as Benitez pulled his shirt down to reveal the rows of crosses branded into his brown skin. Three scar-formed crosses on his chest, four on his back, and one on each of his shoulders marked him as a *palero*, a high priest in *Palo Mayombe*.

Although he had the right to kill, Elio said that it was Constanzo who sacrificed Kilroy. Elio did admit to the press that he had performed human sacrifice in the past.

Cult rituals were used to weave spells to protect a lucrative drug business, which moved more than a ton of marijuana each week.

At twenty-six, Adolfo Constanzo was only a few years older than the fanatical followers who blindly obeyed his orders to kidnap and kill in drug-cult rituals. An American of Cuban descent, he was born November 1, 1962, in Miami, Florida. Neighbors often complained of dead animals on their doorsteps after offending the family. They also complained of strange rituals and a terrible odor coming from the building. None of the children on the block were allowed to play with Constanzo or his two brothers and sister.

Constanzo attended high school in Miami, and audited at least one year of college. In 1981 he was arrested for shoplifting, convicted, and paid a fine and court costs before dropping out of sight. He resurfaced in Mexico City in 1984 where he worked as a model and soon became a favorite of the rich, famous, and powerful for his alleged ability to foretell the future. American officials said that Constanzo made weekly trips to Matamoros from Mexico City to oversee the drug business he had taken over from the Hernandez family.

"He had a wealthy lifestyle," Gavito told the press. "He paid cash for a 1989 Mercedes. All these men drove new cars or trucks equipped with telephones."

"This guy wore fur coats," Neck added about Constanzo.

His followers acknowledged that Constanzo had an unnatural hold over them. Charm, intimidation, and fear of death were the tools used by the pied piper of sacrifice. His power was the occult. Once they had murdered in the name of *Palo Mayombe* the cultists were even more bound to Constanzo, who convinced them that the victims became "spirit walkers" who would report directly to the *Padrino*. Nothing his drug cult members did could go unknown. His disciples said that Constanzo was a stern taskmaster who rarely laughed.

"He would get the spirits or something to kill you," Sara Aldrete would say later after her capture, explaining the followers' fear. "[He] was a strong personality. If he told you to do something, you would do it. We were his servants. . . . I didn't love him. But I followed him."

This was not the only inconsistency for twenty-four-year-old Sara Maria Aldrete Villarreal. She led a bizarre double life as a witch in Mexico and a college student at Brownsville's Texas Southmost College, a two-year college of approximately sixty-five hundred students. She was well-liked by students and teachers there who described her as cheerful, helpful, and friendly.

At six-feet, one-inch tall, she carried 143 pounds with grace, and was a well-proportioned physical education major with a charming smile. She was a member of the faculty-nominated "Who's Who" and president of the college's Soccer Booster Club. Sara was once honored as the "Outstanding Physical Education Student."

But Oran Neck found a disturbing note attached to her college records. It warned that she should be kept under observation because she was known to recruit fellow students to join the *Santería* cult. A Mexican national, she lived in Matamoros but maintained an address in the United States.

Aldrete had met Constanzo by chance when they stopped side-by-side in their automobiles. After a brief fling which included a shared interest in *Santería*, she introduced Elio to Adolfo.

"Sara told Elio that she could introduce him to someone who would protect him, make him a millionaire, and bring him to heights he hadn't known before," Benitez said.

The suspects claimed that Sara often lured young men to their deaths and that she was the main recruiter for the drug cult. It was Sara, they said, who turned the group from the more benign *Santería* to the malevolent *Palo Mayombe*.

When Mexican police raided her Matamoros home they found a room with ritualistic altar standing against a blood-splattered wall, with lighted candles still flickering. Carefully placed on the altar was a bowl of fruit which officers later learned was an offering to a *Santería orisha*, or saint. Infant's clothing, some torn and speckled with blood, was found near the altar.

"My God, do you think they are sacrificing children?" Neck had asked when he and Gavito investigated. Police had found a pair of children's sneakers at the tarpaper temple on Rancho Santa Elena.

"Could be," Gavito said. "The reports from Mexico City say that a few pieces of children's clothing were found in Constanzo's house near a couple of marble altars."

It had been discovered that a fourteen-year-old boy had been found among the twelve victims at Santa Elena. He was the youngest reported. Officials were concerned, because to cult worshipers, children represent the essence of pure innocence that needs to be defiled to perfect their worship.

"Why? Why did you do these things? Why gouge out the brain?" one reporter shouted.

"Because it is our religion," Serafin said calmly.

"The Godfather told us that if we did it, bullets couldn't harm us," Elio added.

The suspects denied that they drank blood or participated in cannibalism. They also denied that most victims were narcotics addicts. And they denied that they, themselves, were drug addicts. They denied they were satanists. But by the end of the day, a new word had found its way into the Spanish language. The community had dubbed the drug gang *narcosatanicos*, meaning "drug-satanists."

By the time the exhausted press returned to the United States, Gavito believed they had been properly softened up for the Kilroys.

A hush fell on the normally talkative group as Jim, Helen, and Keith entered, each wearing a yellow ribbon that said "Miss You Mark." Most of the newsmen there had just walked in Mark's last footsteps, had stood at the spot where Mark had last stood alive, and had looked into the depths of his makeshift grave. It had been a sobering experience. For most of these reporters this had become a very personal news story.

The Kilroy family was composed, looking out over the mass of faces and cameras. Jim already knew many of the reporters from the long days of searching for Mark.

What can I tell these people? he thought, looking around the room. *They all wanted us to find Mark, and now that we've found him, what can I say that might make a difference, that could give Mark's death some value? What can I say that could turn evil into good?*

He cleared his throat.

"I want to thank the media, especially the local media," he started. "Everyone has done a very good job.

"Because of the publicity, we were able to keep searching—we were able to find this group of people who did these things to Mark," he said.

"I also want to thank the law-enforcement agencies in both countries," he said. "Because they worked together to find Mark, we can all take comfort in the fact that these men are not killing anyone any more."

He went on to thank the people all over Texas and Mexico for their prayers.

"The reason we're not worried about Mark now is that he was such a good young fellow. He made us proud. We loved him a lot. The Father in heaven loves him more than we ever did and He's taking good care of him now," Jim said.

"I think one of the last things I want to say is that Mark never had any involvement with narcotics. He never even tried them that I know of. He was afraid of narcotics. Yet it was narcotics that killed Mark! So when people stand there next to you and try to tell you that a marijuana cigarette doesn't hurt . . . they're wrong!" Jim insisted.

"Marijuana is what killed Mark. These guys were marijuana smugglers."

As Jim responded to questions from the media regarding possible penalties for those involved in the sacrifice murders, he said, "It definitely is very important that they never be allowed to do again what they did to Mark and the other victims. The problem is that murderers in the United States can get out of prison in fifteen years or so. And I've been told that some people can pay their way out of prison in Mexico.

"I think that what these men have done is serious enough that we should make sure they are controlled."

The composed father went on to ask for financial help for the eleven other families in Mexico who had lost loved ones.

"We don't want to forget them," he said.

Helen looked out at the press. The room was jammed to capacity with cameras, microphones, and nearly a hundred reporters who were hanging on Jim's every word. *It's almost like we're among friends,* Helen thought as the questions continued.

The family had special praise for Juan Benitez Ayala and his cooperation with U.S. police officers.

"It illustrates that countries can and should work together," Jim said. He suggested that the two countries form a joint task force to solve the drug problems along the border. Jim also pointed out that the cult murders were not uniquely a Mexican problem. These are problems that affect both Brownsville and Matamoros—problems that are shared by two countries.

He heard someone ask Helen about her attitude toward the killers.

"I think they must be possessed by the devil. I pray for all of them. I ask everyone to pray for all of them, that they can come to realize how wrong all this is, how terrible it all is," she said. "I look at them and I don't believe they really realize what they've done. I pray that they will be sorry for what they did."

For the third time that day the press was shocked. This time not by evil, but by good. How could this mother pray for the murderers of her son?

"This might sound hard to believe, but I don't feel any anger at all," Jim added his feelings. "I think that the people who did this are so bad, that they will never ask for forgiveness. But I hope they do. I hope some day that they can go up to Mark and apologize in person for what they did," he said quietly.

And the Kilroys?

"We're at peace now," Jim said as Helen nodded her agreement. "We know that Mark is safe."

That night Sergio Martinez stunned Mexican officials by telling them he knew where a thirteenth body was buried at Rancho Santa Elena. The bombshell put Benitez back on the telephone to Gavito. *How many more would be found?* Gavito wondered.

As word of the murders spread, hundreds of Mexican people with missing loved ones surrounded the morgue in Matamoros, demanding the right to view the bodies. Many of the families were critical of Mexican authorities, complaining that without the massive search for Mark Kilroy, the bodies of Mexican nationals would never have been discovered.

Hysteria swept through the Lower Rio Grande Valley Thursday morning when rumors circulated that devil worshipers were launching a counterattack by kidnapping children in retaliation for the arrests at Rancho Santa Elena (what the media were now calling the Devil's Ranch). Parents yanked children out of classes, and many kept their children at home behind locked doors. School officials confirmed that more than four hundred children had missed school in three districts.

The press got a firsthand view of Mexican justice as Sergio Martinez was ordered to exhume the thirteenth victim later that Thursday morning.

Sweat began to pour off Martinez as he labored in the heat. He was surrounded by Mexican police armed with automatic weapons—and the police were surrounded by the news media.

A hushed silence fell over the normally glib group, a silence punctuated by sweat-soaked Martinez's pleas, first for water and then, as he began to uncover the body, for a mask to cut the stench which permeated the air. His pleas were met with curses from the police and the threat that if he delayed he would be made to dig with his hands in the manure-laced straw.

The stench finally became so overwhelming that Martinez ignored the armed guards and climbed from the open grave to stand face to face with a television cameraman, who took off his mask and gave it to the suspect. It proved of little value, however. The mask dropped from his nose as he bent to his labor. A mortician's aide, wearing red rubber gloves, helped in removing the body which was wrapped in sheets of plastic.

Perhaps it was the realization of what he had done or perhaps it was the stench which pierced even the strongest masks; or perhaps it was a superstitious fear of an unleashed spirit that caused Martinez to leap from the grave and run backwards, cowering near the fence as the body was removed. An autopsy would later reveal that the heart had been cut from the body.

Within a few minutes the area was virtually deserted. Mexican officials marched Martinez past the cauldron and pots that were supposed to make him invulnerable at the cost of human lives. In their haste to leave, officials overlooked the skin off the bottom of one of the victim's feet. Like the bottom of a small house slipper, heel still intact, it lay on the edge of the putrefied pit, now covered with flies.

That afternoon Mark Kilroy's body was returned to the United States and driven to Mission Park Funeral and Cemeteries in San Antonio for cremation.

"We have created our own demon, and the demon is drugs."

The Rev. John Nicolau sought to reassure the standing-room-only crowd at the Mass of Resurrection at Saint Luke's Catholic Church that night in Brownsville. More than a thousand people were jammed under the arched wooden ribs of the cathedral.

Christian love, Jim Kilroy thought as his family was escorted to the front row. *That's what this is all about.*

He saw Oran Neck and George Gavito; faces from Santa Fe also dotted the congregation. The Rodriguez family sat with the Kilroys. Jim's brother Ken hovered over the family, prompting reporters to seek the identity of the towering, authoritative figure with the brown mustache.

Jim was struck by the outpouring of love. For four weeks this congregation had become another family to him. Many of them had called to say, "You don't know me, but I want you to know I care, and I hope you find your son." As the Mass began, Jim felt the power of the prayers that had been said all over the United States and Mexico and he believed that power had culminated in this service. He knew it was being broadcast live across the nation on CNN, and although it could not erase his tremendous sadness, he felt a measure of peace within his soul at the power of the prayers now being added to those already said. He turned to Helen and asked, "Do you feel it?"

"What?"

"The love in this building. The power of prayer."

Helen clasped his hand.

"Yes!"

"This has been selfless prayer," he whispered to his wife. "It was love from afar, but now we stand in the middle of it."

"That's what has given us the strength to continue," Helen said.

Father Nicolau reached out to his congregation that night with a soothing message of love and dedication colored with a strong anti-drug and anti-cult stance.

"Drug addicts and criminals may kill the body, but they were not able to kill Mark's spirit," he said.

"We have had four emotions: Anger, fear, love, and joy."

He went on to describe the emotions. Anger because of the type of crime that claimed Mark's life, fear that it will happen again, love as demonstrated by family, and joy at the thought of resurrection.

"The emotion of joy is the result of the first three emotions," he said.

"Mark doesn't have a problem. We have the problem.

"We have the problem because of satanic cults," he continued. "I've been hearing about satanic cults for several months from teachers, counselors, and parents.

"One ten-year-old told me that 'If I give my soul to the demon I'll be rich.'"

He paused to let the impact soak in.

"We all have a desire to worship. These people chose the wrong deity to worship."

"Mark deserves an apology today," he added. "And I apologize to him.

"Mark, you came to the Valley for a week, but you will stay forever," he said. "We will miss you."

Then Jim and Helen mounted the podium, where Helen bravely choked back a mother's tears to beg for prayers for the men who had killed her son.

"Pray for the people who have done this thing. Pray that the Lord will enter into their hearts so that they will know they are wrong," she said, her voice barely above a whisper. Helen still wore her bright yellow "Miss You Mark" ribbon which glowed against her red polka-dot dress.

In living rooms across the nation people watched, and marveled at this family, asking themselves, *Would I be able to have that kind of forgiveness?*

It was the same tone of forgiveness that the family had set the day before in the press conference. But it is forgiveness that will forever be tinged with an admonition against illegal narcotics. For the Kilroys, the battle lines against drug abuse had been drawn. Their son had never used drugs, but their family had suffered the ultimate horror of drug abuse.

George Gavito and Oran Neck were among the first to embrace the Kilroys following the service. Then Don Wells of the U.S. Consulate in Matamoros approached Jim and hugged him. "I've learned a lot these past few weeks," he said. "I'm very sorry for your loss."

Jim Kilroy:

We had both learned a lot.

This man's job required a delicate balancing act. On one hand he is charged with the responsibility of promoting good relations with Mexico; on the other hand, he has the responsibility to help U.S. citizens with problems there. It is a difficult task.

In our search for Mark I had learned the great need for diplomacy, especially cooperation. I had become more aware of the difference a muddy river can make in how men live. I also learned the need for two nations to work in harmony.

I couldn't help but recall what Joe Rodriguez had said earlier in the day.

"Basically two positive things came out of this, if anything positive can be said about a beautiful human life being lost.

"It has put an end to a satanic cult, and it has cemented two nations. They are working together in a way they have never worked before," Joe said.

Senator Lloyd Bentsen has talked of creating a federal border agency with Mexico to deal with problems common to both nations. Texas Attorney General Jim Mattox is in favor of creating a state task force to study what could be done to promote cooperation between the neighboring countries along the Texas border.

Whichever plan is followed, something needs to be done!

The outpouring of affection continued long after the service ended, as hundreds of people passed by to embrace family members, or give a flower or a poem.

Helen looked deep into their eyes. She could see love there, and shared grieving.

It's like a reflection of my own sadness, she thought.

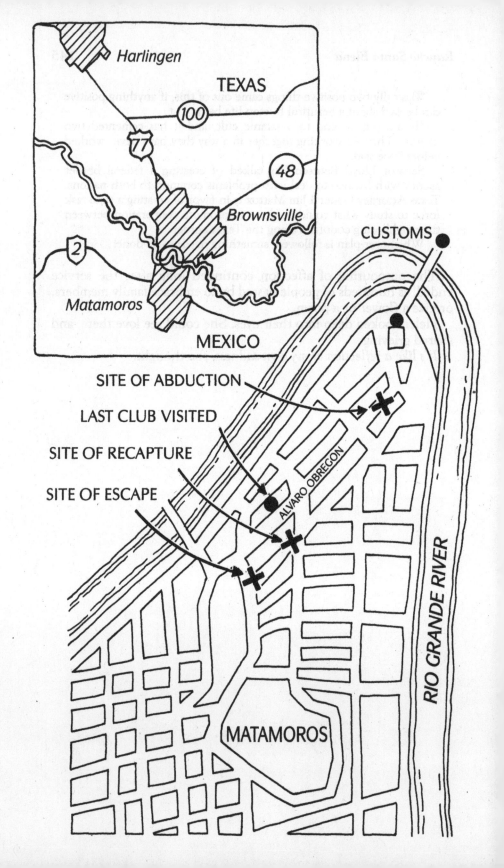

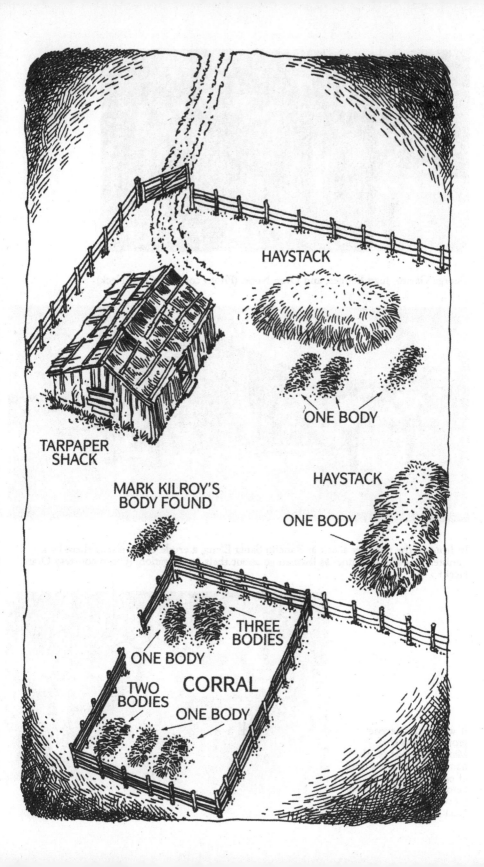

HAYSTACK

ONE BODY

TARPAPER
SHACK

MARK KILROY'S
BODY FOUND

HAYSTACK

ONE BODY

THREE
BODIES

ONE BODY

TWO
BODIES

CORRAL

ONE BODY

George Gavito, Juan Benitez, and Oran Neck. (Photo courtesy Oran Neck)

In front of the tarpaper shack at Rancho Santa Elena, a crude cross, placed there by a minister, is a silent sentinel as lawmen go about their investigation. (Photo courtesy Oran Neck)

It was in this serene grove of trees that Mark Kilroy sat on the hammock and ate a meal of eggs just minutes before he was murdered. (Photo courtesy Oran Neck)

(Left to right) Elio Hernandez Rivera; David Serna Valdez; Serafin Hernandez Garcia, Jr.; and Sergio Martinez Salinas stand handcuffed behind the killing shack the day Mark Kilroy's body was recovered. (Photo courtesy Oran Neck)

Nine bodies uncovered at Rancho Santa Elena have been encased in body bags and three covered with sheets. Later a thirteenth body was found. (Photo courtesy Oran Neck)

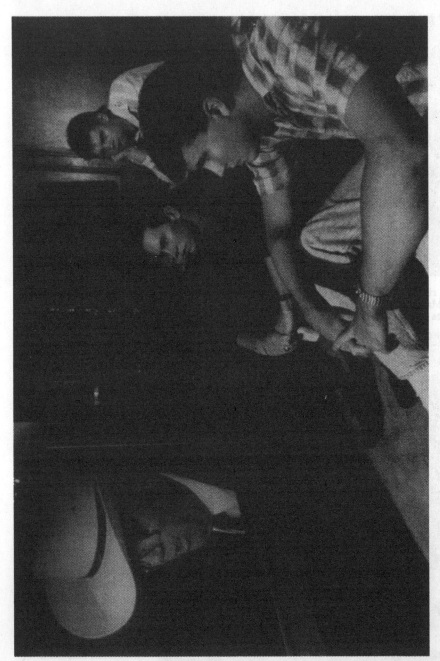

The three friends who were with Mark Kilroy when he disappeared in Matamoros—Bill Huddleston (left), Bradley Moore (foreground), and Brent Martin (background)—watch a news conference concerning the discovery of Mark's body. (Photo: *Houston Chronicle*)

ABOVE: Several weeks after the tarpaper temple was discovered at Rancho Santa Elena, it was destroyed by fire to show that the black magic practiced there was ineffective.
BELOW: The nganga (upper left) with four smaller pots in which sacrifice and offerings were made. In the foreground, a pot with pennies. (Photos courtesy Oran Neck)

ABOVE: The nganga—which supposedly contained Constanzo's warrior spirit—is charred and nearly destroyed after being engulfed with flames. (Photo courtesy Oran Neck)

BELOW: Dr. Charles Wetli, Dade County Medical Examiner, holds two examples of an Ochosi. The one on the left was discovered in the nganga at Rancho Santa Elena.

LEFT: Adolfo de Jesus Constanzo.
CENTER LEFT: The photograph of college student Sara Maria Aldrete Villarreal that was used on wanted posters.
CENTER RIGHT: Mug shot of Sara Maria Aldrete Villarreal the day she was captured in Mexico City following a shootout in which Constanzo died. (Photos courtesy Oran Neck)

A *Santería* altar discovered in Sara Maria Aldrete Villarreal's home. (Photo courtesy Oran Neck)

BOOK FOUR

THE HOMECOMING

REMEMBERING MARK

On the night before Mark's funeral Mass, his friends wanted one last evening with him, sharing the kind of time he enjoyed, filled with fraternity and laughter. About fifty of them gathered in the home of Mark's classmate Diana Alexander to reminisce about their slain buddy. Maybe they realized it, maybe they did not, but each wanted a chance to collectively deal with his or her own outrage over the profane death and loss of a young man with such promise.

"The one thing about Mark that really stood out," said his friend Michael Heygood, "was that he was a good guy and a good friend. He was always there for people who needed him."

Richie Kuebler added, noting that friends often turned to Mark for advice. "Sometimes he'd say, 'Gee, I don't know, I don't think anyone listens to me.' But they did. Many of his friends have told me how much they followed his advice."

"He could always make you laugh," chipped in Mitch Tully, a member of Lambda Chi Alpha, Mark's fraternity.

Rick Rezek fondly recalled the day Mark tried (unsuccessfully) to surf.

The friends spent the evening watching home movies of Mark's high school basketball games and a film of the 1986 Senior Class Follies in which Mark had appeared. But Bradley could not bring himself to watch the live-action videos and films.

"To look at a picture is one thing, but to see him live, moving on a video, is just too difficult to watch," he told Brent that evening.

A few of the students, including Bradley and Brent, had talked to Anne Maier, a reporter for *People Weekly* magazine.

157

"Mark was a good friend," Bradley said. "It was as if all the good things you find in people you know were put into one person."

"It didn't matter what we did—as long as we did it with Mark, we knew we'd have a good time," Brent added.

Former high school basketball coach Terry Ray was one of the few older people attending the gathering.

"Mark could always make a positive situation out of everything," Ray said, adding a teacher's perspective. "And he was very considerate. Whenever he was in town he would come by the high school to visit me."

Index cards were passed out and each friend was asked to take a moment during the evening to write what he remembered foremost about Mark. The cards would be given to the Kilroy family.

It is Mitch Tully's recollection that Mark decided to become a doctor during his senior year in high school.

"I remember he was always telling us that he'd end up patching us all back together in future years, because we wanted to play sports; but he had already made up his mind to be a doctor. I guess because he liked to help people."

Having to deal with the death of a friend was sometimes too difficult for these young people. Many of his classmates wept as they remembered Mark; they mourned with the full knowledge that on the next day they would bid him a final farewell.

Amid thousands of fluttering yellow ribbons the family of Mark Kilroy came home for his funeral Mass on Saturday.

Ironically, it was the final day of "Yellow Ribbon Week," and the small yellow ribbons which proclaimed "Miss You Mark" were everywhere. The project that had begun as an effort to keep his name before the public now became a golden memorial.

Mourners knew they were nearing Santa Fe when the yellow ribbons began to show up on rural mailboxes along the highways leading into the city. Soon the distinctive ribbons were festooned to telephone poles, fence posts, and even trees, each fluttering gently in a breeze that took the edge off the Southeast Texas heat. At the city limits, automobiles began to sport delicate, joyful yellow bows tied to radio antennas.

The short, main drag of the small community was ablaze with yellow. Planters of yellow mums brightened a street divider in the heart of town. A flag rippled at half-mast on a pole bedecked with a large yellow bow. Each business had a yellow bow of mourning on its door. A business marquee bore the legend: "Our prayers are with you Mark & family." As American communities have done in time of tragedy since the birth of this country, the citizens of Santa Fe banded together to protect and honor one of their own.

The little town, which had enfolded the Kilroy family into its heart, now opened that same spirit of compassion to a mixture of mourners. Many who traveled those distinctive beribboned roads were friends and acquaintances; some were simply curious, and wanted to touch a piece of history. Still others drove hundreds of miles to be in the presence of the exceptional courage and the godly love demonstrated by the Kilroys. For most of the week the Kilroy family had appeared daily on television as the world recoiled from the evil uncovered at Rancho Santa Elena, and it seemed that everyone wanted to reach out to comfort them.

Jim Kilroy:

Everywhere we looked, there was a message for us as we were driven to Our Lady of Lourdes for Mark's funeral Mass. Helen was amazed at all the signs amid the blaze of yellow covering our hometown.

This yellow testimony of sympathy touched our hearts. We had learned the importance of condolences the past few days. Until Mark's death I had never realized how valuable the sympathy of friends was during a time of mourning.

Without the support of our friends and family we would have been unable to endure this ordeal. And now we faced the final public farewell to our son, and it meant so much to us that it would be shared with family, old friends, and new friends who had come from all over the United States to celebrate the Mass of Resurrection with us.

Police Chief Mike Barry secured more than thirty police officers from various local and state departments to handle traffic and security. Area funeral homes donated seven tents to accommodate the overflow from the church. By the time the service began, more than seven hundred people crammed into the church building and another eight hundred watched the service on big-screen television sets under the tents. Loudspeakers broadcast the ceremony.

The grounds were aglow with yellow. The trunk of the large oak tree in front of the church was still festooned with the "Miss You Mark" ribbons put there in the emotional service conducted Wednesday by grade-school children. An occasional mourner would add a ribbon to the tree.

Nearby a large majestic wreath, more than seven feet across and ten feet high, dominated a portion of the lawn. At its base were more than sixty pots of shimmering yellow mums. Behind them, an American flag waved at half-mast.

Large yellow bows decorated the doors at the entrance to the church building. Flanking them were a pair of tables to register mourners. Every nook, cranny, and corner inside the sanctuary was filled with floral tributes. Folding chairs on each end of the pews and down the center aisle added extra seating to accommodate mourners until the building overflowed. The press was relegated to the choir loft, out of the mainstream, but with its own private entrance. Photographers clamped cameras onto the ledge as the loft overflowed, also. The interior of the building spread out before them. Subdued light filtered through the ten stained-glass windows depicting the life of Christ. Above the altar, a crucifix in a marble niche dominated the front of the building. Sixteen empty pews were reserved for the Kilroy family which had gathered from the four corners of the country.

Mark's picture stood on a stand to the left of the altar. Beside it a large table in front of the family pews held scattered mementos of Mark's short, twenty-one years of life.

On the table were pictures of happy times: Mark and his family at the beach, clowning with Keith, teasing his mom, fishing with his dad, dressed in a tuxedo for prom night, group pictures with his baseball and basketball teams, even photographs of Mark with girls he had dated. Several newspaper clippings added the details of his short life. One told of a crucial basketball bucket with only six seconds remaining in a game which secured a 60–58 district victory for the Santa Fe Indians against arch-rival El Campo. Mark was hot that night, scoring eighteen points.

The index cards of remembrance, signed by friends and class-mates the night before, also lay on the table. The cards eulogized Mark as "out-going," "fun-loving," "very kind," "an inspiration," and "full of life." One friend remembered him as the kind of person who always had "something positive to say."

At the end of the table were stacked copies of the circulars—in English and Spanish—which the Kilroy family had determinedly distributed in two countries during those dark days after Mark disappeared. Some mourners took a circular for a memento.

A few feet away stood a wreath shaped in the numerals 86 which was sent in the name of his graduating high school class. At its foot a small Teddy bear lay nestled among yellow mums. It was wearing a tiny Santa Fe Indians T-shirt.

The Kilroy family and friends awaited the start of the service in a fellowship hall at the back of the property behind the church building.

Jim Kilroy:

It was while watching Keith talk to my brother that I came to a realization which seemed to polarize many of my thoughts: The importance of family ties.

Distance made no difference to our families. They immediately offered their prayers and help.

Helen's mom and her three sisters—Rosemarie, Carolyn, and Mary—kept the telephone lines humming.

Family support from my brothers, Ken and Ron, and my sisters, Judy and Diane, was tremendous. My parents were in constant contact with us.

I watched Keith and Ken talking and I was reminded of what Keith said about Mark: "If I had a problem, usually I'd take Mark's advice, and he'd be right. I'd be glad I listened."

I'm glad he did listen while he could; Keith no longer has a brother to rely on.

Yellow was the predominant color of the event and when the Kilroy family was ushered in for the service, they were dressed in light colors, shunning the traditional black of mourning.

The Rev. John C. DeForke, fifty-six, brushed aside his own grief as he mounted the stairs to stand before the altar. He had been pastor there for nine years.

How many times has Mark stood by me as we celebrated Mass together? he thought of his former altar boy as he bowed before the altar. As a priest he daily dealt with death and man's inhumanity to man; but familiarity with evil could never erase its horror. That thought was comforting. He shuddered to think that he could ever be blasé about the reality of evil.

As Father John turned to face the audience, he was struck by its youthful composition. It seemed that more than half the participants were teen-agers. He said a silent prayer that his sermon would touch those youthful hearts and perhaps prevent future tragedies.

Secreted in his hand was a yellow ribbon of mourning. It, too, bore the legend "Miss You Mark." No one noticed as he slipped it under the lectern.

It will always remain here, he promised.

As he looked at the suffering in the faces of the young people he realized that Mark's death had reawakened the need for decision-making. *I pray their decisions will be wise,* he thought.

Once again he brushed aside melancholy, knowing it could so easily descend upon this group. It was a time of joy, not mourning, so he smiled as he looked at the congregation, then very warmly turned to the Kilroys.

"Welcome home."

It was a simple greeting, returning old friends back into the warmth and love radiated by their home church. It was the first time the family had returned to Santa Fe since Mark's body had been discovered.

"You are home now.

"We are your family.

"We are your friends."

The parish priest explained the rituals and symbols of the Catholic Mass as he conducted a service of "homecoming" during the Mass of Resurrection, which he called a celebration of new life.

He compared the Kilroys' search for Mark to that of Mary and Joseph when their son, Jesus, disappeared and was later found teaching in the temple. For "three days they were heavy of heart as they made their way to Jerusalem searching for him. Like Mary and Joseph, Helen and Jim knew the heavy heart of searching.

"And now, like Mary, the Kilroy family understands what it means to treasure all these things in the heart.

"So often we lose ourselves in the horrors of this world," Father John said, changing to another subject. "God allows us to see the ugly, the depraved, the senseless killing. We must never turn away from this."

But the priest suggested that the audience remember instead the death of Christ on the cross and His last words: "Father, forgive them, for they do not know what they are doing."

"We must forgive in our hearts? Yes, just as this beautiful Kilroy family has shown love and forgiveness."

Next, Father DeForke challenged the audience to disdain the use of drugs. "Is it worth it?" he asked the audience before urging them, "Repeat after me: Never. Never. Never."

Three times he asked "Is it worth it?" and three times he called the audience to repeat "Never. Never. Never."

In discussing death, the priest affirmed that some of the most difficult words to follow are recorded in the Lord's Prayer: "Thy will be done."

But he warned, "It has no meaning if we have no faith and trust."

Father John was joined by Bishop Joseph Anthony Fiorenza of the Houston-Galveston diocese. Dressed in red, and carrying the staff of his office, Bishop Fiorenza praised the family's courage.

"You have taught us how to face adversity of the worst type. And you have taught us how to face it with dignity," he said.

Addressing the congregation, the bishop continued: "They have been able to see beyond the grief. The Kilroys have been evangelizing us while they endure their suffering. They have indeed lived their faith. Of course, they seek justice, but they do not want revenge," he said.

"They show us love instead.

"They show forgiveness rather than vengeance.

"It is their attitude which can break the vicious cycle of vengeance in the world," he concluded, then once again addressing the Kilroys: "For days to come your eyes will close in sleep, but your hearts will weep as you turn sorrow into joy."

Three friends from Mark's graduating class—Rick Rezek, Richie Kuebler, and Michael Heygood—spoke briefly after presenting a single red rose to Helen which Richie plucked from the wreath sent by the Class of '86.

"Mark was a friend to everyone," Rick said. "Many friends considered him their best friend; he didn't single out one person. He had a way of making everyone feel special."

Richie took his cue from Father DeForke, focusing his remarks on the evils of drugs, and ending with the same challenge: "Never. Never. Never."

As the Mass drew to a close, it was time for Jim and Helen to address the mourners. Standing side-by-side at the altar, Jim first thanked the news media for restraint.

"I'm proud and thankful because the media could have focused on the sheer madness of all this. Instead it chose to focus on love," he began. Then he zeroed in on the work and dedication of police officers in two countries.

"These men worked night and day and weekends," he said of all the officers, but singling out his close relationship to Neck, Gavito, and Benitez.

"And I believe they all came to love Mark. These are tough men. They have to be hard to do what they do; but they were always there to console us.

"And when they went to the killing grounds they all cried—all of them," he stressed.

Next, Helen thanked both sets of parents for instilling religious faith.

"They showed us God's love," she explained.

The tragic events of the past month had helped her gain new appreciation of a great truth she had known all along: God is the center of life. Her parents and Jim's parents had taught them to know God's love and they, in turn, had taught Mark and Keith of God's unconditional love.

"That is what has gotten us through all this," she said.

And Mark, too, she thought.

It was a beautiful affirmation of the importance of parents in the faith-development of their children.

Jim concluded: "We are proud of Mark, and we thank God for the way Mark was—and the way we were when we were with him. Mark is with God. Do not be sad for Mark; be sad for yourselves and us because another good man is missing from our world."

Unable to contain themselves any longer, the congregation gave the family a prolonged standing ovation.

When the applause died down after several minutes, Father John invited everyone—all fifteen hundred people attending the service—to be guests of the parish in a communal meal that had been prepared by the women of the community.

"We have enough food to feed all of you and twice that many more," he said. "So share love and joy today."

(That prediction would prove true and the next day the parish took a three-day supply of food to Daily Bread, a shelter for the homeless in Galveston, which, ironically, had no food the day the donation was delivered. Also, the flowers and potted plants were sent to cheer the sick in the surrounding hospitals, with only one arrangement left over.)

The love feast was designed to allow the family to greet old and new friends as the fellowship hall behind the church filled with people.

Seated at one table was Helen J. Steier, sixty-six, Mark's maternal grandmother who had traveled from Springhill, Florida, for the service.

Wearing a yellow dress accented by pearls, she clutched the teddy bear that had been on one of the wreaths. The last time she had been with her grandson was Christmas—which also happens to be her birthday.

"Mark would tell me not to worry, that when he became a doctor he would take care of me when I got sick," she said, smiling at that and other fond memories of her first grandson. She remembered times with Mark when he was a baby, holiday times and special occasions as he grew older, even a trip to Disney World when he came to visit her and his grandfather in Florida.

But there was one jarring note. Amid all the yellow ribbons of remembrance were long police barrier ribbons—also yellow—to channel the crowds and provide privacy for the family. These ribbons bore the legend, "Crime scene. Do not cross."

Somehow, those words seemed to come too late; the line had already been crossed.

A policeman guarded the gate to the cemetery Monday morning during a private family service and interment. He was not needed. The family had requested privacy for this precious moment, and the news media honored that request.

Father John placed the ashes of Mark's body in a small rectangular bronze funeral urn with a scene depicting the Lord's Supper etched along the front. He brought the urn to the Kilroy family, placing it in Jim Kilroy's arms.

The father carried the remains of his son to the burial site, with the priest leading the way and the family following.

At the gravesite Jim gently handed the urn to Helen.

It looks just like a treasure chest, she thought as she tenderly kissed it before handing it to Keith.

Keith looked around the cemetery. It pleased him that his brother was to be buried next to a little baby.

Mark would like that, he thought.

Jim took the urn one last time before handing it to Father John. As the priest started to take the urn, Jim hugged it tight to his body.

It is so good to be able to hold you one more time, he thought.

Then the ashes of Mark's body were buried in the consecrated ground of a Roman Catholic cemetery.

A large wreath, more than seven feet across and ten feet high and surrounded by sixty pots of yellow mums, dominated the front lawn of Our Lady of Lourdes Catholic Church on the day of Mark's funeral Mass.

Jim and Helen Kilroy address the congregation at Our Lady of Lourdes Catholic Church during their son's funeral. Mark Kilroy's picture is at right. (Photo copyright 1989 by the *Houston Post*; used by permission.)

ABOVE: President George Bush hears Jim and Helen Kilroy express concerns for tougher controls on illegal-drug use. (official White House photograph, Aug. 1989)

BELOW: Keith Kilroy, Father John DeForke, Helen Kilroy, and Jim Kilroy stand in front of a tree which Mark and Jim planted on the church lawn several years before Mark's death.

THE
DEATH OF A CULT

BOOK FIVE

THE
DEATH OF A CULT

CONSTANZO

Within hours of finding the bodies at Rancho Santa Elena the search for the elusive Adolfo de Jesus Constanzo had spread worldwide.

Swift reportage by the news media caused a deluge of information, including telephone calls from frustrated former neighbors in Miami, and even a Constanzo family member who telephoned to talk to Oran Neck and George Gavito.

Just as it had done with "America's Most Wanted," the switchboard lit up. Telephone calls from Honduras, Costa Rica, and Guatemala could have been anticipated; but sightings were also reported in New Zealand, Australia, Japan, England, Italy, and Canada.

Perhaps the most unique inquiry came from an earnest state trooper in Kansas.

"I'm talking to you on a highway near Kansas City," he said when finally put through to Gavito. He had used his radio to contact home base, and they had dialed in the Cameron County Sheriff's Office. "I have a suspect who looks like this Constanzo."

He went on to describe a man who neatly fit Constanzo's description. Gavito could not think of anything else to tell him—then he remembered.

"Does he have tattoos on either arm?" he asked.

There was a brief pause.

"No." George could hear the disappointment in that single word.

"That's not him, but thanks for calling."

"Anytime. We have to look out for each other."

It pleased Neck because all the publicity and interest was spontaneous. No longer did they have to rack their minds for story ideas

171

that would entice the media to keep Mark's name before the public.

Instead of going into hiding as others might have done, the Kilroys expressed their gratitude to the press by remaining available for interviews. It would have been easier on the family to avoid the glare of publicity in this time of intense grief. But for weeks they had begged the media to help keep the search for their son in the news; now they would not refuse to cooperate with men and women who had helped them.

Suddenly, the whole world seemed to have become aware of the occult and drugs, and their twin threat to society.

"America's Most Wanted" contacted Neck. They wanted to do another program, with the focus on Constanzo and Aldrete. This time Deputy Ernesto Flores and U.S. Customs Agent Willie Canant went to Washington, D.C., to field the telephone calls.

"You know, George, this has become a community problem," Neck said as they sifted through leads. "There is no flag, no border, no river that divides this community on this issue. It even crosses international boundaries. The whole world wants Constanzo brought to justice."

Warrants were issued for the arrest of Constanzo and Aldrete as well as Ovidio Hernandez Rivera and Malio Ponce Torres. Airport records revealed that Constanzo had fled into Mexico on tickets purchased by Aldrete.

Raphael Martinez, an Afro-Caribbean occult expert at the University of North Florida, believed that Constanzo would seek out his *Tata*, the spiritual godfather who had initiated him into *Palo Mayombe*.

"He has fallen so far that he probably believes that only baby's blood can purify him," Martinez told Gavito. "And that might even require a bathtub full of baby blood in which he can immerse himself."

In an effort to sort out the religious practices, the Mexican government invited Martinez to survey the tarpaper temple and the killing grounds.

Benitez was upset with the cult "evidence" lying around his office. And just as disturbing to him was the tarpaper shack, a sinister reminder of the cult's vile activity.

"Why don't you do something about it?" Martinez suggested. "Why don't you burn it?"

Burning the shack would be another spiritual blow to Constanzo, Martinez explained, especially putting a torch to the *nganga*. It would send a message to Constanzo that his black magic was ineffective. But, Martinez urged that the temple not be destroyed until he could come to Matamoros and dismantle the vile *nganga*. There was much to be learned that could be passed on to law-enforcement officers whose lives are always in jeopardy when dealing with *Paleros*.

When Martinez arrived several weeks after the shack was discovered he found a partially looted crime scene; but there was enough there for him to verify the existence of *Palo Mayombe*.

As the anthropologist began to examine the *nganga*, he accidentally tilted it, nearly spilling the contents.

"Don't spill it," Gavito cried out, fearful of the Mexican policemen's reaction. Although these men deal daily in the realities of crime, often putting their lives on the line in gun battles, this killing ground had them spooked.

Martinez looked up to find three submachine guns trained on his mid-section by nervous officers.

Martinez was surprised to find more than the prescribed twenty-one sticks in the *nganga*. He also found seven railroad spikes, seven horseshoes, Mexican coins, a cat skull, the backbone of a chicken, turtle shells, *otanes* (a smooth stone sacred to *Santería* worshipers), and an *Ochosi*. Several bindings in which names were written on virgin (or unused) paper and attached to bones were also recovered, but the names could not be read. He was told that pathologists had removed a skull, brains, and a human heart from the *nganga*.

Also missing was the *Elegguá*, the *orisha* of the pathways. No rite can be performed without the round, fat idol with seashell eyes. Since it was missing, Martinez speculated that a member of the drug cult—perhaps its leader, who would understand the special meaning of the *orisha*—had visited the shack after police had discovered the "Devil's Ranch."

A similar *Elegguá* would later be found in Sara Aldrete's house in Matamoros.

Martinez was also unable to locate the delicate bird's nest of human hair that had been reported, or the full human scalp that Ernesto Flores reported hanging at the back of the shack.

Perhaps a pot of tiny gold-colored beads held the greatest mystery. Martinez told Gavito that he feared that each bead represented a sacrifice. There were thirty-seven gold beads in the pot. At first it was believed each bead was from a necklace, but a number of the beads did not have holes drilled in them. Since fifteen bodies were discovered, it led to speculation that another twenty-two are buried in that area. Mexican citizens have since dug dozens of holes at the killing ground. Police suspect they are seeking missing kinsmen.

Benitez also gave Martinez a chance to review Constanzo's *liberta*—a diary written in Spanish and Bantu, the African language from which *Santería* originated. Constanzo kept a meticulous account of spells, cleansings, and divinations for clients in Mexico City and Matamoros. Two ritual cleansings called for human sacrifice; one stipulated a girl child and the other called for an unspecified adult.

The diary had been discovered in Mexico City when police raided Constanzo's plush home. It was obvious that several pages had been torn from the diary. Police speculate that these were pages which would incriminate Mexican leaders. An overlooked page contained the name of a Matamoros police officer. Some of the entries show that Constanzo was paid up to fifty thousand dollars by drug dealers for a ritual cleansing, a *limpia*, in which he would pass an egg over the believer's body. He would then crack it open into a glass of water to discover the source of evil or to see if the spell had been broken. Superstitious believers have told police they thought they saw eyeballs drop from the egg into the water, a sign that the evil spell had been broken; or perhaps it was testimony to Constanzo's ability at sleight of hand. Routine *limpias* cost around eight thousand dollars.

The day after Raphael Martinez dismantled the *nganga*, a *curandero* asked Gavito and Benitez to sign a picture of Constanzo which he carefully sealed in an envelope and placed inside the tarpaper temple. After performing rituals, then sprinkling the shack with a flammable liquid and adding hay from the corral, the *curandero* set the building afire by throwing a torch inside it. He then tossed packets of a white, powdered material at the burning building. Flames quickly engulfed the wooden shed, spreading to the sticks in the *nganga*; soon it was a churning, fiery mass. When the fire had run its course, the charred *nganga* was contemptuously overturned by the *curandero*, it contents spilling onto the ground.

"I hope Constanzo is watching this on the news," Gavito grinned at Benitez.

When only ashes remained, the *curandero* took a white dove from a cage and released it. It flew away, carrying with it whatever evil had escaped the fiery exorcism performed by the *curandero*.

Gavito watched the dove fly as he got into the patrol car.

I'm leaving this place and I'm never coming back, he vowed to himself as he drove onto the highway.

A *corrido* called *Tragedy in Matamoros* had begun to be played on Mexican radio stations. The plaintive ballad told the story of death and drugs on the border. It was followed a week later by another traditional folk song titled *El Rancho de Elena*.

Panic swept across Southeast Texas, especially in the coastal plains surrounding Santa Fe. It was an especially difficult time for the

Santa Fe school district. Already that school year one student had died of drug abuse, cancer claimed one life, another had had a heart attack, and a motorcycle accident killed still another. Mark's tragic death compounded a feeling of calamity, and by year's end the teachers were concentrating more on holding students' fragile psyches together than on teaching.

Then the rumors began. Someone said the head of a black cat had been rolled down the hallways at junior high; still another heard that Sara Aldrete had threatened to send a cult hit team to Santa Fe to grab children in retaliation for the arrest of its members. Several students were spotted carrying satanic bibles on the school grounds. The principal's investigation discovered nothing sinister in the students' actions. They had heard so much about satanism, they were just curious. But parents were encouraged to be alert and not to take curiosity too lightly, because that is one way kids can be drawn into satanism.

Worried parents began to spot what they considered satanic signs. One turned out to be an advertisement in Spanish for a local church. Still other parents began a secret patrol of the schools, spending hours driving around the school block, eyes peeled for sinister-looking characters. It would be weeks before the community could settle back into its normal routine. But they now realized that they were not immune to the evils of drugs and cults.

For four long weeks the lawmen helped in the search for Constanzo. At times the frustration of following fruitless leads had almost reached the same levels of stress as the search for Mark. Only this time, there was an additional concern: Constanzo and his band had killed twice after sacrificing Mark Kilroy. Would they kill again?

Once again, Neck and Gavito found themselves working against time, as Constanzo proved elusive. At one point, Mexican authorities were only minutes from capturing him in his plush home protected by a modern security and lighting system. But he eluded them. They did find Sara Aldrete's passport and a purse filled with money. Lawmen speculated that he might have killed Sara because of her startling physical presence. Where do you hide a six-foot-tall woman whose very height calls attention to herself?

In Mexico City a team of detectives quietly worked on the case. Juan Miguel Ponce noticed that the Matamoros murders had some of the same characteristics as a group of savage homosexual murders in the Zona Rosa in 1987. Doggedly contacting snitches and walking the streets with pictures of the suspects, Ponce and his detective colleagues traced Constanzo to an apartment only one block from the British Embassy and three blocks from the U.S. Embassy.

On Saturday, May 6, almost four weeks from the day Benitez had picked up Serafin, Mexico City police officers surrounded the apartment and waited. A carefully planned raid was about to begin when Constanzo spotted a pair of officers checking out a limousine which had stopped in front of the apartment. He opened fire.

During a forty-five-minute gun battle, Constanzo started throwing money and gold coins out the window; perhaps he was sacrificing to his gods. He also started burning thousands of dollars on a stove.

"'If I can't have it, no one can,'" Sara later quoted him as saying during his last minutes of life.

Then Constanzo allegedly wrapped his arms around Martin Quintana Rodriguez, later identified as his homosexual lover, and ordered Alvaro de Leon Valdez—*El Dubi*—to kill the pair as they squatted on raised partitions in a clothes closet.

When *El Dubi* refused his leader's order, Constanzo slapped him twice in the face and threatened: "Do it, or it will go bad for you in hell!"

El Dubi sprayed the two with machine-gun fire.

"He said he wanted to be killed, that everything was finished," a sobbing Aldrete told police only moments after Constanzo issued his last order. "He said, 'Let's all die.' But I didn't want to die."

Neighbors said they heard a woman screaming "Shoot him! Shoot him!" Then a blast from a machine gun had followed.

After Constanzo was killed, Aldrete went screaming for police to cease fire. Newspapers quoted her as saying: "He's dead! They killed him! He's dead!"

Also arrested was Omar Francisco Orea Ochoa, twenty-four, another one of Constanzo's homosexual partners, who later died of AIDS. Omar said Constanzo had introduced him to "black magic" six years previously. He told police that he helped launder the gang's drug money. He denied any participation in the Matamoros murders, although he did hint that the body count might be "seventeen or eighteen dead" instead of the fifteen that were recovered.

"Constanzo used to say that every human being is like an animal," *El Dubi* said later, noting that the *Padrino* considered human sacrifice on the same level as animal sacrifice.

El Dubi also displayed ritualistic V-shaped tattoos on both his arms which were found to be similar to those found on Constanzo's left shoulder. He said he was working as a laborer on a northern Mexico ranch when he met Constanzo, who "marked" him for divine protection because he had killed someone in Matamoros.

The ignoble end of the gang only stirred the controversy.

Slowly a picture emerged of a privileged life that had been carved from the depths of poverty through the manipulation of superstition. *Santería* and *Palo Mayombe* appeared to be Constanzo's mother's legacy to him, although Cuban refugee Delia Aurora Gonzalez Del Valle denies she taught her son the rituals of *Santería*.

"That's a lie. I'm not a *Santería*, or anything. I have my saints, my Virgin Mary, my Santa Barbara, and I put my candles up," she said on a Miami radio talk show. "That's not *Santería*, We are Catholic; my children are Catholic." (Santa Barbara is the syncretism of the *orisha Chango* in *Santería*.)

But the denials failed to convince her neighbors in a predominantly Cuban neighborhood in western Dade County. In published reports, one neighbor reported finding a dead goose wrapped in a red handkerchief on her doorstep. And once she saw the family leave pieces of hacked up goat in the street, she said. Another neighbor found six headless chickens on the doorstep of his home after a quarrel with Constanzo's family.

Constanzo's younger brother, Fausto Rodriguez, confirmed that his brother was paid $30,000 to $40,000 for a cleansing. And although Fausto refused to be interviewed, unless paid, he did deny that his brother was a homosexual or that he practiced *Santería* or *Palo Mayombe* as claimed by the police. (Mexico City officials had depicted Constanzo as a bisexual who was having affairs with members of his cult.)

No one knows how deep the tentacles of the *Santería* cult have driven into the Mexican political structure.

"We suspect the list of those who asked him to use his powers in their behalf includes more than just entertainers," Federal District Police Comandante Ignacio Flores said of Constanzo. Within a few days of Constanzo's death, more than 500 pages of testimony were gathered and 450 people linked to the cult.

By the middle of the week, Flores had tied Constanzo to the deaths of nine men and women in the Mexico City area. The spine had been cut from each of the bodies, a trademark found on bodies at Rancho Santa Elena.

"I estimate that they must have killed at least one hundred," Flores added.

A love of money fueled the bloodlust, according to Frederico Ponce Rojas, a district attorney in Mexico City.

"He was crazy about money," Ponce stressed, noting that Constanzo wore rubies and diamonds on every finger, owned several late-model, expensive automobiles which he purchased with cash, and twice went on ten-thousand-dollar spending sprees in Brownsville to clothe a boyfriend.

"I don't think that it will end with us," Sara Aldrete said in a press conference. "Because this religion has a lot of people." She also claimed that a similar drug cult exists in Monterrey, a steel city in Northern Mexico approximately two hundred miles from Matamoros.

Aldrete had cut her long hair, darkened it, and lost more than twenty pounds during her month-long flight from authorities. Most of the weight loss was attributed to the inability to keep food in her stomach. Sara told lawmen that she had posed as Constanzo's girlfriend or wife during the month they eluded capture.

She has exhibited a dual personality, Neck said. Then he explained that whenever she is approached by lawmen, she becomes the hardened criminal. But when she is approached by reporters, she "reverts to this nice, young, clean-cut kid from Texas Southmost College."

Neck and Gavito were invited to Mexico City to help clear up loose ends after she was captured. Who knew the case better than these two men who were working without authority?

"We're having difficulty breaking Aldrete," District Attorney Frederico Ponce Rojas told Neck and Gavito upon their arrival.

The young college student found herself in a unique position. Texas law allows the death penalty while Mexican laws forbid it. She might receive a long prison sentence, but she would still be alive. And often—through the power of money—Mexican prison cells are turned into living quarters that rival the plushest hotels.

"I think we can do something to help," Neck said to Ponce, "if you're willing to try."

A few minutes later the men approached Aldrete who was being questioned in a large interrogation room. Nearby El Dubi stood in a stupefied state, the right side of his face swollen.

It was the first time Neck and Gavito had been face to face with Sara Aldrete. She was gaunt and drawn, with disheveled hair, nothing like the smiling young girl on the wanted posters that had gone around the world.

"Pack your things," Neck said without ceremony.

Sara became alert, her eyes darting from one man to another.

"What do you mean?"

"Just what he said," Gavito joined in. "Pack your things; you're going back to Texas."

Ponce just shifted his shoulders.

"You can't do that," she said. "There's no extradition treaty; you can't take me back to the United States."

"Oh, but I can. And when we get there, I'm going to turn you over to the police, and they're going to give you a trial, and then they're going to fry your butt," he emphasized the last words. He realized that the death penalty in Texas was by lethal injection, but the reference to the electric chair was more dramatic—so he repeated it: "They're going to fry your butt because of what you did to Mark Kilroy and all the others."

"And if they'll let me, I'll watch," Gavito snarled.

"I really don't. . . . " Ponce began.

"She's ours and we're taking her with us," Neck cut him off.

"No. You can't take me back," Sara said, by now her voice shrieking, profanity lacing every other word.

She had turned into a snarling, screaming criminal, fighting for her life.

"I wouldn't let you take her." Ponce's voice was low, but piercing, threatening.

Neck and Gavito heard the click of weapons around the room.

"She won't talk to you, but she will to us, right before they fry her," Neck shouted, his face only inches from Ponce.

He wheeled on Sara.

"Are you going to talk to them?"

She nodded in the affirmative.

"You go in there right now and talk to Ponce. You give him a full confession or you go with me," Neck threatened.

"I'll tell him everything he wants to know," she whimpered.

Ponce nodded at the interrogator, who led Sara to another room. Downstairs Neck looked at Ponce and laughed.

"Man, you're sure some actor," he said.

"I'm an actor?" Ponce said. "I forgot you were acting a couple of times. I thought you were mad at me."

Soon rumors began flying that Constanzo had yet again confounded the authorities and escaped. Was it really Constanzo that Mexican authorities loaded into a silver casket that was topped by a crucifix and shipped to Miami, Florida?

Dr. Charles Wetli confirmed identification during an autopsy May 22, 1989, at the ultra-modern Dade County forensic facilities.

Although the body had already been embalmed, it was in a decaying state when it arrived. The chief medical examiner worked swiftly. First he took fingerprints and palm prints from the corpse for comparison to arrest records.

"I have heard that he is very strict about not using drugs himself," Wetli then told an assistant. "I understand he killed a gang member for using drugs. Let's check his brain for drugs, just to see if he had used any."

The autopsy's routine visual examination revealed that Constanzo had a mustache and short hair dyed reddish brown (probably part of a disguise). The rest of his body hair was black. His body bore sixteen bullet holes in the chest, arms, and head.

A tattoo which represented the evil god *Kadiempembe* was found on his right arm. Another tattoo on his left shoulder appeared to be a straight line with V-shaped inscriptions.

Constanzo also bore tiny tattoos about one-quarter-inch high in the shape of a cross. A few looked incomplete. None of them were fresh, but had faded with years. They were on his shoulders, front, and back; in the middle of his chest and on the back of the calf of each leg.

Unless someone knew to look for the tiny markings, it would be impossible to realize that he was marked as a high priest in *Palo Mayombe*.

No drugs were detected in Constanzo's brain.

Fingerprint records matched those on file with the Federal Bureau of Investigation.

Cause of death: multiple gunshot wounds.

Constanzo's body was released to Rivero Funeral Home which took it to the Grove Park facilities for cremation. The ashes were packed in a cardboard box and given to the family. The remains of the coffin were dumped in a garbage heap.

In Austin, Jim and Helen began the painful task of retrieving their son's possessions from his apartment.

Jim Kilroy:

When we arrived at Mark's apartment we unlocked the door and found the door latched from the inside. At first it was very eerie because we thought someone was in the efficiency apartment; but then it became obvious that the door had been jimmied once before and Mark had latched it in an attempt to protect his meager possessions.

One of his friends crawled through the window that Mark had left unlocked. There were several piles of papers and notebooks on the floor that at first looked messy. This turned out to be the way Mark kept his papers sorted because he did not have enough file and drawer space.

We found his homemade cockroach trap in the middle of the kitchen floor: sticky syrup on a paper plate circled a piece of cake, which had dried out. Even with all of his innovation, not one cockroach was in his trap.

The dishes in the kitchen were all washed and stacked in the drying rack. The place was cleaned up nice, as any parent would like to find it.

It was especially good to see the picture on the kitchen wall of the Good Shepherd holding a little lamb. A neighbor and friend from Santa Fe had given Mark this picture. I didn't realize that he had taken it to college. We also found his Bible lying open on the table next to his bed.

One of Mark's neighbors said that one night, shortly after Mark's body had been discovered, someone had tried to break into the apartment. The neighbor called the police and the burglary was stopped. Actually, I don't think the burglar took anything, but all things considered, the news made Helen and me feel as if someone wanted to violate Mark one last time.

Parents work with their children to instill goals in them so they do not slip aimlessly through school, through life, thinking that only material wealth means happiness.

With the goals come some successes, because you try to orientate your children toward their talents and abilities. But now as I think back on all of Mark's achievements, they are not important.

The way he was, the way he acted, what was in his heart are all that is important now. To be with God forever, that is the only success of everlasting value. And the most important goal of any parent should be the goal of everlasting life for their child.

EPILOGUE

The irony surrounding the macabre link between Mark James Kilroy and Adolfo de Jesus Constanzo is astonishing. They lived at different ends of the spectrum of life, yet they shared a number of common traits, each using them to different ends as one chose good and the other evil.

In life, each was a leader of men, each possessed an intellect that was above average, each had a special ambiance that won friends easily, each was sought out by people seeking advice.

In death, the link was forged on the searing anvil of pagan religion and drug abuse in which both died violently. Mark was an innocent victim brutally murdered and mutilated in a sacrifice to appease pagan *orishas* whose favor was sought to protect a drug ring. Constanzo was machine-gunned down in a moment of screaming frenzy at his own order as police closed in, his drug empire tumbling down around him, abandoned by false and ineffective *orishas*.

Both were returned to America where each was cremated. Mark's ashes are buried in sacred ground. Constanzo's ashes were said to have been scattered at sea. And with those two final acts, the brief link was broken; but because these two men shared a moment in history they will forever be a part of a common legacy in the battle between good and evil.

The legacy of Adolfo Constanzo is one of terror. His name has become a modern-day symbol of the malevolence inherent in drug smuggling and pagan worship. His name has already joined those of Jim Jones, Charles Manson, and Richard Ramirez on a growing list of serial killers who performed atrocities in the name of religion.

In contrast, the legacy of Mark Kilroy is one of hope and love. Although he was only twenty-one, he had already devoted his life to the service of humanity, and that service continues, although not in a way he or his family would have ever guessed.

The events surrounding Mark's death have thrust the Kilroy family into the public spotlight, and they have seized the opportunity to fight a national plague which killed their son and continues to erode the foundation of this country and threatens the very lifeblood of its youth.

Despite demands of a job, family responsibilities, and school, all three Kilroys find the time to speak at rallies organized to combat drug abuse and its attendant evil. Jim and Helen have met with President George Bush and drug czar William Bennett at the request of these national leaders.

This dedicated family knows—as do thousands of others touched by the evil of drug abuse—that the battle with Satan has only begun.

Jim Kilroy:

By Mark's waterbed on the nightstand in his apartment was his Bible turned over on the pages to keep the place, awaiting his hand to resume studying. The fact that Mark had been studying the Bible meant a lot to Helen and me. I marked the place and closed the Book.

A year later as we were writing this book, Bob Stewart asked me what part of the Scriptures Mark had been studying. Helen brought the Bible to us, and we scanned the facing pages on either side of the marker. I was thunderstruck.

"Listen to this," I said, reading the passage from 2 Samuel 22:4–8 in which King David is singing a song of thanksgiving.

> Praised be the Lord, I exclaim, and I am safe from my enemies.
> The breakers of death surged round about me, the floods of perdition overwhelmed me; The cords of the nether world enmeshed me, the snares of death overtook me.
> In my distress I called upon the Lord and cried out to my God; From his temple he heard my voice, and my cry reached his ears.

—THE NEW AMERICAN BIBLE

M.A.R.K.

by Jim Kilroy

"All that is necessary for the triumph of evil is for good men to do nothing."
—Edmund Burke

I have often thought about the biblical story of Simon of Cyrene and what a great honor it must have been for him to have helped Jesus carry the cross. Simon was selected out of the crowd. But now as I think about it, he could have asked, "Why me?" as he struggled with the weight of a burden that was thrust on him without warning. Struggling under the cross, Simon could have been overcome by too great a personal anguish at his circumstances. We don't know if he asked "Why me?" but Helen and I do know that many times we have asked, "Why Mark?"

After Mark's funeral, we finally had the time to begin to sort through the more than three thousand letters that had arrived during the weeks we searched for him. Almost all of the letters were special because they were written from the heart. But the ones from children were especially precious.

Telephone calls and letters that we received from across the country helped us realize that many people are struggling under the weight of a heavy cross, and that the battle is not only of flesh and blood, but of powers and principalities. We know now, more than ever before, that in times of trouble and tragedy one should move closer to God, because it was the Word of God which strengthened us when we easily could have given up.

When Helen and I lost our future with Mark, we learned the importance of comforting the sorrowing. The condolences—especially the prayers offered on our behalf—lifted our spirits and helped us through our deep grief. But our greatest source of comfort was in our religious beliefs, where we found an inner peace that helped us accept what had happened. This, plus the loving concern of others, protected us from the anger and the bitterness that might have engulfed us.

As time passed, more and more of the letters we received contained not only condolences but also heart-rending stories of parents fighting to win their children back from the depths of drug abuse or from the clutches of cults or gangs. As we read those letters, we felt the hurt and understood the grief of those parents. We had not experienced the particular pain and anguish of the drug addiction they described, but we, too, were victims of its far-reaching devastation.

People continued to write and talk to us about drug abuse, and we continued to listen and learn. It was clear to us that drug abuse was causing much needless suffering. One father whose son had committed suicide because of a drug problem called and wanted to know what he could do to stop the use of drugs. As he was going through his son's possessions, he had found satanic items and literature. My heart went out to the man, but I had no answers for him.

Before Mark's death I never thought much about the power of the Devil, but since then I have seen his great powers of deception. I believe that the basic cause of the alarming expansion of satanism in the last twenty years is illegal drug abuse. The fun and the riches promised through drug use is one of Satan's greatest deceptions.

The satanic cult leaders actively recruit young people with the pledge of unconditional acceptance, drugs, sex, and protection against authority. Once they are drawn into the cult, these kids are kept quiet with death threats, secretive blood rituals, and by implicating them in criminal activities. One young boy told me that his own brother threatened to kill him if he left the cult.

Some people wanted Helen and me to begin working directly against satanic cults. But we wanted to distance ourselves from any evil that would remind us of our son's death. At the same time, we believed that we had been given a responsibility to make others aware of the hideous dangers of these evil cults and drug abuse. We just didn't know exactly what to do.

A few days after Mark's funeral Mass, we had a visit from two women. One woman's eleven-year-old daughter had almost been pulled into the clutches of a satanic cult in a nearby town. The other woman is a dedicated school teacher who deals with student drug problems daily. When these women asked us to help in the fight against drug abuse, we realized that by controlling the explosion of illegal drugs the spread of cults and gangs could also be controlled.

A meeting with other concerned citizens revealed two major ob-
stacles in the fight against illegal drugs—apathy and a lack of awareness. While most acknowledged the problem, many were not aware
of its depth, nor that the future of this country is being destroyed by
a handful of people intent on turning the tragic addiction of others
into personal wealth. Others felt the fight was hopeless—that drug
abuse was so rampant that victory over it could never be won.

Before Mark's disappearance Helen and I had not been aware of
the severity of the drug problem. We knew that there were foolish
people who used illegal drugs, but we assumed that the government
more or less had drug abuse under control with its various anti-
drug programs. This meeting helped us to understand that successful drug control will only come if people get involved and demand
reform. That's when we decided to establish the Mark Kilroy
Foundation.

Two things were clear to us: (1) Drug abuse is not a victimless
crime; if nothing else, the addict himself is a victim. (2) The first step
on the road to addiction is casual use of drugs. By addressing these
two issues, then perhaps new programs could be established and
existing successful programs expanded.

The Mark Kilroy Foundation would be our platform. It was char-
tered in the State of Texas as a non-profit foundation on May 22,
1989. At first Helen and I did not want to use Mark's name in the
foundation's name. Mark had never liked having public attention
focused on his successes; he preferred to enjoy them privately. I
remember once, Helen had called the local newspaper when Mark
had made the Dean's List at Southwest Texas State University. The
news article embarrassed Mark. When he was awarded a scholastic
scholarship to Tarleton State University, he made a point of asking
his mom not to put it in the newspaper.

However, the founding committee of the Mark Kilroy Foundation believed that we could be more effective if we used Mark's
name. Helen and I realized this was true. We also like the acronym
of M.A.R.K. (Make A Responsible Kommitment).

We talked with many experts and began to understand what
needed to be done. Soon, the People's Solution was developed, and
the foundation began a national awareness campaign, as Helen and I
began speaking to many groups around the state about drug abuse
and its associated problems.

The People's Solution set forth goals that require political and
individual action by concerned citizens:

1. *Drug-free workplaces and schools.* Employees and taxpayers
should demand their right to a safe workplace by requiring employ-
ers to include random drug testing in their policy.

2. *Enforcement.* By voting and through personal contact, the people should encourage local police, judges, and district attorneys to enforce drug abuse laws.

3. *Casual user laws.* We are now experiencing the result of the lack of deterrent to drug addiction and are fully warned of the dire consequences of further inaction. We the people should demand that our elected officials legislate stiff laws against the purchase or use of drugs.

For example, the penalty for the purchase or possession of small amounts of illegal drugs should include mandatory, daily attendance at meetings of a twelve-step program, such as those used by Narcotics Anonymous and Alcoholics Anonymous. In these free, group-support programs the casual drug user could see addicts admitting that they need help, getting honest with themselves about their addiction, talking it out with someone else, making restitution to the people they've harmed, and praying to their own conception of God.

Each drug user would be screened by trained health professionals to determine his rehabilitation needs. However, a minimum of 500 hours of rehabilitation should be assessed to help stop drug users from traveling the road to addiction. If a first-time drug user, for example, does not need 500 hours in the twelve-step program, the biggest part of his time could be spent in anti-drug education and mandatory work projects that would benefit the community. Assignments for community service projects and education hours would be based on each drug user's needs. The community projects could range anywhere from routine maintenance of roadsides, parks, and other public grounds to menial work in emergency rooms and hospitals for the mentally ill. The trauma observed in the latter experiences might begin to open the casual user's mind to the dangers of drugs. Not only would these mandatory programs of community service be a deterrent to experimentation with addictive drugs, but they could also help those who go through them become more responsible citizens.

4. *Education.* Citizens should step forward and get involved in the drug education programs of their schools, churches, and community.

5. *Rehabilitation.* Charitable organizations, churches, and business leaders should make it one of their top priorities to expand the successful rehabilitation programs for drug addicts by providing meeting rooms, jobs, living facilities, volunteers, and other encouragements.

It is difficult and expensive to recover from drug addiction. There are few charity-sponsored live-in programs, and most of them are short-term with long waiting lists. The longer-term programs have much higher success rates, but even fewer are available.

These long-term rehabilitation programs can become self-supporting through a coordinated business program.

A long-range ambition of the Mark Kilroy Foundation is to establish businesses in live-in shelters. The products made by these businesses would be sold through other nonprofit groups and churches. Funds obtained from the sale of these products would sustain and expand the programs.

Volunteers would teach the business skills needed, as well as other living and coping skills which are necessary for everyday life. By directly involving the live-in residents in such enterprises, the rehabilitation programs would help participants develop greater self-respect and community spirit.

6. *Prison Reform.* Too many prisoners simply return to their criminal past and old habits. An alternate lifestyle in self-supported halfway houses is needed to provide a positive influence to keep prisoners from returning to their old environment. Probation and parole policies should also include mandatory attendance in a twelve-step program to reduce the recidivism rate of the prison system.

Like a shotgun blast, drug abuse is spreading a devastating pattern across the country: child abuse, crack babies, drug orphans, school dropouts, emotional problems (depression, anger, rapidly changing moods), family conflict, runaways, burglaries, Acquired Immune Deficiency Syndrome (AIDS), robberies, assault, prostitution, murder, suicide, etc.

The dropout rate is especially alarming, because without an education in this age of knowledge and technology, failure is almost guaranteed. Many of the reasons students quit school are directly related to drug abuse which causes rebellion, memory loss, and the lack of concentration and motivation.

Another startling trend is the number of children who are contacting law enforcement agencies to report addicted parents. Every day fearful children seek to escape the abuse or neglect of a parent on drugs, a home without electricity or gas, or even the basics, such as food and clothing.

Almost weekly a prominent American admits to drug abuse as he walks through the doors of a rehabilitation center. Entertainers and sports figures lead the parade and are joined by politicians, national personalities, and business leaders. Virtually no segment of the national community is immune.

The Texas crime rate has doubled in four years. Law enforcement officers confirm that 85 percent of those crimes are drug related. Yet, there is debate about the legalization of drugs. The logic used by legalization proponents is that the wave of crime would crest as profits slowed. But it seems to me that they do not understand chemical dependency. Because illegal drugs alter the mind and emotions, the paranoia and depression that result will inevitably lead to violence and suicidal tendencies. History verifies that legalization of drugs is not the answer.

Drugs were legal in the late 1800s. Medical problems and violence by addicts escalated to such extremes that Congress was petitioned, especially by the police, to enact laws against drug use. By December 1914 Congress passed the Harrison Act that tightly regulated the interstate distribution and sale of drugs. By the beginning of World War I, the District of Columbia and forty-six states had also enacted anti-drug laws with varying requirements and penalties. When the Volstead Act of 1919, prohibiting the manufacture, sale, or use of alcohol was repealed in 1933, alcoholism greatly increased. Will legal drug addiction follow the historical pattern of legal alcoholism?

To overcome the devastating problems that result from drug abuse, we must prevent the casual use of drugs. Casual drug users are the addicts of tomorrow. Helen and I have been surprised to discover that many young people actually think that they can choose to use drugs for recreation and fun without any fear of addiction. This kind of thinking makes about as much sense as saying that they occasionally choose to jump off a cliff without getting hurt.

We need to teach both young people and adults what drug addiction really means. If they use drugs, they will continue to use them because they will not experience the terrible grip of addiction until it is too late. They will use drugs first for fun—to get high—then to forget their problems for a few hours, and finally they will use drugs to satisfy the terrible craving, to temporarily remove the depression.

Today, many young people who use drugs try to escape their problems by running away. In fact, there are so many missing young people that it is very difficult to get officials to look for them. Often, only the family and friends search.

A very worried mother called us one day for advice on how to search for her daughter who had been missing for five days. The father of this girl had found the door of their house wide open and the girl missing, even though her purse was still there.

The mother told us that the girl used drugs and was surly and unhappy. She had an identical twin sister who was just the opposite, smiling and pleasant. Physically the twins were identical, but mentally they were completely different.

Within an hour after we received the call, the girl was brought to the hospital, suffering from a drug overdose. This girl was so chemically dependent that she had run out of her house without any concern for anything or anyone except her next high. We need to teach kids about addiction—the terrible craving that enslaves.

When a basically good person starts to use drugs, the deceptions begin to take hold. Gradually, that person rejects more and more of the good and starts to choose the bad as he or she continues on a downward spiral toward evil. Finally the drug user gets to the point where he or she just does not care.

A big part of the problem is that we allow it. We treat drug abuse casually. We need to have laws that will allow law-enforcement agencies to take action the very first time someone is caught using illegal drugs. This action is needed to immediately help that person stop using drugs. Instead, we allow the casual use of drugs by our young people and consider it only a minor offense. It is not surprising that kids from good, loving families are being lost to addiction.

We must concentrate on preventing drug use before addiction occurs. For that reason, I favor random drug testing in the workplace and in schools, because it will greatly reduce the casual use of drugs. Random drug testing in the schools gives the kids a good excuse to say no and will help them resist peer pressure.

Young people need to realize that their future is at risk. Less than a generation ago, it was the drug user who was ostracized as being outside society's norm. But within the reality of today's peer pressure, it is often the non-user who is ridiculed. We must encourage them to be drug-free role models for younger boys and girls. Our young people must reclaim their heritage. And we can help by letting them know they are important to us, by telling them we love them, and by showing that love with our actions.

Low self-esteem and the lack of good role models are always cited by the experts as the major cause of drug abuse. Since an older youth's attitude or actions can influence younger kids for good or bad, we need to find ways to promote healthy role models through our church youth groups, scouts, and other organizations that can offer a positive support for at-risk kids.

By our actions, we are responsible for the future. We can make a difference. In the great commission, Christ sent forth His followers to go into all the world and spread the good news. Undoubtedly the rapid growth of early Christianity was due to the principle of each-one-teach-one. Look at the compounding effect if each person just taught one person and that person just taught one person, etc. Perhaps we need a return to simplicity. If each person helps just one person to abstain from drugs, it would have the same compounding effect. So pray, have hope, and bring the people to God—one by one.

A friend that I have known for years came by to offer condolences and to visit with us shortly after Mark's burial.

"Can I talk to you privately?" he asked.

"Sure."

As I led him out the back door, he said, "You always tell me that we're alike."

"We are. We like to garden, to play golf," I replied, remembering the good times we had on the golf course or talking about our gardens.

"No, I'm not like you," he stressed. "I'm going to give up smoking," he added, a slight pause between each word for emphasis.

"It's okay, you can smoke if you like."

"No," my friend insisted, gently placing his hand on my shoulder. "I'm not going to smoke marijuana anymore."

I was stunned. I didn't know what to say. I looked at him as I considered the implications of what he had just told me. Painful memories flooded my mind—*Mark was dead because people buy and sell drugs. There are thousands of families, millions of people suffering directly or indirectly from drugs.*

Here is a man who I had known for years. At least I thought I knew him. Here is a friend whose hand on my shoulder is a welcome gesture of condolence; yet here is someone who, in one sense, is partially responsible for Mark's death because he had been a casual drug user.

For a brief instance, I felt a sudden surge of anger, but then I felt calm, a sense of peace. My friend had just said that he would *never* smoke marijuana again. A slow smile began to form as I looked deeper into the eyes of my friend.

There is hope! We will win the battles . . . one by one.

THE RELIGION *SANTERÍA*

by Bob Stewart

Mexican authorities are living with a nightmare.

Somewhere under the fertile, life-giving soil of their country there may be a field of tiny corpses: children sacrificed to Stone Age gods in the name of religion. Rumors abound that more bodies are buried at Rancho Santa Elena where Mark Kilroy was killed by a cult of drug smugglers which practiced its own version of *Santería* and *Palo Mayombe*, a pair of intertwined Afro-Caribbean religions. Dozens of holes, dug by desperate families seeking a missing relative, dot the corral and surrounding area of the ranch.

George Gavito believes the sect was just beginning its bloody reign when it was stopped. Oran Neck would not be surprised to find the rumor true. Benitez speculated that nearby Rancho Los Leones was to be the new burial grounds for the cult. All three, however, believe that numerous graves have yet to be found in Mexico City, Constanzo's home base.

North of the border, American police officers are living with a threat that most citizens do not even know exists because the secret world of cult worship seldom rises into public view. When it does, it is only because the case involves extreme violence or desecration. Normally, the symbols of worship and the telltale signs of pagan gods go unnoticed.

The citizens of the world are living with a cancer that has spread it tentacles across the globe through a unique blend of crime and religion that reaches from the depths of poverty to the halls of politics to the spheres of the rich and famous.

Santería, Palo Mayombe, Brujeria—In the aftermath of drugs and death (and human sacrifice), a startled country is just beginning to hear these words and struggle to grasp their sinister meaning.

Is *Santería* a form of satanism? The debate rages. Parts of *Palo Mayombe* resemble satanism (evil is worshiped); parts of *Santería* resemble satanism (a goat's head is commonly used). Many practitioners and anthropologists believe *Santería* is an alternate benign religion—benign because it is a "white" or good religion.

Santería practitioners call it simply "The Religion." After years of study, experts still have differing views on the legitimacy and the impact of the practice of *Santería*, which literally translated means the "worship of saints." Although some anthropologists consider it to be white magic, religious leaders may not be so charitable. *Santería* relies upon the perceived power of magic spells to manipulate the life of both its followers and the people surrounding them. Therefore, *Santería* denies the Christian principle of free-will choice through a practitioner's right of manipulation. In the believer's mind, a young maiden may lose her free-will because a male believer casts a spell on her, forcing her to love him. Likewise, in *Santería* a businessman has the right to manipulate a catastrophe on a rival's business, thereby removing competition.

A *Santería* prayer entitled "Revocation to St. Michael Arcangel" demands "Let my enemies suffer as Jesus suffered on the tree of the cross; bitterness, torment, kicks and slaps like those he suffered. Let him go into a desolate world. Let him take the three falls that Jesus took until he comes to my home asking pardon for his sins. The stars in heaven bear witness to my pleas."

This *Santería* belief in spells that can cause a person to suffer an injury, possibly even death, because of the anger of a spellbinder, directly clashes with the Christian principle of "love thy neighbor as thyself."

There is another, perhaps more subtle, sphere of *Santería* influence: the concept of using evil for good. It is a difficult concept for Christians because nowhere in biblical teachings is Satan used as a direct force for good.

In the *Santería* "Prayer to the Intranquil Spirit," the worshiper calls for help from a spirit in hell, who is shunned by everyone but the person seeking favor. Thus, both good and evil are to be manipulated to benefit the believer. *Santería* is an amoral religion, permeated by an attitude of self-service. Most experts agree, however, that *Santería's* malevolent extension, *Palo Mayombe*, is even more evil.

"With *Palo Mayombe*, the very basis of the religion is that there is no moral code or respect for the law whatsoever. All spells are evil; but the key element is the use of human remains," says Cynthia

Burgin of the Bexar County Sheriff's Department in San Antonio, Texas, who specializes in the occult. "They believe that with the power obtained from the spirits and the cauldron, they cannot be touched by the law, bullets, or anything."

Palo practitioners rob graves—but only graves which contain decaying flesh, according to Burgin. The *Paleros* want skulls that still contain brains so the *nganga* (which to them becomes a living spirit) can think better. When police discover a grave that has been robbed of body parts still bearing flesh, it is generally believed to be the work of *Palo Mayombe* believers; if a grave is robbed which just contains bones, it is believed to be the work of satanists.

"They believe that they can control the soul or spirit of the dead person, and have it do evil deeds for them or protect them," Burgin explained. Fingers and toe bones are taken so the possessed spirit can walk. Sometimes a fibula is wrapped in black and used as a scepter."

While grave robbing seems to be a common practice among *Palo Mayombe* believers, there is general disagreement on the practice of human sacrifice in the believer's routine worship. Raphael Martinez, a highly respected expert on *Santería* and *Palo Mayombe* at the University of North Florida, maintains that human sacrifice is a deviate form of *Palo*, rarely practiced. Felix Jiminez, a Dade county homicide detective in Miami, Florida, disagrees.

"I'm surprised that these mass murders were discovered in Mexico and not Miami. I expected it to happen here first," he paused before adding, "Of course, they may have already happened and we just don't know it."

A native-born Cuban who is now a naturalized American citizen, Jiminez was brought to the United States when he was three years old. The thirty-two-year-old detective says an aged grandmother has told him that as a child in Cuba he was routinely hidden by the family a few weeks before Easter, the traditional time of sacrifice by *Palo Mayombe*.

"They knew that *Palo* practiced human sacrifice, and they hid the children," he stressed.

"*Palo* is often used by criminals for protection. Its magic is used to inflict misfortune. Believers often wear the symbol of *Ochosi*, who is a hunter, jailer, judge, so they have those forces in control," he said.

"I come from the very rural southern part of Cuba where there is a large population of *santeros* and *paleros*," he continued. Jiminez was not surprised to find Constanzo practicing a possible deviant form of *Palo Mayombe*.

"The religion is changing as it moves across the country," he explained. "It would be difficult to find the exact twenty-one woods

that are needed to build a Cuban *nganga*. The strict guidelines in
Cuba may not be followed here.

"Constanzo was in Matamoros, and that's even further from
Cuba than Florida," he explained. "Worshipers are starting to create
different things and changing the religion to fit their needs."

Martinez estimates that there are more than forty thousand *Palo
Mayombe* practitioners in the United States. He considers it the
religion of choice of drug smugglers, who use it to protect themselves and put curses on their opponents.

Brujeria is the practice of magic in all its forms, but most generally
the dark-side forms. Sometimes it is practiced in connection with
Santería and *Palo* and at other times it takes on an existence all its
own.

Curandero is another term (well-known in South Texas with its
strong Hispanic culture) which often surfaces when dealing with
these cults, although it generally applies to a single individual who
casts spells and practices herbal cures within a Mexican community
and has little or nothing to do with Afro-Caribbean cults.

Santería is a Stone Age belief practiced in a modern world. Believers worship in a manner not seen since the fall of the gods of
Greek and Roman legends. Like the characters of these legends,
Santería orishas (or saints) have mothers and fathers; they fall in
love; they war against each other; they bear children; they toy with
the emotions of the humans; they kill each other, and they must be
appeased by a variety of sacrifices. Worshipers believe that a pleasing
sacrifice to these deities can affect their own worldly fate.

Highly stylized rites of worship are carefully followed by the
Santería believers. Hundreds of herbs are painstakingly categorized
for use in spells and cures, and each *orisha* has a preferred herb. One
herb-based elixir is the *omiero*, a drink mixed with the blood of
sacrifice.

Besides a favorite herb, each *orisha* also has a day of the week, a
lucky number, a color, a function or power, a force in nature, and a
weapon or symbol. Finally, each *orisha* is identified with a Catholic
saint and is worshiped on that saint's feast day. The *orisha's* favorite
sacrifice—living or inanimate—is used to obtain favor.

Santería originated more than five hundred years ago when slave
traders would kidnap whole villages in Africa and transport them to
the Caribbean. There, the terrified slaves would be told by Jesuit
priests to worship according to the Catholic religion. Slowly the
slaves began to hide their woodland gods within the superstructure
of the Roman Catholic Church. If a Jesuit found a black praying in
front of a statue of Lazarus, it was assumed the slave was invoking

the saint on account of the benefit to be obtained from God through the saint's intercession. Instead, the slave—in his own mind—might be praying to *Babalu-Aye*, a woodland god. Eventually, however, their duplicity was discovered, and it drove the *orisha* believers even further into underground homage. The secrecy which surrounded such worship still permeates the religion.

Today many *Santería* practitioners embrace both *Santería* and Roman Catholicism. Martinez maintains that faithful *Santería* practitioners *must* also be Roman Catholics. In *Santería: The Religion, a Legacy of Faith, Rites, and Magic*, author Migene Gonzalez-Wippler concurs with Martinez: "Traditionally, all *Santería* initiates should be baptized Catholics."

Gonzalez-Wippler further states, "*Santeros* are among the most assiduous worshipers at Mass services, and they always recommend to their followers that they attend Mass as often as possible." But *Santería* is not Catholicism. It is a separate entity created by superstitious African natives in Cuba who blended two beliefs into a new entity, a new religion.

While Christian beliefs teach self-discipline through service and love with a greater reward in the afterlife, *Santería* is self-serving through domination of the worshiper by the *orisha*, or domination of events or people by the believer through manipulation. In *Santería*, there is no greater reward in the afterlife.

There is no dogma in *Santería* that teaches good for the sake of good. Believers are amoral, living situation ethics to the fullest. For example, a drug dealer will evoke the blessings of *Ochosi*, no matter that he is breaking the law, and then believe the successful completion of the illegal transaction occurred because the gods were pleased with him.

Besides being amoral, *Santería* practitioners have no concept of heaven or hell. There is a concept of a spirit world, and a need for the spirit to peaceably leave the physical world. Great lengths are taken to assure that a *santero* does not roam the world. Burial and attendant rituals take a full year before the spirit is at rest. They believe that spirits do continue to exist within the confines of cemeteries where the *orisha Oya* reigns.

Four elements are the corner stones of *Santería*, with a fifth serving as the glue which holds the sect together. They are stones, seashells, herbs, and water—plus sacrifice.

Sacrifice or propitiation is the act which bonds *Santería* into a cohesive unit. Nothing can exist without sacrifice. No favor can be dispersed, no venture begun with hope of success, no daily life lived without sacrifice to soothe the saints so they will smooth life's pathway. Sacrifice ranges from a few pieces of fruit to money tucked into a tureen (police have found thousands of dollars during drug raids), to a glass of wine or to the ritualistic death of an animal.

Santería is a favored dogma for Hispanic and Caribbean drug smugglers. This became obvious in Miami, where for years law-enforcement officers had difficulty infiltrating undercover agents into known drug operations. The agents were easily spotted and rejected by the drug smugglers. Perplexed law-enforcement officers finally solved the puzzle when agents began wearing the bow-and-triple-arrow medallion representing the *Santería orisha Ochosi*, the god of the hunt and of justice. They believe that his blessings make them immune to law-enforcement officers and to jail. And anyone wearing *Ochosi's* sign was accepted as a member of The Religion and a drug smuggler. (An *Ochosi* had protruded from one of the smaller pots at Rancho Santa Elena.)

"I've never seen a drug dealer without an *Ochosi*," Jiminez said.

Concern over criminal activity and its effect on police enforcement has resulted in educational brochures warning officers of potential danger. The practice of controlling drug smugglers through Stone Age worship explains many acts that otherwise would be considered irrational. For example, it explains the attitude exhibited by the four suspects that day the twelve bodies were disinterred on Rancho Santa Elena.

It is difficult for law-enforcement officers to comprehend a religion which has little or no moral values, in which a practitioner actually evokes the blessings of the Seven African Powers for an illegal undertaking. The attitude of believers is making it more and more dangerous for officers on the streets. Surprisingly, only a few have received briefings on The Religion. And when they do, some scoff because they find the idea of a living Stone Age religion in modern America to be totally unbelievable.

The Texas Department of Public Safety has reported 226 instances of possible cult activity since 1985, the year it began keeping such statistics. Most of them were reported in 1989. The incidents range from suspicious activity to actual discovery of cauldrons.

Perhaps the essence of occult worship is found in the human trait of "magical thinking" so vividly explained by religious writer Richard Vara in a column published April 15, 1989, in *The Houston Post*. Vara believes "magical thinking" is basic greed in the form of instant wish fulfillment that denies reality and tries to control life to avoid hardship. He points to weight-loss advertisements on television that pledge to melt the pounds off (you do not have to work at it), or state lotteries which promise instant millionaires, or New Age religions which promise communication with dead spirits. He cites Karl Marx's theory of a classless workers' paradise as classic magical thinking.

"Mainstream, traditional religion deals instead with moral behavior, duty to others, and self-discipline. Religions recognize the destructive power of evil and its allure through magical thinking," he writes.

To most Christians, the evidence at Rancho Santa Elena would qualify the cultists' activities as Satan worship, in violation of the first of the Ten Commandments: "Thou shalt have no other gods before me" (Exod. 20:3, KJV). Centuries later, Christ added "He that is not with me is against me" (Matt. 12:30, KJV). Under these biblical guidelines, anything that is not God worship is Satan worship.

But while *Santería* and *Palo Mayombe* may be considered "of Satan" by some, it is not satanism in the traditional sense of worshiping Satan himself. There is a fine line that needs to be negotiated here.

Under the umbrella of Satan worship can be found two broad divisions which serve the same devious master. First and foremost would be the direct glorification of Satan as creator and rewarder. The growing trend among America's youth to glorify satanic symbols has spread consternation among parents. Teens are wearing devil symbols on clothing and taking delight in satanic references in hard rock music. Often these teens are just ignorant, participating in lip service to Satan more as part of the rites of rebellion than in actual hard-core Satan worship. Most of these unsuspecting teens have never attended a satanic worship, but they use the possibility as either a threat to parents or a means to belong to an unincorporated group of equally naive peers who smoke pot and flash satanic signs at rock concerts.

Many others, though, understand the true depths of degradation generated by drugs, lack of self-discipline, and hate—the central doctrine of satanism. These worshipers answer to and glorify Satan in ritualistic worship that includes uninhibited sexual conduct and the bloody torture involved in human sacrifice.

The second satanic category is not as narrow in its object of devotion, but offers numerous other paths to Lucifer that do not go by the name of satanism, although the end result still separates man from God. It is the age-old conflict that highlights beliefs which disregard the great love found in the teachings of Christ. These pagan beliefs are rooted in ancestor worship, woodland gods who participate in mythic battles, spells, magic, witchcraft, reincarnation, and sacrifice of animals or humans.

Anthropologists have conveniently decided that all these various beliefs are religion in one form or another. And perhaps they *are* religion if you accept the definition of religion as veneration of something a human considers more powerful, or spiritually higher than himself.

"Man desires to worship something higher than himself," Father Nicolau said in his homily at the Mass of Resurrection for Mark Kilroy in Brownsville. "Unfortunately, these people made the wrong choice. They chose the demon!"

All but two of the suspects in the Matamoros murders remain in jail. Sara Maria Aldrete Villarreal, Elio Hernandez Rivera, Serafin Hernandez Garcia, Jr., Sergio Martinez Salinas, David Serna Valdez, and Alvaro de Leon Valdez face a number of charges in the Mexican State of Tamaulipas. Domingo Reyes Bustamante, the caretaker placed in protective custody by Comandante Juan Benitez Ayala, also faces the same charges.

According to a spokesman for the Mexican Consulate in Brownsville, the charges translate into English as follows:

Felony against public health; murder in the first degree; illegal use of weapons reserved only for the army, navy, and air force; carrying of firearms without proper license; the use of authority without rights; unlawful storing of firearms; unlawful association; and violation of inhumation and exhumation.

When first arrested, all the accused—with the exception of Reyes—confessed to the crimes committed in Mexico. Since then, all have recanted their confessions and maintain they are innocent of the charges. Aldrete and de Leon, who were captured in Mexico City, are now in separate prisons there. Aldrete was convicted of "unlawful association" and sentenced to six years in prison for charges brought against her in Mexico City. It is anticipated that eventually she will be transferred to a prison in Matamoros where she will face the state charges previously listed. (Mexico does not have a death penalty.)

All the suspects, except Reyes, also face charges in the United States of smuggling more than 1,800 pounds of marijuana into the country between March 1 and April 11, 1989.

Two additional suspects face the same charges in Mexico and the United States, but have never been arrested. Police in two countries are seeking Ovidio Hernandez Rivera (Elio's brother) and Malio Ponce Torres.

Since solving the Matamoros murders, the lawmen have moved on to other challenges.

Juan Benitez Ayala has been assigned duties at an undisclosed location near Mexico City.

Oran Neck is serving as a liaison officer in Mexico City on a special task force which is designed to stanch the flow of drugs from South America.

George Gavito is a criminal investigator with the Cameron County District Attorney's Office, assigned to the narcotics division.

Ernesto Flores is now lieutenant in charge of homicide at the Cameron County Sheriff's Office.

9 780849 990984

www.ingramcontent.com/pod-product-compliance
Ingram Content Group UK Ltd.
Pitfield, Milton Keynes, MK11 3LW, UK
UKHW020816120325
456141UK00001B/100